What People Are Saying About Hubba Hubba

"Hubba Hubba is a novel which should make it to the international best-seller lists for it pure entertainment value. Hilarious! (The book) has a well-developed plot, plenty of excitement, sex and romance…make an effort to get it."

—Ken Jones, editor The Visitor

"Hubba Hubba is a highly amusing romp through a dreamlike paradise. Cody is a talented writer."

—Allene Blaker, editor The Bocas Breeze

"This book is the Don't Stop the Carnival of the next century— a feel-good tale about a guy who breaks with his past and starts over. Hubba Hubba could be just about anywhere in Latin America, but looks a lot like Panama and Bocas del Toro. Really funny."

—Bob Applegate, editor The Bajareque Times

"Hold onto your piña colada and strap on your seatbelt—there's not a stagnant moment in the whole book. A feel-good novel and just what the doctor ordered—Hubba Hubba rehab!

—Deborah Carter, jazz diva

"Escape artist Cindy Cody draws from real-life experiences in Hubba Hubba. Writing in a light-hearted tone, Cody has created a novel that has adventure, comedy and drama."

—The Patriot Ledger, January 2008

"No comment."

—Former mayor, from his jail cell in Guabito.

Hubba Hubba

ACKNOWLEDGEMENTS

Though writers spend an inordinate amount of time living inside their heads, no one can create fiction without material. *Hubba Hubba* would never have materialized without Bocas del Toro, or the the creative spark—like a bolt of mental lightning—that shot through my brain one night and showed me this story from beginning to end.

Deepest thanks to the Bocatoreños whose personalities and names were an inspiration for many of the characters in this book.

To Bill Contardi, my almost agent, who took so much time and gave me so many valuable suggestions about the early *Hubba Hubba* manuscript. And to my actual agent, Richard Curtis, who has never lost faith in me.

To Jim McCarren who mowed some impressive lawns on the Gold Coast as a young man, and who helped with early brainstorming.

To Monica Randall for talking with me in-depth about her book, *The Mansions of Long Island's Gold Coast,* and who pointed me to the real gems.

To the staff at the Piping Rock Club for not having my husband and I arrested when we pretended to be members' guests and were found out.

To Nelson DeMille, for his book, *The Gold Coast,* one of my abiding favorites, and another inspiration for the NY setting.

Thanks to Lear Jet for providing details of their aircraft; to Paul Roberts, ex-Navy and commercial pilot who helped me create the realistic airborne event contained herein. And to his wife, Linda, who promised to flog this book on the street corners of Panama as soon as it is in print.

To Niels Sundel who always made sure I had great vacations, whether in Denmark or Spain, and whose generosity knows no bounds.

My deepest gratitude goes to my husband Paul who created the writing casita of my dreams on the hill on the farm we call Heaven-on-Earth. It was from here, looking out to sea, and plugged into a car battery, that I wrote most of *Hubba Hubba*. A more inspirational setting or a more supportive husband simply does not exist. And to trusted readers Elaine Allan, Laurie Kelliher, and my mother, who always tell me what they really think.

Thank you all from the bottom of my heart.

This book is dedicated to the memory of David Jackson, one of Ft Lauderdale's most memorable and successful yacht brokers. Often as I wrote this book, I could picture David, salty dog in hand, exhorting me with laughter to keep it up.

my neck and went out to greet Marty Kahn, my business partner and best friend, who was sitting outside the glass enclosure with his new wife, Melanie. They'd come to join us for a drink.

Looking at the two of them sitting there, I had another sobering jolt. My marriage might not be perfect, I told myself, skittering back into denial, but God help me if I ended up like Marty!

Melanie was the denouement from the end of Marty's first marriage to Marlene—a Gold Coast doyen and mother of Marty's two sons. It had cost him tens of millions to get out of his marriage to Marlene, and all he had to show for it was this surgically enhanced creature whose taffy hair and glossy lips made even the most broad-minded social registrant shudder. Norma Schram (pen name Melanie Muse) wrote children's stories about a band of fugitive teddy bears who lived in the wooded areas around the big North Shore estates and were always being chased away by rich, cranky, shotgun-toting owners.

"Why don't you play at home if you're going to let her humiliate you like that?" Marty asked me as I came towards them.

Hillary had gone directly to the ladies' changing rooms, so I was spared the need to publicly defend her, a role Marty enjoyed thrusting me into at times.

Marty had known me for so many years, I'd lost count. No explanation of my life with Hillary was necessary, nor his with Marlene. The one that still mystified me was his relationship with Melanie.

Hillary might have her faults, I thought, but at least she didn't look at my ear like it was a won ton.

"Hi, Mel," I greeted Marty's wife. "Are we going up for a drink?"

"Oh hi, Richard," she said dreamily. Maybe like her protagonists, she was just coming out of hibernation.

Marty's decision to divorce Marlene and marry Melanie was so much in the "not done" category, that everyone in both Jewish and Gentile circles on the Gold Coast still had trouble coming to terms with it. Though Marty's old money prevented them from becoming complete social pariahs, his status had irrevocably changed. No one knew quite what to do now that Marty had a new, tacky wife that he had met at a book signing at the Barnes and Noble on 25A.

We walked as a threesome up the hill to the clubhouse and sat down under green and white umbrellas with all the other millionaires and billionaires and I ordered a Grolsch.

Hillary was not long in joining us, nodding at us with a tight-lipped smile that meant she still hadn't forgiven me.

I watched Marty watch her, wondering how long it would take him to set the bait and hook her. The Kahns and the Goodmans had an unrelenting competition on the Gold Coast that seemed antediluvian. Maybe in past lifetimes they had also belonged to different clubs, attended different places of worship, and still thought they each lived in a better cave neighborhood—who could say for sure?

Hillary ordered a Perrier from the waiter.

"So, you won," Marty began in the gentle tone that meant Hillary would be kosher dog meat in less than five minutes.

"Marty, if Richard refuses to take even *one* lesson, of course he's going to be a poor loser," my wife said blithely, watching Melanie fondle Marty's ear with a suspended reaction that spoke volumes.

I said nothing.

"At least next Saturday he'll be off the hook," Marty added.

"And it's for a good cause," I said eagerly, trying to keep everyone in their corner, like a good referee. If Hillary and Marty got stuck into each other, it would be like trying to separate two overgrown cacti—and I'd be the one left bleeding in the middle.

"The French Poets?" Marty said disparagingly.

"How much has been raised so far?" Melanie asked. Her blue mascaraed eyes always looked opaque and innocent. I wondered—not for the first time—if she was stoned.

"Actually Melanie, we cannot speak in terms of *cash*," Hillary said, as if the very word was beneath her. "But I have a total of twenty-five items for auction, so the prospects for success on Saturday are excellent."

Melanie looked properly chastised, which seemed to further inflame the defense mechanism already ignited in Marty's brain. "Hillary," he sighed in the manner of a sage to a wayward acolyte, "aren't the French Poets just a bunch of overwrought dilettantes at the end of the day? I'm sure there are more meaningful causes for someone with as much energy as you have..."

Score one for Marty. I thought Hillary would pop a cerebral blood vessel when he'd said this.

"I hardly think scholarships for *deserving* French students..."

Marty did his weary Jewish bit and pushed back his chair. "Don't worry, though, Hill. I'll give something. I know how much it means to you. Let's go, my little schnitzel." He and Melanie got up before Hillary had a chance to react to this, and behind her back, Marty did a perfect imitation of Hillary rolling her eyes. "We'll see you both on Saturday then? At Harbor House?"

"You will," I answered, glad that my old friend's survival instincts were still intact and that we wouldn't have to witness Hillary's wrath decorously unleashed.

"I'll be sure to bring my checkbook." He winked at me. "For the French Poets."

"Bye-bye," Melanie said, doing a little flutter at us with her long, pink nails.

Hillary had her Perrier by the neck and looked as if she would crush it. Good breeding won out, though, and the bottle stayed in one piece.

I let out a sigh, and ordered another Grolsch, wishing I could transport myself to some faraway place. If I did, would Harry Goodman hunt me down and carry through on his promise? The thought gave me the first real diversion I'd had all day.

2.

Our home is modest by Gold Coast standards: a smallish twenty-six room English Tudor of mullioned windows, ancient timbers and imported fireplaces. Placed artfully among the fifteen manicured acres that surround us are a gardener's cottage, a five-car garage, a pool and pool house, a pair of tennis courts, and a small pond stocked with carp. There is also a wooded area, and maybe bears too...I'll have to check with Melanie on that one.

Foxglove Hollow used to belong to Harry Goodman, Hillary's father, but Harry and Beverly prefer Palm Beach now, and so we got the old family homestead for a modest ten million, gutted it, spent another five on renovations and voilá!

The kitchen is state of the art, though Hillary doesn't like to cook.

There is also a gallery where people are put out to pasture before dinner; a Jacobean style dining room that could comfortably accommodate thirty knights and their ladies in medieval regalia; a billiard room; a formal salon; a great hall and a library/study. We have an English pub called "The Old Rose" in the basement which was bought in its entirety by Harry Goodman's father, Harry B. Goodman who brought it over from the West Country panel by panel and had it reconstructed here, right down to the lager taps in solid brass. We have some steamrooms in the basement, a bowling alley, which no one in our generation has ever used, and about fourteen fireplaces throughout the house. The fireplaces were also imported from England and put into place, crests and all.

Upstairs we have the bedroom wings. Elizabeth has one, I have one, and Hillary has the biggest one of all. There are also two guest suites, though I couldn't really describe them to you, as it's been so long since I've stepped into one. Each suite has its own bedroom, dressing room, sitting room and bathroom. My bedroom connects to Hillary's through an outer corridor that is little used these days, and the whole upstairs has been carpeted, at my insistence, against the stone and slate floors for which Harry B. had a particular fondness.

Of the whole house, there's a spot in the kitchen I like best next to a shiny green Aga with an easy chair beside it where Daniel, the chef, and I, share the turf. When I feel like a little human companionship, I go down there and sit and Daniel gives me a snack or sandwich, and I can just relax and read the paper and not have to talk to Daniel or anyone else unless the spirit moves me.

Tonight though, there would be no contemplative silences. Hillary was in one of her talking moods, and being her husband, it was my duty to listen.

"I don't know *who* I feel sorrier for," she began, coming in through the door. We had arrived in separate cars from the club, and so came home that way, too. In spite of my many attempts to get Hillary to hire a driver, she refused. She had numerous tickets to show for her speed-loving ways. In her latest diversion, she staked out the local cops' positions via radio and drove around them— that's why she was late getting home—she was speeding around radar traps instead of taking the most direct route home.

"What do you mean?" I asked.

"*Melanie*, Richard, who else? And Marty. They are just *so* pathetic together. If I were Marlene, I'd move to the West Coast before *ever* suffering the sight of those two together."

"Mmmm," I said.

"And would you tell me *please* why some people just can't seem to check their emotions in public?" she asked, though I knew she wasn't looking for an answer. "There are times when I *honestly* feel embarrassed to be with them." Hillary Goodman Darlington, I thought, Truthsayer Extraordinaire.

She took a breath.

"Love has many strange faces," I said, and immediately regretted my insouciant reply. Hillary gave me a look as if I were a few stocks short of a portfolio.

"How would *you* know?" she asked, at which point Daniel crept out of the room and down to the wine cellar. Coward.

"Well," she said, shoving her tennis things into the waiting hands of Cecilia, the personal maid who had been caring for her since she was ten. "Thank you, missus," Cecilia said, taking the dirty laundry, a small cat smile on her face. Cecilia has had more entertainment value from my marriage to Hillary than most people get from going to the movies. She also has an almost surreal knack for showing up just at the most opportune moments and saving my ass.

"There's no real point in continuing *this* discussion," Hillary said, meaning she would not continue in front of Cecilia. "I'm going up to bed."

I got up and kissed my wife goodnight on the cheek, and went back to my chair and read the *Journal*.

Eventually, Daniel came bravely up from the wine cellar, gave me a glass of skim milk, and made me a crabmeat croissant, which he passed to me saying: "Here you are, sir." No other words were necessary, nor would Daniel ever presume to pass a comment on the lady of the house no matter how cozy we felt together in the relative sanctuary of the kitchen.

After an hour or so of reading, I went upstairs and checked on my wife who was already fast asleep in her Egyptian cotton nightgown. Hillary loves her sleep more than anyone I know, and God help anyone who interferes with it. Sometimes she'll read for awhile, and she secretly loves *The Sopranos*, but mostly she goes directly into a half-hour ritual of cleaning and creaming herself before putting on her Lone Ranger mask, and departing the world for at least nine hours.

On the nights that my wife is interested in having sex, she does not wear the nightie, and turns on only the bedside lamp. This is her signal to me, and has been for years, and every night I check in on her just to see whether I am being welcomed, or not, and more often to see Hillary in a state of repose.

Next I went down the hall to say goodnight to my daughter Elizabeth. Elizabeth is what is commonly known as a geek. In my day we never had girl geeks, only boys. Now all the roles have changed, and it is acceptable for girls to be bookish, computer-crazed and intellectually driven. In my opinion, she simply spends far too much time alone in her room, and though I don't like it, she and her mother have colluded to let me know that my opinion on this subject is not necessary.

I wonder for the hundredth time: How can my daughter who I think is beautiful with her dark hair, creamy complexion and deep brown eyes and who doesn't look like either one of us, sit here alone night after night? Whatever happened to giggling girlfriends, and pajama parties?

"Hi honey," I said, trying to keep my voice neutral, wanting her to turn on a light.

"Be careful you don't strain your eyes."

"Oh, Dad," she said, world-weary. "My eyes are wrecked already, and pretty soon I'll have laser surgery, so don't worry about it." Her perfect complexion had a bluish tinge from the computer screen.

I moved behind her chair in time to see the words: *Pierre, mon amour* on an outgoing e-mail document. Did my little girl have a French pen pal, or was this some grown up man, the kind you read about, who preys on minors over the Internet with a view to achieving something more subversive? Furthermore, was this obsession with French-speaking men only happening in my house, or was it a national plague? Surely there was a chat room for concerned fathers of teenagers whose only relationships were electronic and whose wives had a proclivity for French poets.

"Corresponding with a friend?"

"Yes," she sighed, a signal for me to vacate her space.

"Anyone I know?"

"Dad!"

I tried smiling.

"Stop hovering, okay?" She clicked on the little red X that made the document disappear from view.

"People are not always what they seem, Elizabeth."

"You're telling me!" she snorted, making a pointed reference, I felt, to her mother and me.

"At least we're real, in the flesh people. Not some Internet invention." The words spilled out before I could stop them. Why did I always seem to get off on the wrong foot with my daughter?

"Dad," my daughter said, in the tone of an adult speaking to a child; I had questioned her judgment, and now she was going to get even. "The people I talk to on the 'net, are not inventions, OK? They are some of the nicest people...much nicer than a lot of people I could name."

"Elizabeth..."

"I'm fine Dad, perfectly fine. Really."

Really! If I didn't leave soon, there would be a scene, and scenes with my daughter were never pleasant. I knew I had to choose my battles carefully, for underneath Elizabeth's toughness I knew there was an acute vulnerability, and as her father my instinct was to protect and comfort her first. Confrontation was a distant second.

"OK, I'm leaving."

"Don't worry so much, OK?"

Did my daughter find me as neurotic as I had my own parents at her age, I wondered? And what role did I have around here besides parental trespasser and inept tennis partner?

I closed the door on my daughter's secret life, and went along the vaulted corridor to my own rooms.

Cecilia had already turned down my bed, and warmed the towels, and I stripped down and stepped into the shower where I could be massaged by the pummeling water from six thermostatically controlled showerheads.

I watched myself in the wrap-around mirrors—a fit, wealthy man nearing his fiftieth birthday—and thought back to the scene at the Piping Rock. If I wasn't happy, who did I have to blame but myself?

3.

Hillary could have had her French Poet's benefit at the Seawanhaka Corinthian Yacht Club which is named for the extinct tribe of Native Americans who lived in Long Island before the socialites. But no. Hillary wanted to do her benefits on a grand scale, and the Seawanhaka is just too small, and the Piping Rock and The Creek are too clubby.

So she convinced the Nassau Historical Society to rent her the ballroom from Harbor House, a French chateau which sealed its reputation as "most desirable venue" when the former owner hosted a party in 1924 for the Prince of Wales and the entire British and American polo teams. About a thousand others made up the guest list.

The estate is immense, and only partially open to the public due to limited funding, but for five bucks at certain hours you can still see the resplendent Marie Antoinette bedroom, and a Napoleonic master suite that reputedly belonged to the great, little man himself.

They say the gardens once rivaled those at Versailles, though the fountains no longer sprayed perfumed water into the air, and the marble nymphs were looking a bit slimy, to be honest. Still, Harbor House was a stunning edifice, even by Gold Coast standards, and my wife had her heart set on it.

The ballroom, with its crystal chandelier seven feet across and a rococo ceiling adorned with cherubs in flight—what could be more perfect? It could easily accommodate a crowd of two hundred, and if anyone got tired of donating money, they could just head up the $2,000,000 pink marble staircase and lie down on an Empire-style bed for awhile.

On the big night, we were all in attendance. This was one of the times when Gold Coast WASPS heartily embraced their neighbors, be they Jews, Iranians, Koreans, or simply new billionaires from Silicon Valley. The color of a buck was still green, after all.

Hillary, as one of the area's most prominent residents, backed up by four generations in the New York Social Register, was a world class fund-raiser, and knew instinctively that the best way to *get* the green was to invite the very rich to an imitation French castle where they could dress for their peers, and then bid against each other in a "private auction" that was actually very public.

As a former resident of upstate New York, where my father owned the now defunct Darlington Tannery, I guess you could say I'm still a little incredulous at how these people who have so much money could be so childish. Then again, maybe that's what happens when you've grown up with nannies and ponies, and your own managed portfolio from the age of one.

So, the French chateau at Harbor House it was, an event where cocktails and entertainment would be followed by an auction, then dinner and dancing. A prepaid donation of five hundred dollars per plate had already been solicited with the engraved invitation, all proceeds to benefit the French Poets Society with Michel Depaulier, the head French Poet, leading the charge with my wife.

The theme of the evening was "I Love Paris in the Springtime," and the ballroom did indeed resemble Paris in the spring with opulent displays of dogwood and rhododendron, and some very big hanging scenes of Paris strung up around the perimeter to give the waiters behind-the-scenes maneuvering room.

Marty was there with Melanie, of course, and Melanie was wearing a shocking décolletage that had everyone craning their necks. For old money representation, we had the Astor-Smiths, the Hubbard-Joneses, and a couple of just plain Posts. Milton Kahn, a big fan of Hillary's in spite of the competition of years with her parents, represented the Jewish contingent along with the Goldapples, the Goulstans, and a solitary Guggenheim. For new money, sportswear made by slave labor in Malaysia, we had Bill and June Henniker. I was a little surprised to see that Aubrey Coulter, the man responsible for more Gold Coast interiors than any other, was also in attendance with his companion, a blond-maned stud named Leonard Stuveysant whose ancestors had once owned The Bowery.

The "Girls" were also there, a bevy of seventy-ish widows whose husbands had left them all fortunes. Who would ever believe that this innocent-looking group of four wealthy matrons representing the quintessence of good breeding, would play such a big, rowdy role in my future?

There was Helene du Pont, who could buy and sell everyone at the table at least ten times over; Shelley Wurst, an old B-movie actress with an unfortunate name; Martha Stuart, with a "u" as she is constantly saying these days, and Frances Porter Dodge. These women had lived lives of nearly limitless privilege. Every one of them was well- educated, and was either born or married into some of the wealthiest families in the United States.

On that evening, they simply commanded respect, so I went over to do the correct and gracious thing, and welcome them to my wife's benefit.

"Richard!" Helene du Pont cried, as I came close. She is the Girls' ringleader, and an old flirt who's had at least two face-lifts. She looks to be in her late fifties, though I happen to know from Hillary that she is actually seventy-two.

I went over and took her hand, and kissed it.

"You devil you," she said, beaming up at me.

"You all look wonderful," I said to the table at large. And it was true. Each woman was fit and glamorously turned out; they nearly gleamed with all the pampering they received.

I learned that they had just returned from a cruise, the consensus being that it had been a "little tedious" and "too long."

"The problem is, we're bored," Shelley Wurst told me. "Too many of the ports look the same these days. I'm trying to convince everyone to go up the Amazon, something along those lines."

"So you can pretend you're Kate Hepburn?" Helene shot at her.

Shelley had actually played a bit part in one of Bogart's movies.

"The world really *is* getting incredibly small," Martha said. "We've done every corner of Europe from the Grand Canal to the coast of Norway. We've already been to Africa, Alaska and the Outback. I'm thinking I'd rather stay home and read a good book."

Helene pursed her lips in disapproval. "We'll have none of that," she said.

"We need an adventure," Shelley repeated.

"Would anyone like a drink?" I asked, after a pause. Obviously, this was an ongoing discussion with dissension on all sides. I was better left out of it. I hailed the waiter, then said my good-byes. Marty and Melanie and our new neighbors the Hennikers were waiting at a round table near the stage, and as I sat down a trio of violinists began strolling through the audience playing, *I Love Paris*.

My wife came onstage mid-song looking lovely in a couture strapless gown of peach silk with a woven bodice and trailing scarf that floated behind her.

She greeted the audience with great charm, then introduced Michel Depaulier who came onstage looking both devilishly handsome and a little deviant in his black beret, collarless shirt, and rented tux. A mime was also part of the act, a creative adjunct to give the spending of hundreds of thousands of dollars a light-hearted touch.

Michel went offstage and came back carrying an oil painting, a small Delonnay donated by the Guggenheim family. A professional auctioneer appeared at the podium, and asked for an opening bid of $50,000. The auction had begun.

With everyone's attention firmly on the stage, I excused myself and headed for the men's room, choosing to walk behind the hanging murals that formed the service passageway instead of interrupting the cream of New York society in the midst of the bidding process.

I was halfway around the room when a waiter rushed past, and I pressed myself against the hanging mural to let him by. As I did so I quite clearly heard the voice of Stephen McNead, the tennis pro who was responsible for Hillary's killer serve.

"When you're hot, you're hot," he said in a lewd undertone that obviously did not include the table at large.

I stayed in place, waiting for more.

"Yeah," someone else, a man's voice, agreed, sounding equally lusty.

"She's a looker, our Hill," said McNead.

"A looker *and* a doer," added the other man, and they both chuckled deeply.

The same waiter rushed passed me again with an empty tray, giving me a harassed look that indicated his displeasure at finding me *still* standing in the servants' passageway. I waved him past, feeling myself go from hot to icy cold in seconds. McNead and his companion found no need to say more on the subject of my wife, however, and I could not continue to stand there waiting for more fodder like a big, dumb animal.

I walked into the men's room, moving and smiling, as the words turned over in my gut like hot coals. Had McNead really been talking about my wife? And the other man—I was sure it was Tom—the strapping thirty-ish something man who was now in charge of the pro golf shop. The scenes in which Hillary was "doing" something—and I was sure he was not referring to her golf swing—didn't bear thinking about.

I walked back through the ballroom to my seat, and watched as the mime came out dressed like Napoleon, carrying an antique scabbard that was item number four.

"And what have we *here?*" Hillary asked, hamming it up.

Which was precisely the question I planned to ask her myself, as soon as we were alone.

4.

There are some married men who are serial sex addicts, and those who just dabble. But for some reason, men tend to downplay the fact that many of the women they're getting it on with are married themselves. Therefore, being confronted by the extramarital activity of one's own spouse shouldn't be that much of a shock. But it is, trust me. It is.

Now let me state for the record, that although I won't say I've *never* been unfaithful to my wife, I'm not like some of the men I could name around here who go from one woman to the next like dogs in heat. It's just not my style.

Maybe it was my father's grilling back at my days at Exeter Academy: "If you have to screw around, do it privately. Don't go looking at other women in public, either. Girlfriends and wives hate that sort of thing, and they always find out!"

I've had my share of offers, still do. Some are from women right here on the Gold Coast—their names would surprise you. And their husbands, who think their wives are being faithful while they play sink the salami with their mistresses in the city, would also, I'm sure, be shocked to know how common this kind of activity is here—though it is handled very discreetly, of course, like everything else.

Hillary had been spending at least two evenings a week in the company of the French Poets for the past six months. Marty had said jokingly that Michel Depaulier looked like George Clooney in a beret, which gave us a few laughs over drinks one afternoon at Harry's, but gave me no cause for concern.

If Hillary was one thing, I was sure she was faithful. And even after the comments from McNead and company, I was reluctant to see it differently.

Maybe they had been talking about someone else, and I had misunderstood. Maybe they had said Jill. Jillian Sanders had been seated close by. Or 'Lil—though the latter was doubtful. Lillian Mordecai was eighty years old, and seated across the room.

I also realized that apart from a two-sentence exchange, I had absolutely no proof that my wife was screwing around.

And how could I ever accuse Hillary, my highbred wife of twenty years, on such thin evidence?

I see now in hindsight that I'd also begun to weave a tightly knit cocoon of justifications around our marriage by simultaneously forgiving Hillary any indiscretion, while denying any indiscretion had occurred at all. I was also enjoying a certain degree of superiority in our relationship, like a high-ranking diplomat who knows how to keep hostility from developing into an armed conflict. I was just taking the elevated road, being the bigger person.

She continued to go to the club, and come home looking happy, even bouncy, and I remained mute and celibate as a gelding.

Little did I know that the coconuts were going to start falling, and I was going to be standing right underneath.

5.

When I look back at my life before discovering Hubba Hubba, everything makes sense, as it tends to do with the advantage of a restored sense of humor. For example, today I can see that events seemed to conspire to make me transform my life, even as

I resisted the change, like a dog in front of a fire, drowsy and inert.

After the French Poet's benefit, I began to feel as if nothing mattered: not the house, the cars, the clubs, any of it. I was firmly in my cocoon, and like a drugged pupae who might vaguely wonder what's going to happen next, I was too enervated to pull back the layers of safety and have a good look.

Was it any surprise, then, that an outside force would attack my apathy in the form of my best friend? And that as a result, my life would never be the same again?

On that fateful Monday, about two weeks after Hillary's highly successful benefit, I was headed, as usual, to the offices I share with Marty Kahn and his father Milton at One New York Plaza.

Raymond, the brooding Pole, drove me into the city in the black Lincoln Town Car as he had for years. Maybe it was from a sense of duty, or maybe it was the great view of the Sound from the offices that Milton leased from Goldman Sachs on the fifteenth floor, that I went there at all. Mostly, I think it was just a habit, plain and simple.

Unless travel or health interferes, Marty and I worked from ten to one Monday through Thursday, mostly meeting with our analysts to consider new investments and review existing ones.

At just after one, we'd head over to either Harry's or the India House for lunch. Afterwards we'd have a half-hour meeting with Milton to keep him updated, and I was headed back over the Throgs Neck Bridge well before four in the afternoon.

On this particular Monday, we had a morning meeting with the analysts. As I opened the door to the conference room, I heard Marty: "Come *on*! There's only one way to market an *herb*, for God's sake! The boomers only want to feel like they're back in the sixties, anyway. Find one of those hippie companies in Maine and let them handle distribution. If we try and go through the FDA, I'll be in an urn on somebody's mantel before we get approval."

"Hi everybody," I said, walking in and taking my seat. "What's up?"

"Our resident genius has found some Venezuelan doctor who has made this plant infusion that reduces high blood pressure in less than 24 hours, all naturally. We've got his studies here, and it looks real enough. Put a little bag of this dried herb in boiling water like tea and bingo! No more high blood pressure."

"How much?"

"Could be cheap, could be expensive, depending how fast we get down there. Thing is this: The plant grows wild in Venezuela in quote, regrowing pastureland that is partially wooded, unquote. But it's also pretty common throughout Central and South America. It just so happens our doctor is Venezuelan and has done his research there."

"A common plant that's a miracle drug? Sounds like morinda," I said. I still regretted not having invested in the French Polynesian farms which were now churning out the latest touted cancer "cure" and anti-oxidant through their processing plant in Utah. The worldwide market for morinda—or "noni" juice—was huge, and growing.

"Exactly," Marty told me. "You know how the boomers are. We could be flavor of the month for awhile like Cherry Garcia, then the market will become saturated with other brands, and we'll want out." Marty, at forty-eight, was solidly in the boomer category, but liked to pretend otherwise. Hillary had a photo of Marty at Berkeley, a Chicago Seven groupie, with long hair and an annual mid-six-figure trust-fund income while he was still under twenty-one. He didn't fool me for a second. I knew how radical Marty had been, and still was, even if his custom-made Italian wardrobe and family income seemed to contradict this.

"So market it as a maintenance thing for people with chronic high blood pressure?" I asked.

"That's one way to go," the analyst was enthusiastic. "You could do a whole range of products, actually. A blood pressure maintenance pill, a three-day treatment for intervention, and a one-pill special like they do with Viagra. You know? Pop goes the weasel." He laughed at this, and Marty looked at him.

"Who needs Jim Carrey when we've got you?"

"A few articles in *Mature Living*, and pretty soon you've got the whole senior population taking it as a supplement," I said ignoring them. "What about a name?"

"LBP?" the analyst asked, suddenly shy. "You know, an acronym for low blood pressure."

"Rhymes with LSD," Marty said, nodding his head. I could tell he liked the idea.

I liked it too, though I thought the name still needed work. What I didn't know was how much this conversation, and where it would lead me, was going to change my life.

"Let's do lunch," Marty said after the meeting, giving me a meaningful look which meant he had information for me he didn't want to share with the room at large.

So, we walked over to India House around one, a sedate members' club on Hanover Street and sat at our usual table. Before I could object, Marty ordered a Wild Turkey on the rocks for himself, and a Speyside for me. We didn't normally drink at the club during the day, it was just something we weren't in the habit of doing. We'd have a drink at Harry's to celebrate a venture, or split a bottle of wine, but today was a Monday. There was nothing unusual to celebrate. No problems that required a stiff drink—at least that I knew of.

Our drinks came; Marty remained pensive and silent, something very out of character for him.

He took his drink and half drained his glass, indicating that I should do the same. The single malt, meant to be sipped, was raw on my throat. I raised my eyebrows, feeling tense. What was this all about?

"We need to talk," he began, as dread flooded my bloodstream. Just how bad was it? And was it business, or personal?

"You've been a good friend to me, Richard," he began. He was talking now about all the times we had talked about Marlene, Melanie and his choice for a new life.

"You're smart, caring, and give excellent advice," he went on, looking at me with brown, basset hound eyes. Marty's eyes, which turn down at the corners, have always looked a little sad to me. "I don't know how I would've survived my divorce from Marlene without you."

I wanted to scoff at this, but was too busy wondering where he was leading. I hadn't seen Marty so serious, or deliberate in a long time.

"Do you remember how you told me to follow my heart about Melanie?" he asked. "I know that wasn't easy for you. I know you never approved of Mel, probably still don't."

I started to protest this, but knew it would sound phony. He was right; I'd never thought Melanie was a good match for him, but it wasn't my life, it was his.

"The thing is you didn't judge me for my choice, and that is rare, very rare, Richard." He took his glass, jangled the remaining Wild Turkey against ice, and threw it down his throat. He waved his hand, and ordered us two more.

"That's why I don't want you to think that what I'm about to say is about me standing in judgment of *anyone*. It's very important you understand this."

"Christ, Marty. Stop torturing me!"

"Okay, alright." He fixed me with this look, as if still making up his mind, then decided to proceed. "If I told you your wife was getting it on with the Frenchman, what would you say?"

"What?" I asked, nearly choking. A sudden vision of Hillary laughing with pleasure, her long, creamy neck arching the way it did when we made love, shot into my head like a clip from a movie. McNead had been right! Christ, how many men *were* there?

"You know—the guy onstage with her?"

"Michel Depaulier?" I murmured, as if saying his name aloud would help me get the reality of it. I had another flash, this one of Michel Depaulier banging my wife *sans* his little French hat. Where had they done the dirty deed or deeds? The possibilities grew exponentially; the clip was becoming a mini-series in less time than a subway stop.

"Are you sure?" I continued. But I already knew. If Marty Kahn was telling me this about Hillary, he had incontrovertible proof; this was not a little bit of gossip overheard behind a curtain.

"How do you know?"

"I saw them," he stated, "that night after tennis? He kissed her goodnight in her car; they were in the shadows and thought they were alone." He looked angry just thinking about it.

"Hell, Marty, a kiss…"

"So I had them followed," he continued, looking grim. "I hired an investigator and he has been tailing Hillary for two weeks: at the beach, in a motel on the south coast in a wig and a rental car…I'm sorry Richard. I wouldn't be surprised if you never forgave me." He passed me the photos.

"Shit," I said, and drained my drink, too. "I never thought she'd stoop so low."

"Stoop so low?" Marty seemed to find this amusing.

"Yes!"

"Hillary may be rich, Richard, but she's still flesh and blood. Just another human being wanting to get her ya-yas out."

"Her ya-yas?"

"Just like you."

"I have ya-yas, too?" I could feel the hostility building. How dare another man fuck my wife!

"Do you still love her?" Marty asked, swirling his drink. I found it strange he would ask.

"That seems beside the point right now," I told him.

"Is it?"

"Yes it is."

"That's not what you told me about Marlene."

"What exactly did I tell you about Marlene?" The sarcasm in my voice was as thick as the veal chop on the plate in front of me.

"You told me I should follow my heart."

"I said that?"

"You did. And I quote: If you love Melanie more than Marlene, you should leave Marlene."

"How profound!"

"Don't kid around," Marty said, fixing me with those rabbinical eyes. "It *is* profound. Profoundly simple. And that's why I decided to do what I did."

"Have my wife followed?" I still wasn't sure how I felt about this.

"Yes."

"So I'd know if I still loved her when I found out she was fucking someone else?"

"Exactly. And do you?"

"Of course," I said. But *did* I? Even as I came out with this knee-jerk response, I wondered if it was true.

And what about our daughter Elizabeth?

I sat across from Marty, and stared out the window wondering if anything more than my pride had been wounded. Wondering if after twenty years, I still loved my wife, and if I did, what I was prepared to do about it.

6.

I went back to the office in a stunned state. Marty met with his father privately, and I sat in my office rolling my Montblanc between my fingers. The view outside my window was gray and drab. What the hell was I doing here? My young life had been spent outdoors on hard playing fields, in trees, running through the deep woods that bordered our house.

Now I sat in a big box in a five-thousand-dollar leather chair and reflected about how I'd gotten here. Years before, while Marty was still smoking dope full time and dabbling with his third unfinished dissertation, Milton read the *Business Week* article, and made me an offer I couldn't refuse.

I'd made millions for Milton and a healthy percentage for myself before Marty came on the scene, a West Coast rebel who Milton thought I could tame and train.

Marty's dark wit had been a balm to my WASP soul, and we became friends. I'd taught him everything I knew, and we'd had fun. But accumulating money with Marty and Milton had moved way beyond fun, challenges, needs, wants or even future security. It had evolved from a challenge into a predictable, deadening, moneymaking habit.

Was my marriage to Hillary in the same category? Michel Depaulier had put on a little beret, written some poetry only other French poets could understand, and slid into home base with my wife. Had I been neglecting Hillary? Or had I simply stopped caring a long time ago?

My reverie was broken by Elaine, who buzzed to tell me Helene du Pont was on the line. Now this was a surprise. Helene was in that circle of social contacts we had dinner with twice a year. We occasionally met at event like my wife's recent fundraiser, but it was most unusual for her to call me at the office.

Curious, I picked up the phone.

"*Richard*!" she greeted me warmly. "Wasn't it a wonderful evening the other night? I can't tell you how much we enjoyed it. Hillary certainly has many talents, doesn't she?"

I agreed she did.

"We all enjoyed ourselves *immensely*."

"I'll be sure to tell her." *The cheating bitch.*

"But that's not why I'm calling," Helene du Pont told me.

"No?"

"Richard, you know that you have an *excellent* reputation for making successful investments. I daresay you have quite a lot of notoriety in this regard. In fact I know a good many people in our circle who would *love* to know your secrets."

"That's very kind of you Helene," I said, feeling tired. I knew she hadn't called to flatter me; Helene also knew that we did not handle anyone's money but our own. Our business was strictly a private affair.

"The thing is, I'm looking for a little advice, and thought you might help."

"You know I'm happy to help." How many more platitudes could I squeeze into this conversation?

"Thank you, Richard. I know that is sincerely meant. Regarding my financial situation, I'm happy to report that I'm on solid ground. It's just that I have had a most annoying development regarding a family member who has a personal problem and needs some protection for her assets."

I wondered what "family member" she could mean. And how serious was it if she was calling me instead of relying on her well-trusted and well paid team of advisors? I had a suspicion that the "family member" was Helene herself, and that for some reason she didn't want to consult with her own people.

"Offshore is really not my specialty," I told her. If I'd done anything right in my life, it was to have a complete above-board, trouble-free relationship with the Feds. "But there are many ways to go. Remember though, there are risks. The IRS recently forced the Bahamian government to name names through U.S.-based corporations like American Express. You might suggest a Nevada corporation, or a corporation in the Caymans held through a trust in Belize. The problem is getting the money out of the country."

"I didn't realize it had gotten so *complicated*." She sounded genuinely distressed by my news, and to cheer her up, I referred her to a group of lawyers in Baltimore who specialized in something called offshore asset protection. I gave her a thumbnail sketch: There were family limited partnerships, limited liability companies, revocable and irrevocable trusts, all designed to protect the assets of high net worth individuals.

"If you use them, you won't have to put the money on a sailboat, and sail the cash away. Remember Helene, there's always an electronic trail when you move money today. But if you move it around the *right* way, you'll have a firewall around you."

"A firewall?" she asked, sounding confounded.

"Just call them. Tell them I referred you." I pulled my contacts list up on the screen, and gave her the details she wanted. I wanted the conversation to end; talking about money had seriously started to bore the shit out of me.

She thanked me and asked if Hillary and I would be free for dinner soon.

"Of course," I said, trying to sound cheery at the prospect. An evening at Helene du Pont's was nothing if not memorable. At one dinner party in the mid-eighties, Adnan Khashoggi, the Queen of Denmark, and Henry Kissinger had all been present. In spite of the radical mix of guests, the evening had been a resounding success. That was Helene du Pont. She was a world-class hostess whose fortune and social standing made her impossible to ignore. I was therefore mystified to hear something that sounded like insecurity in her voice.

"You know Richard, if these offshore consultants really can do the job, I have several friends who will also be interested."

"Good luck, Helene."

"I'll call your wife," she told me, "about dinner plans."

My wife. Those two little words, so commonplace, now infused me with a righteous anger that I could hardly wait to divest myself of.

I called Raymond to bring the car.

7.

I drove across the Throgs Neck Bridge feeling like the photos might burn a hole in my lap, right through my leather briefcase. Marty had walked me to the elevator, practically cheering me on: a Hillary come-uppance, at last!

But how should I begin? *So, are the beds comfortable at the Strawberry Bankes Motel?* Or: *Gee, Hillary, I never realized you liked French poetry quite so much.*

Would she become tearful? Filled with remorse? What penance would I extract? What threats to make her stop? At the back of my mind, the question haunted me: Did I really care if she stopped at all?

Imagine my surprise when I pulled into the driveway ready for the biggest confrontation in my marriage, and saw an ambulance parked next to the front door at Foxglove Hollow. Red lights revolved and flashed, and I watched dumbfounded as two men carried someone out on a stretcher.

Hillary dashed out behind them, and even as I got out of the car, I could see she was crying, nearly hysterical.

"It's Cecilia!" she cried, running towards me. "I found her collapsed in the middle of the hall. Oh God, Richard. They said she had a heart attack!"

Cecilia died several days later in the intensive care unit of the hospital, and my wife remained distant and inconsolable.

After the funeral, I simply went back to work.

And made plans to go to Caracas to meet Dr. Herb.

On the Sunday before my departure, I told Hillary about my plans. I even invited her to go with me as a kind of sick joke.

She was red-eyed and looked exhausted. "Caracas, Richard? Where that horrible dictator is, and they just had all those mud slides? No thank you." She sipped black coffee, looking at me over the gold rim of Lenox china. "When will you be back?"

I knew what she was planning, of course: lots of uninterrupted *rendezvous* and solace from you-know-who.

"I'll be back on Thursday," I said, pretending to read the paper.

Elizabeth came down and put her arms around my neck, and I felt my body infuse with righteous indignation again. How dare Hillary put our daughter's reputation in jeopardy? What if Elizabeth found out about Depaulier? What if someone else did?

When I got back, I'd confront Hillary about her affair and make sure it ended, whatever it took.

That night I headed into the city and stayed at a hotel near the airport. I needed to get out of Foxglove Hollow.

DISCOVERY

1.

Our Lear 45, Marty's, Milton's and mine was a private aluminum tube ideal for escape. At ten years old it had cost over three million dollars; and we spent another five hundred thou a year in maintenance and crew salaries, but it suited us perfectly for our international travel needs. If the Minister of Finance in the Dominican Republic invited me to his home with two days' notice for dinner to discuss mineral leases, I could be there. If the Chinese Ambassador called and wanted to meet Marty the next day in Vancouver to discuss a start-up for a government-sponsored Internet portal, he could be there, too.

We had it on good authority that a major drug company was considering a buyout of our Venezuelan doctor's magic blood pressure herb and his ten years of scientific research. There was also talk of floating it on the stock exchange in Caracas. If we could get there first and cut a deal, we'd have a foolproof winner. My old moneymaking instincts were still firmly in place.

The next morning at six, Raymond brought me to the hangar at La Guardia. My Danish pilot, Eric, and his ample blonde wife and co-pilot Helga had flown for SAS for a combination of thirty years through some of the roughest weather Scandinavia could dish out. Marty and I had decided they would be a perfect team for our new-to-us jet. We headhunted them in Copenhagen one night when we were all staying at the same hotel, and they'd been with us ever since.

As a team, they were capable, intelligent, experienced, and had a solid marriage. Unlike pilots who too often loved to carouse the bars at night, Eric and Helga Damskov, married and childless, kept each other company and went to bed early.

We were given clearance at approximately oh eight hundred and took off from New York into a jewel of a day with no heavy winds and a shimmering blue sky. Our ETA was 15:20, Caracas time, a flight of about six hours.

I kept myself busy doodling on my yellow pad. There were house-like squares with arrows inside, as if I could control the problem by putting walls around it. Without really thinking about it, I began making a list about my marriage to Hillary.

It looked like this:

Sex sucks
Pompous bitch
What conversation?
Adversarial relationship
FUCKING DEPAULIER!!! (And how many others?)

On the plus side, I had:

Good mother
Financially independent
Well educated
Twenty years is a long time.
The devil you know?
Once loved her? Still do?

It reminded me of one of those plus/minus lists I'd make before going ahead with a business investment.

I thought back to the early years of our relationship. How Harry's reluctance turned into grudging support about our getting married. Virtually overnight, I'd gone from pariah to Anointed One, and suddenly there were all these parties. I was whisked along, giddy and happy. It felt like I'd been chosen. But did I love her? Did I love her even then? I looked outside the plane into seamless blue skies...

And heard one of the engines shut down.

What the...?

Around us lay miles of empty Caribbean Sea, and right below, an island looking like a big errant golf green surrounded by white sand traps and pale blue water. I went forward to the cockpit, my stomach tight with fear.

"It's the oil pressure, sir," Eric told me, looking tense. "We need to make a precautionary landing."

"Where?" I wondered aloud, trying to keep a grip on my fast-disintegrating control.

Helga pointed to the island on the chart, but Eric said the landing strip was for small craft only.

He then asked me politely, but firmly, to return to my seat. We started our descent. Helga—who was now totally concentrated on the charts—announced that we were headed for a private runway in a place called Platanillo. It was used by corporate jets for visiting banana executives, I heard her say.

We changed course.

"Please strap yourself in, sir," Eric told me over the PA.

Anxiety began closing my throat like a vise. What if we had a loss of oil pressure in the other engine, too? What if I died without having done any of things I'd wanted to do?

Eric and Helga conspired in intense voices, and my imagination spun into overdrive. Suddenly, I wanted to live, to be alive with an intensity I'd never known. My whole body seemed to ignite as I listened to Eric talk on the radio, first in Spanish, then English.

"We're seven miles from Platanillo," he turned around and told me. "They're clearing the decks for us now."

"Clearing the decks?" I asked. Neither Helga nor Eric could hear me with their earphones on.

I heard the word "cows."

"Don't worry," Helga turned and reassured me. "It's four-hundred meters long; it's enough to land, but more importantly to take off again."

Eric circled around and as we began our descent to Platanillo, the green island's town revealed itself right in our flight path. I had a flash of blue, pink, and green houses tilting at odd angles, curving palm trees, opalescent water and sugary beaches. I blinked and suddenly we were flying over dense green jungle. Small islets appeared just offshore like green jigsaw pieces that had broken free.

I tried to materialize more solid ground and was rewarded by a little beach, a dusty-looking town, and then more bananas than I'd ever dreamed could be planted in one place. The banana company's runway had to be close now.

"Prepare to land," Eric said to me over the PA, and then we hit the runway with a thump. Eric braked hard, and I was thrown forward against my seat belt as we bounced over uneven tarmac.

We finally stopped, the single engine whining itself to silence. I undid my belt, and went forward to the cockpit.

"Thank God," I said to my pilots, jubilant to be on the ground. Ten yards in front of us, the runway ended; beyond that lay the sparkling Caribbean Sea. In the distance, the green island shimmered like a mirage.

"We're here," Eric said. His normally stoic face was filled with relief.

"Where did you say *here* was?"

"Platanillo," Helga told me. We all seemed to find this quite funny.

"And what's that little piece of paradise over there?" I pointed seaward to the island, which I estimated was five miles offshore.

"That," Helga told me, her finger still on the chart, "is Hubba Hubba."

"Hubba Hubba?"

"I've never heard of it," she said to Eric. "Have you?"

"No."

Eric said, "I never saw the oil pressure decrease so fast, I had to shut the engine down. Let's hope it's a faulty gauge…or the oil pressure transmitter." Helga nodded at this. I patted myself on the back that I'd had the sense to hire Eric who was also a qualified mechanic.

Problems in my marriage to Hillary suddenly seemed very insignificant.

We suddenly heard a siren, and outside the cockpit window an old red fire truck—I later learned it was a vintage 1924 American-

We headed down the airstrip; Shakey avoiding the ruts and bumps like obstacles on a computer game screen. For someone who gave the impression of being laid-back, he drove like a madman.

"Where you from?" he asked me eventually, eyes on the road.

"New York."

"Nice shiny plane. Too bad it got troubles." *Trabells.*

"Yes, well. Eric should have it all sorted out soon," I said with the easy optimism of someone whose "trabells" were almost always sorted out by someone else.

Shakey, a few shades darker and a foot taller than Archibold, spoke English more clearly than the other man. I asked him what his name meant.

"Dat short for Shakespeare," he said, nodding and smiling, like it made perfect sense to be named after a 16th century bard.

We turned off the airstrip and onto a partially paved road, which Shakey drove on like he was a commuter with a tight schedule. He swerved violently around each pothole, honked at all traffic, and at all pedestrians, muttering under his breath the whole time. I thought how the same behavior on the Tri-Borough Bridge would probably get him shot by some overwrought commuter for whom a honking horn was the absolute last straw.

After passing several miles of banana plants, he made another sharp turn and we were in the "town" of Platanillo. I looked around. The one-street settlement consisted of a string of wooden buildings in faded pastel colors. There was a small market, a shoe repair shop that doubled as a radio station, a restaurant with fried chicken in a glass case out front, and a fruit and vegetable stand banged together from some old boards. An immense concrete building with the name "El Turco," blaring calypso music onto the street, seemed to offer everything else from fans and baby clothes to umbrellas and kerosene. A cavernous structure with a tin roof announced the word "Bus" in bold yellow and red letters at the end of the main drag. But there were no buses, only two empty benches and another little restaurant that looked shut down.

"No hotel?" I could no longer contain my surprise at what Platanillo had to offer.

"Oh, ho, ho," Shakey kept shaking his head back and forth. "A hotel in Platanillo? No hotel here."

Helga and I looked at each other. "Well, the Lear will be fixed soon, and we can get back into air-conditioning and be on our way." Even to my own ears, my voice sounded snobby and filled with false bravado. I could not honestly remember the last time I had been seriously inconvenienced in any way.

"Coca?" Shakey asked, eager to please.

"Oh no," I said, misunderstanding. "I don't do drugs."

Shakey laughed. "No drugs, man. Just Coca, you know Coca-Cola? The stuff you drink?"

"Ah," I said. "Coca-Cola. Yes, let's have a cold drink. Why not?"

One cold Coke later, we were back in the jeep headed to the airstrip. Shakey drove up the airstrip at high speed, as if we were diplomats, and came to a screeching halt just short of the Lear's front tire.

Helga and I got out to get the news from Eric, and I couldn't have been more surprised when he said: "I'm afraid it's not good news, sir. I did a boroscope of the engine, and mechanically she's fine except for the transmitter. We're going to have to courier the part down from Kansas, then I can install it."

"What?" I asked, feeling incredulousness sink in. "Courier? If you could see Platanillo, you'd know how unlikely that is."

Both Helga and Eric looked sorrier than I'd ever seen them. I knew that Eric's diagnosis couldn't be questioned, but felt aggravated that such a small thing could cause such a big delay. Shakey listened to all this, smiling and nodding. A man who already had the answer. "You gonna ship it to Concepción," he told us. "Then I gonna pick it up."

"How far to Concepción?" I asked him.

He made a motion with his hands, so and so. "'Bout eight hours. Gotta take da ferry to Rambala, but I drive quick—so maybe we do it in seven."

counterpoint, a petite, white, thirtyish woman, Wanda herself, with blonde, cotton-candy hair and heavy make-up, strutted in a pink sequined outfit with matching shoes looking like a miniature Marilyn Monroe.

The women each had a banner across her chest with her name. Wanda's said 'Wanda Lust' in loopy red letters that sparkled with more glitter and Jim leaned over and whispered, "That's not her *real* name. Real name's Wanda Petrowski. From up north, Manchester, New Hampshire."

"Really?"

"Loves to get all dolled up, does Wanda."

Each woman had a chance to walk in a circle once by herself, while the other contestants stood in a line and politely clapped. The judging was based on audience response, and from the sound of it, Wanda was a big favorite. The audience whooped and yelled as she walked in a hip-swinging circle, though she was as reedy as a broom stick with as many curves.

"Don't look that good at home," Big Jim said. "Keeps the wig for special events."

In the end, after a lot of foot stomping and catcalls, a local woman named Lucia won. She was forty-four, and the mother of seven. A tall, stunning young woman named Seferina came in second, and Wanda came in third. By two a.m., defying every rule I knew about beauty contests, the unlikely Queen and her court stood alone. Each woman received a branch of frangipani blossoms and a bottle of Mi Abuela, and the audience applauded loud and long.

Big Jim eventually went behind the curtain to collect Wanda, and I continued to sit there as the crowd thinned out, feeling the swirling happiness, the good-will-toward-all mood that was an indicator of true drunkenness.

When I thought of Hillary in a Jackie O disguise meeting Michel Depaulier in a seedy motel room, I started to laugh out loud. What a farce my life had become, living on the Gold Coast. All those social registrants conspiring to pretend the old protocols mattered, then behaving secretly without any decorum at all! My wife was fucking a French poet, and probably the golf pro, as well. The prim and proper Mrs. Hillary Darlington was really just a common slut!

Once I started to laugh, I couldn't seem to stop. People stared, some looked worried, and others laughed along with me. I picked up the Mi Abuela bottle and took a long swig. God, it felt good to be free: free of Hillary, Marty, Foxglove Hollow and all the trappings of a gentrified life. What a load of crap!

I couldn't remember the last time I'd laughed so hard. For the past twenty years, my life had been like a long-running comedy act, and I was only getting the punch line now.

Luckily, Big Jim came along and interrupted my one-man show with a gentle reminder that tomorrow was Hubba Hubba Day. We needed some sack time. I got up and looked at Jim, then at the woman by his side with short, spiky brown hair, and no eyebrows. Wanda?

I don't remember getting back to the Boatel, I'll admit it, nor do I have any recollection of sleeping at a 15-degree angle in my bed. What I most definitely do remember, though, is being peeled off the mattress at dawn by The Swinging Dicks, who were going from block to block, rousing everyone from their beds with a short, brassy blast of the island's theme song.

Hubba Hubba Day had begun, and it wasn't even six a.m.

5.

Hubba Hubba Day is really a week-long carnival that starts with the naming of the Queen and her court, continues with drinking and dancing for six straight days and nights, then ends with everybody getting soaked with seawater from a fire hose they attach to a tank truck in the center of the Calle Principal. On my first visit I was only there for three days—thank God.

Hubba Hubba Day requires training, I've learned, and lots of pacing.

As I said, day one burst forth with a brassy blast, which peeled me off the mattress, and at seven I gave up trying to go back to sleep and staggered toward the smell of coffee like a caffeine-addicted Bela Lugosi.

A slight woman with a spiky hairdo, looking like an elf in a kid's story, turned and greeted me with a grin.

"Wanda?" I asked. The blonde hair was nowhere in evidence. Thin little pencil lines accentuated large gray eyes in a pale face.

"You look like shit," she told me. "Siddown, I'll fix you up." She poured me a big mug of black coffee and stirred in a tablespoon of sugar, then added a tablespoon of Mi Abuela rum. "My Grandmother" was following me wherever I went

"Hair of the dog?" I asked, giving her the devilish smile that women always said made me look boyish.

"When you're an alchy, you know all the tricks," she said, ignoring the smile. "Drink up, it'll set you right." Her accent had a New England woodsy twang. She watched me with serious, lucid eyes.

"Jim says you crash landed your jet over in Platanillo."

"Not exactly."

"Stayin' in Hubba Hubba long?" She hummed under her breath, and walked her finger across the counter as if they were legs going somewhere.

"Probably another day or two." She moved her fingers more dramatically now, up and down like the kicking legs of a chorus girl, and I realized she was choreographing something.

"You'll get hooked," she said suddenly, fixing me with those big eyes, which were not gray, but a pale blue with flecks of gold, like a kaleidoscope.

"Really, I don't normally drink so much, I…."

"Not on *Mi Abuela*," she said, as if I didn't have both oars in the water. "Hooked on Hubba Hubba."

Big Jim chose that moment to make an appearance. "Leave the paying guests be, Wanda J," he said as firmly as a father, and I saw that there was at least a thirty year difference between them. Wanda sulked off, and a couple of minutes later a loud version of Ravel's *Bolero* began emanating from the Boatel's forward cabin.

"These alchies," Big Jim said, as he reached in the fridge and grabbed himself a cold Ice. "As unpredictable as a *por*coopine in heat."

Footsteps on the deck above indicated a visitor. It was Shakey, who came down the companionway. A Hubba Hubba girl, amply endowed, followed.

"Hey Shakey, how you be?" asked Jim.

"I be right here, Mr. Jim," Shakey said. "Right here." The girl, she must've been all of twenty-one, smiled at me and I smiled back. Oh boy.

"This here's Julie," Shakey told me. "My cuzin."

"*Hola*," the girl said. Her dimples were big enough for me to lose my finger in up to the first knuckle. She leaned forward to give me a nice limp island handshake and for a moment I thought those magnificent coconuts might break free from that cumbersome cotton dress she was wearing.

The three men in the room held their breath in anticipation, and then the moment passed. Julie stood up, and Big Jim passed around a plate of toast that was brown only on one side.

6.

Happiness is like that. One minute you're riding the crest, the next minute you've crashed into bed in a leaning Boatel having one of the most prophetic nightmares of your life.

Hubba Hubba Day finally took a breather around two in the afternoon, and people wandered off to the shade of the park where dozens of little kiosks offered grilled sausages and chicken, fried yuca and rice and lots of icy Ice and soda. The ice cream vendors and ice cone shavers were doing a brisk business, and I had a dripping mango swirl before heading back to Big Jim's for some sack time.

I had partied, danced, and been in a parade. Two hours' sleep the night before was finally taking its toll.

Jim had gone off to find a guy called Moses, and Wanda and the girls had wandered back to Seferina's to change. Shakey had gone up the road to La Cabaña with Julie and Coralia, Julie's aunt, to "rist up," and so I had the tilting giant to myself.

Inside the Boatel it was hot and stuffy, so I turned on all the little fans that Jim had affixed to the walls and got the air moving. I found a big pitcher of ice water in the fridge, and poured half of it over my head and drank the rest.

My cabin was dark and cooler now, and I shut my eyes as tiredness pushed me down, sucking my head into the dark, moldy, netherworld of the lumpy, foam pillow.

And then the sun came out and was streaming through the little checked curtains. I was naked in a bed with an equally naked Hillary, and we were young and giggling, preparing to make illicit love before our wedding day.

Suddenly the door was flung open and Michel Depaulier was standing there. "I want my hat back," he told me, and grabbed his beret off my head and stood at the end of the bed glaring at me.

"What about my suit?" I asked him, because he was indeed wearing one of my best hand-tailored worsteds.

"Finders keepers," he said, crossing his arms over his chest. He smirked at me and laughed.

Hillary began laughing too.

"What's so funny?" I asked, not getting the joke.

"Losers weepers," he added, tears running down his face. He couldn't stop laughing.

"Wait just one minute…"

"Oh Richard, it's just a game," Hillary told me. "Don't you think it's funny?"

"No," I said. "I don't think it's funny." And to Depaulier: "You French dickhead."

"Sticks and stones," Michel said, wiping his eyes and becoming serious. "This suit is mine now."

Hillary got out of bed looking ill at ease, and put on her red hunting coat—nothing else—and went and stood next to Depaulier. I could only think of how hot she must be, for the room had become stifling. Where were Jim and Wanda?

Marty was there too, standing next to Hillary on the other side. He was wearing a black robe like a judge. Didn't anyone know we were in the tropics?

"Do you love her, Richard?" my best friend asked me.

"Of course I do," I said. But the three of them looked at me with contempt and pity; I was a sicko who couldn't be helped.

"Tell us the truth," said Marty. "We need an answer now, Richard."

I felt panic seize my gut. Who was Marty to judge me?

"I….don't know. But it's not my fault, it's hers!" I pointed at Hillary. "When you're hot you're hot!"

Suddenly, Wanda stuck her head in the door. "Liar!" she cried, and everyone else nodded.

They all looked at me as if I need to be committed. "We could try the bamboo cage," Depaulier said, as sweat poured down my face.

Hillary said, "You never loved me, Richard. I know that now."

"But you're a looker *and* a doer," I announced, as if this would clear up the misunderstanding.

"And you're as phony as my falsies," Wanda said, pointing her finger at me. "Face it."

"I'm going to have to tell my father the truth," Hillary added, looking at me sadly. Everyone nodded again. They knew what this meant: Harry Goodman was going to kill me.

"It's a life sentence, Richard," Marty told me, a reluctant judge. "Marriage is a sacred vow, and you blew it."

"WE HAD TO GET MARRIED!" I screamed at my jury, and woke up drenched in sweat, my heart pounding. The little fans had stopped working, and the cabin was airless, suffocating—but drop kick me, Jesus! At least I was awake.

I pulled myself up with my still hammering heart and went into the bathroom to douse myself with cold water. A red-faced, disheveled man stared at me in the mirror.

I took some deep breaths, trying to bring my adrenaline level back into normal range. With more cold water the flush left my face.

I looked at myself hard in the mirror: Hillary and I had to get married. Had it really taken me twenty years and a nightmare in a tropical sauna to dredge up *that* little morsel from my subconscious?

We were sitting on the pier of the yacht club one evening after cocktails when she told me the truth., that she was pregnant. She'd always been so cool and controlled, but suddenly she was falling apart. A few days later, Harry had called and invited me to meet with him in his study. I sat drinking cognac and waiting, terrified, while he gave me *his* proposal. The rest was history.

But Wanda was right, too. Marrying someone like Hillary had been one in a line of challenging goals that I had set for myself, and then achieved. I was a fake, a phony who had worked for so many years to belong in Hillary's world that I'd even convinced *myself* I belonged there.

As a young man my father had insisted I attend the right schools, play the right sports, and cultivate the bearing that would make me a marriageable prospect for an *important wife*. I had worked my magic on Harry Goodman, won his sudden acceptance, and spent years proving to everyone in Hillary's life that I belonged at Foxglove Hollow as her husband. But did I?

I had amassed my own fortune, been a quick study of the lifestyle, and become assimilated into one of America's most insular old-money communities.

I belonged to the right clubs, drove the right cars, had the right wardrobe and my own jet. I'd learned to chuckle and not bray, clink and not clunk, close and not slam. I learned "the nod"—a slight declination of the head that is the mark of old wealth—and could excecute a passable East Coast "lock jaw" when the situation demanded it.

It had to be the longest running act in the history of theatrics, but this load of crap was never going to win any starred reviews in *The New York Times*.

I had secretly despised many of the uppercrust whom I'd tried, and succeeded, to emulate; Harry Goodman was the ringleader prodding me through the hoops, his friends and cronies our audience.

Somewhere along the line, in the process of trying to fit in, smugly in the beginning, and then simply out of habit, I, Richard Darlington, had *become one of them*.

Looking at myself in the mirror, I knew only one thing with certainty: change was imminent.

My most important life choices had been made long ago, and I saw now with clarity that many of them simply didn't work for me anymore.

It was time to confront the past and start making plans for the future.

After another half hour or so, I got up to stretch. Being set up wore thin after awhile, even if it was to supplement municipal salaries. Even the Hubba Hubbans started to lose interest.

"You can't leave now," the Mayor told me sulkily.

"I thought I'd see a little of your beautiful island while it's still light."

"Oh! Then, you need a special government tour guide," he said, immediately happy again. "Thirty dollars."

"Fine. Where do I find the driver?"

The Mayor picked up his microphone. "Onassis! Onassis!" he screamed, competing to be heard over the cacophony of salsas, merengues, and other people's microphones blaring throughout the park. "*Ven aca.*"

After a few minutes, Onassis, a short, stocky, Latin man with a wide smile, the former driver of the Hubba Hubba Queen and her Court, strutted up to the gazebo and presented himself.

"You speak Spanish?" the Mayor asked me, while Onassis sized me up, and said nothing.

"A smattering."

"Good," the Mayor told me. "Onassis, he don't speak English."

"But you're sure he's official?" I couldn't help ribbing the mayor about a tour guide who spoke only Spanish.

"Oh yes, yes!" the Mayor assured me. "He went to the tourism school in Concepción."

Onassis, deciphering this, nodded vigorously and turned up the wattage.

"Ten dollars for the library fund, twenty for the driver, those be the municipal fees," the mayor told me, smiling and extending his hand. "Please, you pay me the library tax now?" I was beginning to feel like the Mayor had more than a rudimentary knowledge of bureaucratic collection methodologies. Maybe he'd gone to Mafia College in Las Vegas?

"Sure," I told him, peeling off a twenty. "Double or nothing when it comes to the library," I winked at him. "We can't be skimping on education now, can we?"

"Thank you, sir," the Mayor said seriously, folding the twenty neatly into quarters and sliding it into his shirt pocket.

I followed Onassis to his vehicle, which turned out to be the same rack truck that had been in the parade. It was still festooned with palm fronds and crepe paper, with shaving cream on the windshield. Onassis cheerily tore everything off and threw it in the street, and then cleaned the shaving cream off the windshield with a dirty rag.

"*Donde quiere ir?*" he asked, after I managed to open the passenger door and find a space on the seat that was still intact. I couldn't remember the word for north in Spanish, so I just pointed to the road that I knew led out of town.

"*Ah! Las playas!*" Onassis said, then rattled off something else in Spanish that I missed. He laughed, put the old diesel truck into gear, and we lurched forward.

We were going to the beaches, I knew that much, but it took me a few more minutes to figure out that Onassis—who somewhere in his soliloquy had used the word "*hermana*"—also planned to introduce me to his sister.

"I'd love her to see that hill at sunset," I said, wondering if anything so far-fetched could ever happen.

"Ah," George said, "Da hill." He breathed out the words as if they were sacred, and closed his eyes, smiling. "Dat's one special hill."

"Indeed it is," I agreed.

"George's daddy bought the land to plant coco," Ella told me. "They planted hun'reds of trees up yon, hun'reds and hun'reds. Cocos fallen so fast they rolled right in the sea."

George opened his eyes and looked around as if he was surprised to see us sitting there.

"Then the blight came, then the depression. Well," she said, resigned, "no more coco bizness after that."

"Nope," George came back to wherever he'd been and shook his head. "But that hill shor pretty." They both smiled easily, remembering the decimation of the family business, and the collapse of the coconut industry that supported Hubba Hubba as if it were an inconvenient glitch in the grand scheme of things.

"Plenty lobster, though," George said, philosophically. "Could wade right on the reef and pick it up."

"Yes, sir," Ella agreed. "Plenty lobster. Plenty coco rice, too!"

"Wisht I had those cocos now," George said, watching a *panga* speed close by the Wreck Deck in the dark, loaded with children and bananas. "The kids in California have a mind to buy this motel up north. Like to hep 'em out," he took a long, thoughtful pull on his drink, and smiled. "Caint do it sellin twenty loaf a bread a week."

"Couldn't you replant the trees?" I asked, the professional solver of problems.

"Nope."

This was one of those Hubba Hubba responses meant to stop the flow of conversation about a certain subject. As a New Yorker though, I was used to forging on, planting my ego wherever I thought it might take root.

"Why don't you *sell* the land?" I forcefully asked. "I mean, if you don't want to take up coco farming at your age, why not sell the land itself?"

"Don't be reed-i-coolus," said George, waving his hand in dismissal. Ella just snorted.

"What's so far fetched about that? It's possibly the most virgin, pristine piece of Caribbean water frontage I've ever seen."

"Well, I was gone ta say we got us a shortage of land buyers in Hubba Hubba, Dick," George said, in his soft-spoken way, "but you soundin' more like a potential with every passin' minute." He and Ella had a jolly laugh at this.

I sat back in my chair, and realized he was right. Here I was making a convincing case to George that he had a unique and beautiful piece of land while subconsciously coveting it. Marty would be horrified.

This must have been the reason I continued. A part of my brain had apparently short-circuited. I thought of my earlier idea about leaving a legacy for my daughter, and made up my mind.

"Alright then, George," I said. "I'll give you a million dollars for your hill and cove and one mile of white sand beach." I let out my breath, suddenly afraid he'd turn me down.

He smiled at me—the same easy, unsurprised smile he'd worn all evening—and turned to Ella.

"Okay with you honey?" he asked, as if he was going to sell me a loaf of bread, and needed her permission. When she continued to look both pleased and speechless, I knew we had a deal.

"Come along to my daughter's office in the morning then," George told me as calm and poised as one of the egrets I'd seen earlier on his reef. "She's the lawyer here in Hubba Hubba. We'll sign the papers so that hill can be yours, Dick."

"Thank you."

"Don't mention it," George continued, as if people showed up every day and gave him a million dollars in cash. "Well, Ella," he said, starting to laugh. "Looks like the bread tycoon is gonna retire." His laugh was infectious. "Guess we be goin' to California for awhile. Hep the kids with that motel."

CIVILIZATION

1.

Seventy-two life-changing hours after our emergency landing in Platanillo, we took off again into a cloudless, blue sky, heading northeast. Venezuela was not on my agenda now. Being in Hubba Hubba had helped me crystallize some decisions. It was time to head back to New York and deal with the problems in my marriage.

I looked at the digitals I'd taken of Coco Beach and felt a little thrill course through me. When was the last time I'd done something so spontaneous, right from the gut? It felt great. Maybe I'd go back one day, buy up more properties, and add them to Elizabeth's eco-portfolio. Hell, maybe I could even earn her some environmental tax credits into the bargain!

I also knew it was time to confront Hillary, and make some decisions about our future together. I still wasn't sure what lay ahead. A lot would depend on her reaction to the photos of her and Depaulier. Would she feel remorse? Or charge me with neglect? Being away had helped mellow my position. Maybe Hillary was simply lonely. Maybe we needed to spend more time together, travel more. Elizabeth was going away to school, and was hardly ever home now. Hillary was, naturally, going through an empty-nest syndrome.

That's when I hit on the idea of a cruise. I'd charter a big luxury sailboat and we'd go off, just the two of us. Depaulier would be history.

After that, I'd go back in person to close the deal on Coco Beach. What was the point of spending any more time at the office? Between Hillary and me, we could support decades of Darlingtons on interest alone. Marty would be pissed, of course. He'd always relied on my instincts to make the biggest investment decisions for both of us. I'd sit down and hash this out with him when I got back. Eric had already advised the office we were heading back to New York.

I pressed the intercom key and asked Eric to make a stopover in Baltimore. Who would believe only a few days after my conversation with Helene du Pont, that I too would need the services of Xanadu Financial Services? If I was going to be transferring a million dollars into an offshore account for personal reasons, I needed to know all the rules.

I made an appointment with accountant Jarald McVey for later that afternoon.

We flew through more cloudless blue skies and I typed "luxury sailboat charter" into my search engine, and came up with Felder Yachts in Ft. Lauderdale.

David Felder emailed me back almost immediately and told me he had just what I was looking for: an 85-foot luxury sailing yacht sitting right at Pier 66 called *Nemesis* that was available for two weeks on short notice. He uploaded all the photos, and it was perfect. I sent instructions to my bank to give him a deposit, and the deal was done. I was on a roll.

I sat back feeling glad to have the old clarity back, the old in-charge feeling. It would all work out, I felt sure of it.

I envisioned taking Elizabeth to her hill; the look on her face as she tried to take in the overwhelming natural beauty of the place.

I imagined Hillary, remorseful about Depaulier, agreeing to sail away with me. Even if we didn't feel a burning passion for one another, at least we had a lot of common ground, a daughter, and twenty years of a (mostly) monogamous relationship.

But oh—what a difference between those visions on the Lear, and how reality twisted itself into a knot of gold chains which had to be unwound, and untangled with a watchmaker's patience.

You see, I, Richard Darlington, thought I had my future all perfectly mapped out.

The Big Guy, as usual, proved to have other plans.

2.

I sat in Jarald McVey's plush offices in Baltimore, and thought of Veronica. Like a dark angel, she kept reappearing in my mind: her long fingers pointing at the contract, the way she moved her head to the side to look at her father, the way she looked at *me* with a steely glaze that could not completely cover the hurt in her large, brown eyes.

In striking counterpoint, I now sat across from this large, pasty man who looked like he lived underground. Jarald—"with a J, please call me Jerry"—McVey cut right to the point by immediately renumerating the many different, all legal, ways that I could achieve "offshore asset protection" through his company.

"Mr. Darlington," he said, "we would be happy to form several offshore corporations through our associate offices. We handle all the paperwork here, of course. It's not necessary for you to actually *go* to the Bahamas or the Cayman Islands. Oh no!" He laughed with a barely suppressed thrill.

"Our methods, of course, are strictly legal. We would never *ever* recommend an action to any of our clients that would put them in jeopardy with the US government. In fact, many of our employees formerly worked for the IRS!" He showed me a document that mentioned something called "reduced-fee legal representation" in case of difficulties with the Feds. The phrase gave me heartburn.

I told Jerry with a "J" about my plans to purchase property in the country of Concepción—a big offshore tax haven—and this pleased him so much, his pasty white face actually flushed to a light shade of pink.

"Oh well! That makes everything even easier!" He began to enumerate rules which included freedoms most tax paying citizens hadn't enjoyed since before the Income Tax Act of 1913.

He talked about the costs for forming offshore corporations in Concepción, and also suggested I turn part of my assets into a digitized gold account. "And then you can have a credit card which you use just like cash, but is debited against your gold account, instead of in US dollars!" The exclamation points were starting to get to me.

"Now, if you will just fill in these forms," Jerry said smoothly, taking a fat gold pen from his pocket and passing it to me. "Strictly confidential, of course and absolutely legal! The information is transmitted electronically within half an hour to one of our associate offices in Switzerland and then all these print applications are put through a paper shredder." He smiled at me, and I wondered if he'd gotten his training as a used car salesman.

"We ask for your social security number, of course, but only for purposes of our own financial evaluations: it is never kept. We also have a company that does an independent investigation for any felonious activity; not that we'd worry in *your* case!" He chuckled affably at the implied vision of cigar-smoking mafia dons trying to use *his* service as a high-class money-launderer. Imagine!

I filled in the blanks and turned the application his way. "Ah, the North Shore of Long Island, is it? We had a lady contact us from there last week." He smiled, looking at me with a new gleam in his eye. "In fact, if I recall correctly, she gave *your* name as a reference."

"The lady wasn't Helene du Pont by chance?" So Helene had followed up on my information. I was amazed. Helene simply did not seem the type who would seek offshore asset protection; she had a whole staff of CPAs and generations-old trustees to manage her vast fortune. Why would she need someone like Jarald McVey?

"Well, since you recommended her, I can admit to you that this indeed was the lady in question." He smiled at me like we were all part of one big, happy family.

"That's great, Jerry," I told him. "But I hope that you will never, under *any* circumstances, tell Helene du Pont about my association with your office. Otherwise, you will be forced to put your reduced-fee legal team to its most stringent test." I gave him a smile that was not boyish in the least, and he seemed to understand.

"Of course not, sir," he said. His eye had caught the multi-digit sum I'd entered into the box marked: "Amount to be invested."

"We will maintain strict anonymity, of course." The armpits of his starched shirt were starting to darken with sweat. It was time for me to go.

"I'll be in touch." I shook his proffered hand, and went immediately into the men's room to wash the stickiness off my hands.

White people in general were starting to give me the creeps. I can't imagine why.

***

Landing at La Guardia was easy, and timely. It was past 6 p.m.; the traffic would have thinned. I could be home earlier than I'd planned.

I called Marty to tell him myself about my change of plans.

"So the Lear was fine, but you still decided *not* to go to Venezuela?" his voice was incredulous. "Mind if I ask why?"

"Um...personal reasons," I told him.

"Personal as in...what? Are you sick? Sick of making money?"

In one deft unconscious comment, he had hit the proverbial nail on the head.

"Personal as in Hillary."

"Oh."

"I need to address the problems in my marriage, Marty," I told him soberly.

"So, you're sneaking up on her?"

"Not exactly."

"Shit, Richard. Good luck, man." He sounded happy.

"Thanks."

"And don't worry about Dr. Herb. I'll run a conference call with him and the translator tomorrow. Smooth everything over."

"You're a pal," I told him, meaning it. How much of a pal he might be in the future was up for grabs.

"I might be taking off for awhile," I told him, scattering the bait to see how he would react.

"A vacation?"

"Something like that."

"You can run, but you can't hide," Marty told me half-seriously, and I suddenly saw that he'd never support my decision to leave my old life behind. It would mean his life would have to change, too. I also realized that Marty—having carved out a new life for himself with Melanie—was actually very attached to the status quo.

"Lucky it was only an oil problem," he said about the Lear.

"Lucky, yes."

"Eric said you were in some tropical backwater with no hotel."

"I found a place to sleep."

"The Cockroach Motel? " he laughed.

"Something like that."

"Well, you're back on solid ground now. Let's do lunch next week."

"Gotcha," I said, and hung up the phone, feeling like early retirement might be a whole lot easier than I ever dreamed possible.

***

And so, an hour after landing, I pulled through the gates of Foxglove Hollow, and up to my front door in a Yellow Cab driven by a garrulous Armenian who laid out a very neat case for the impeachment of the vice president.

I tried to ignore him, concentrating on my confrontation remarks to Hillary. The photos were still in my briefcase. I looked forward to having this talk with her and moving forward. We'd had too many years of lies and obfuscation. Too many years of Harry Goodman's interference. Too much rote behavior, and not enough communication. It was all going to change.

I walked in through the front door, and called out a big hello.

Daniel came out to greet me looking startled, wiping his hands on a tea towel.

"Welcome home, sir!" he told me with loud bravado. What was that about?

"Keep your voice down, Daniel," I told him, sensing something wrong. "Is my wife is at home?"

"Yes, sir." He was getting more nervous by the minute. As I approached the stairs leading down to the pub, he almost started to shake. It was like the kids game, where the closer you get, the "warmer" you are.

I cocked my head with a downward direction. "Is she down in the pub?"

I went to the top of the staircase, and then I could hear it: the strains of Edith Pilaf singing in her smoky voice, along with some familiar giggling.

"Is she...entertaining?"

"Entertaining, sir. Yes."

"Jesus," I said. "How long has this been going on, Daniel?" I had the sinking feeling again, just like I'd had behind the curtain at the fundraiser, but magnified.

Daniel managed to look me in the eye. "For years, sir. It's been going on like this for years."

I felt my insides turn to stone.

"Fine. Don't disturb her. Get me a drink, and let my wife know I'm home...when the giggling stops."

"Yes, sir."

"And Daniel? You did the right thing by telling me." He nodded and turned away. I pulled off my tie and began heading up the stairs. It took a supreme act of will not to race down the stairs and strangle them both. This was no dalliance, but a serial activity probably involving a number of different men. Everyone else probably knew all about it, and I was the last to know.

It was the last straw. There would be no cruises now, no soul-baring talks. I had never been clearer about anything in my life: my marriage to Hillary was over.

I walked into my bedroom and the adrenaline began to ease. I looked around at the walls covered with Thai silk and the coordinating hand-painted curtains. Hillary had spent hundreds of thousands redecorating my suite and had flown in some famous Oriental artist living in St. Paul de Vence who specialized in this technique. I had a sudden urge to rip down the drapes, stuff them into the marble fireplace and have a bonfire. Instead, I parted them and looked out to the back yard where a security light illuminated everything. I realized I hadn't seen the view from here in years.

I walked into my wardrobe and took in the walls of suits, the stacks of shirts, the shoes, and hundreds of ties. It was a fair-sized room with enough apparel to supply a Wall Street brokerage house.

I thought about throwing in onto the lawn; maybe the Portuguese gardener could find some use for my clothes now that I was through with them.

I felt like I'd entered the stage set of an "esteemed" gentleman. My life had been reduced to living in a cold-hearted house, with a wife who fucked other men in the basement while I was away.

I knew I'd be free, then—whatever it took. Free of the clubs; my so-called friends; the long commutes into the city and the money that seemed to hem me in on all sides. Mostly though, I'd be free of Hillary and a marriage which had been nothing but a big, fat lie.

But I'd need to handle it carefully, too. I didn't want Harry Goodman ensnaring me in some messy divorce proceedings that might have me tied in place for years. I needed to formulate a plan, give myself some maneuvering room while I moved my assets around, and got my ducks in a row.

I needed time and space to think it all through and it wasn't going to happen in the Big Apple.

I decided that a cruise was just what I needed, after all.

3.

I came out of the shower wrapped in my towel to find Hillary perched on the end of my bed and felt a preternatural calm. She too was freshly showered, all hints of the Frenchman having been washed away, compliments of Crabtree & Evelyn.

"You're back," she said, smiling at me. Such bravado! I thought. She must have been terrified to think how close I came to catching her in the act.

"Yes, the Lear broke down. We had to wait for parts, and so I decided not to fly on to Venezuela."

"I see," she said in her usual warm, concerned voice with nary a word about what kind of breakdown we'd had, or where.

I continued to towel myself off. "How's Elizabeth?" Amazing how quickly I too could switch to role of Great Pretender.

"She's gone on a date with a new boy."

"Anyone we know?" Given Elizabeth's age, lack of experience, famous grandfather and net worth, Hillary and I had established some firm policies about our daughter's social life. Having an introduction from someone we knew was the first requisite.

"Actually, he's a nephew of Michel DePaulier, a boy called Pierre." *Surprise, surprise.*

"Really?" I said, swallowing my anger. That he was a nephew of my wife's paramour seemed to plumb a new line of contempt for me. Would Hillary ever hit bottom?

Sex had blinded her, apparently. DePaulier was definitely not of a class that Hillary would have accepted in the past, and now she was allowing our daughter to date a member of his family. Fucking someone changes all the rules, I guess.

I looked at Hillary sitting primly on my bed, blinking at me innocently, a vision of hypocrisy. I was sure my daughter Elizabeth could do better than either of us, if we only gave her a chance.

"It's such a coincidence, really," my wife continued. "They are the same age and really seem quite compatible. I invited them for dinner here last night. Pierre is very charming and is going to Mt. Holyoke in the fall. According to Michel, he comes from an excellent family. His brother married one of the Cointreaus."

"Oh well, as long as he's rich..." I began, but my sarcasm was lost on Hillary. I wondered how long I could keep pretending I was her loving, dutiful husband.

"We've been invited to the du Pont's tomorrow evening," my wife told me, changing the subject. "I hope you haven't made any plans."

"No, no plans," I said, thinking: Except for leaving you, my work, and my entire life behind, I've got no plans at all.

"Good. Helene says she wanted to thank you for something." My wife got up and gave me a perfunctory kiss on the cheek.

"You must be tired from your trip," she added, which in wife lingo means: You're not going to get laid tonight.

"Exhausted," I said, which is a husband's retort meaning: I didn't want to fuck you anyway.

At least after twenty years, I'd learned all the translations.

4.

Hillary and I went to Helene du Pont's the next night in the same car. In a perverse way, I was looking forward to the evening. It would be my last social engagement with a group of people who'd been a constant in my life for the last twenty years.

Inside I felt completely altered; giddy with thoughts of independence and almost silly. I wondered if anyone would notice the difference and guessed they would not. If wealth had given these people one thing, it was a genteel self-centeredness which anticipated attention like hothouse flowers. No one at Helene du Pont's would notice a difference in me because they were inured to everyone else, and in any case obvious prying was considered very bourgeois.

In the car Hillary was her usual composed self in shantung silk the color of mayonnaise. I poured myself a single malt from the Daimler's bar and in response my wife grew chilly and turned to stare out into the darkness through tinted glass.

"Finished?" she asked as Raymond pulled under the portico of Helene du Pont's and came to a stop. The quintessence of non-reaction, Raymond raised not an eyebrow to the palpable tension between us.

I smiled, threw down the rest of the pale gold liquid and winked at her. She looked appalled at this, an old put-down trick she'd learned from her mother. I was through hooking into Hillary's upper class rebukes though, and when I saw the confusion in her eyes, I sensed she felt the balance of power shifting ever so slightly.

"Ready?" I asked, as our doors were opened simultaneously by Raymond on her side, and the du Pont butler on mine.

She set her face into a mask of serenity and took my arm, digging her nails in, and we followed the butler inside. What would Hillary ever have done without finishing school, I've often wondered? Flashes of mud wrestling on cable TV have persisted in my imagination for years.

We were shown into the library where the guests were already gathered in little clusters and I saw it was the same old-money faces with a smattering of the movie crowd brought in like fresh meat from the Hamptons. Helene really was slumming it, I thought, to mix it up like this. I could hear the gossip now.

What would any of the gathered make of Hubba Hubba, I wondered, and smiled picturing it.

Between new money and old, there was probably enough hard currency in the room to refloat the entire Social Security system.

I waited for my turn to greet the hostess, and after I began sipping another drink I began to feel unearthly, like an alien who wakes up and finds he's on the wrong planet.

Helene du Pont, having made us welcome with a quick air hug, returned to her conflicting memories with Frances Porter Dodge about some man they had known more than forty years before.

I looked around at the various ensembles: the movie people—a director, a producer and their glamorous wives; The Girls, frisky behind well-practiced poses of languorousness, facing each other on plush settees, leaning forward like hungry birds as Hillary came forward to join them; the older men were also gathered in a closely-knit group, looking like well-dressed turkey vultures with their long, rubbery necks and hooded eyes; Aubrey and Leonard, the interior designer and his boyfriend, off by themselves—insensible to anyone else. Aubrey kept brushing invisible lint off Leonard's sleeve in a possessive gesture that made me wonder if Leonard was roving.

Left to my own devices, I wandered off to the periphery near the bookcases to take it all in. Like watching a foreign movie, the actors' mouths moved, people gesticulated, but I was no longer a part of their milieu. I wondered how I had endured the lack of reality for so long, how anyone had. But of course I knew the answer already.

Money, and lots of it, could be a wonderful buffer against loneliness, insecurity, boredom, and other depravations. Money could be a great facilitator, an insurance policy for future generations, or simply be used to provide endless diversion.

Everyone was different. In Harry Goodman's world, money was power; in his daughter's case it was used as an aphrodisiac, among other things.

But in spite of their fortunes, most of those present had lived lives predestined since birth; the schools, cotillions, fraternities, chairmanships, careers, even their future mates were often earmarked in advance. Like mine had been to Hillary.

As if in rebellion though, many had private eccentricities. Helene for example collected primates and kept the whole menagerie in her back yard in huge cages with two full time keepers; Shelley had a full movie theatre and thousands of reels of black and white movies from the fifties, many of them reputed to be pornographic. Frances had a steady stream of young Cuban lovers that she brought into the States through Mexico as domestics. One of them, Chulo, had been with her for more than ten years, since he was 19. Martha, being more of a traditionalist, had a huge hoard of silver she kept in a vault off the kitchen. Like three generations of Stuarts before her, twice a year it was all brought out and laid across the Oriental runner in the hall, inventoried and polished by a staff of five.

My wife, of course, had her own recreation, though I don't really think it could be squeezed into the "hobby" category any more.

In any case, of all the Gold Coast residents The Girls seemed the most independent. They shared a genuine camaraderie which had kept them traveling, playing bridge, and keeping tabs on each other like an extended family.

The married men seemed the worst off. Having been born into wealth, then married into more of it, most had been deadened by decades of elitism and passionless marriages. Unlike their forefathers, the F.W. Woolworths and J.P. Morgans, men who dreamed big and played hard—especially in the days of Prohibition—today's gentry seemed to be nothing so much as a generation of clingers. Most of their familial estates had been turned into colleges, museums, tax-exempt monasteries and parks, but still the Old Guard hunkered down in lesser mansions, surrounded by others of their kind.

That night at Helene du Pont's I saw how much safer it was for these people to live in a community surrounded by their peers. Predictable and deadening. Had I really lived here all these years, and not seen the insularity of it?

"Dinner is served," the butler announced, and I walked like a well-trained actor toward a head haloed in wisps of flame-red hair, and offered my arm to Frances Porter Dodge. She happily took hold, gnarled hands anointed with rings, and began flirting with me. Frances Porter Dodge had been a famous stage actress whose affair and subsequent marriage to hotel magnate E.J. Dodge had been front-page news many years ago. Like many once beautiful, wealthy women, Frances still had a coy self-confidence that I'm sure was kept bolstered by her domestic staff of young Cuban men.

Maybe Hillary could become her trainee.

"A penny for your thoughts?" she asked. "I saw you sitting over there deep in contemplation."

"Hmmm. Just some business pending," I told her, smiling to reassure her that this was true.

"A very far away look, too," she continued.

"Marty and I have a deal pending in Venezuela," I added, hoping she would take the hint. I did not think it politic to share with Frances Porter Dodge my neoteric notion that the room we had just vacated was full of rich zombies, or that my wife the sex addict would make a great apprentice.

"E.J. and I went to Caracas once, years ago," she said looking into the distance. "A cruise. Very romantic, too. Are you a romantic, Richard?" she asked me, as I pulled out the fully-skirted chair, and slid her into it.

"Of course."

"That's what I thought." With a squeeze of my hand, she turned to face the table. Helene's butler then escorted me to my seat between Shelley Wurst and one of the movie wives. Charlie

Schwabb Hubble sat across from me, the expanse of linen, crystal and hedge of tiny pink roses entwined in English ivy not enough of a barrier for my liking. A financier from the famous Schwabb family, Charlie could take the most exciting takeover and make it sound like slow death by hemlock poisoning. He had a deep voice, which was utterly without inflection and a cast-iron Eastern lockjaw. A droner in the worst tradition.

The soup was served. Vichyssoise, a du Pont standard, was first on the docket with a beautiful little Riesling. The wine began to work its magic, and then Charlie spoke in his sonorous voice through lips that barely moved.

"So, Richard. How goes the VC battle?"

"Admirably well," I told him, taking another sip of wine. Hint, hint.

"Glad to hear it," he answered, reminding me of a ventriloquist. "Anything new and exciting we should know about?"

Now this was a departure. Normally any talk of money or business was reserved for after dinner, and then away from the ladies, usually over cognac and cigars.

"Not a lot." I smiled at him and focused on my soup.

"Richard's going on a trip," Frances said coyly, and the table seemed to enter a suspended state as nineteen faces turned my way.

"Just doing some research," I said, looking at my wife, who sat several seats away on the opposite side of the table and had a brilliant, hard smile turned my way.

"Richard is scavenging," she told the assembled, with a light-heartedness calculated to take the heat off me.

"Salvaging?" Martha Stuart said. "Did you say salvage?"

"Richard's not going into the sanitary landfill business," Helene said, and everyone twittered. "We don't live in New Jersey, dear."

Martha looked perplexed, and my wife, perhaps out of pity announced, "Richard has a new herb he's looking into." She pronounced the word with correct American usage, leaving off the "h" and I thought how odd it was that she had decided to share this detail with the whole table. Some of the most moneyed people in the country were seated within earshot and there was not one of them who wouldn't want to know what was about to make me—and possibly them—richer.

"An herb, Richard?" Charlie repeated. *Urb.*

"That's right," I said, putting on a cheery face. Since when had everyone become so interested in my livelihood? First Helene du Pont was calling me at the office and now I was being grilled by Charlie Schwabb Hubble at her dinner table.

"'Like herbs and trees that bring forth fruit and flourish in May,'" the new money movie producer—his name was Robert "Buck" Langley—quoted to the table at large.

"Anything organic looks tasty to me," said the new money director, Vincent-something. Now here was a little jargon from the LA/Hamptons to enliven the conversation. Helene, of course, did not react at all to "Vinny's" use of the vernacular. She merely dabbed her lips with an heirloom napkin.

"Yes, organic *is* interesting," Aubrey Coulter said. He was another one who talked through his nose, which in his case was very long and narrow with a knob on the end, making it look like a small penis.

"Do tell," Leonard Stuveysant prodded.

"It seems there is an herb that can reduce high blood pressure nearly instantly," I told them. I was wondering how to wriggle out of all this attention when a devious thought sprung to mind. "Or so says a doctor in Venezuela," I added, dipping my spoon into the cold, chive-speckled soup plate in front of me. "Caracas, actually."

"Caracas," Charlie repeated, looking like a parrot who has finally cracked the husk of a sunflower seed to get to the tasty morsel inside. Around me I saw faces nodding in polite interest. Bingo.

"Now you have us all curious, Richard," Helene said. "I hope you'll tell us *all* about your adventure when you get back." Around her, everyone smiled and nodded their encouragement, then went back to their own conversations.

Soup plates were cleared, and sautéed *foie gras* on a bed of red lettuce was presented with a Chateau Lafite-Rothschild that was thirty-five years old.

I swirled the wine, feeling happy with my ruse. I could imagine them all jumping online as soon as they got home, trying to pull up any information they could find on my Venezuelan cure. Marty would be furious at my disclosure. Oh well.

I'd be turning myself into gold dust soon enough. The next time Helene du Pont called the office, she'd have to talk to Marty, not me.

5.

Monday arrived, and with it the need to start implementing my plan. Escaping from America and Fortress New York would be my first step, and that meant going on my "Caribbean cruise."

Being secretive had never been my strong suit, but I needed to learn if I was going to preserve my future freedom. Marty was too close—and too tied to the status quo—to be a safe repository for my secrets. Elaine was also on my list of casualties, as were Milton, Eric, Helga, and the entire office staff. If I was going to successfully extricate myself from my old life, I had to make my leaving look, at least in the beginning, like nothing out of the ordinary.

Everyone had their stake in Richard Darlington staying the Richard Darlington they knew, from Harry Goodman, right down the line to the IRS. I was about to become a boat rocker, a misfit, and a non-resident alien of the United States. Everyone might forgive me in time, but I was certainly not going to let anyone spoil my plans before I'd even left the country.

Over the next few days, I decided what I would do: Hubba Hubba was remote, beautiful, and as different from New York as any place could be. It was a good place to make a fresh start, if only temporarily. I'd keep my whereabouts a secret, and ask Hillary for a divorce when I was damn good and ready and my assets were all secure. I would not, under any circumstances, become a financial casualty of divorce from Harry Goodman's only daughter simply because I let her see all my cards in advance.

My daughter would be at freshman indoctrination at Smith College in a few short weeks, and would be off the scene when the chips fell. This was also important to my plans. I didn't see any reason for Elizabeth to suffer because of problems between her mother and me that were simply not her fault.

Marty, unfortunately, would probably suffer the most from my leaving. But ever since our fateful lunch, the photographs he produced from the private investigator he'd hired to run Hillary to the ground, I'd begun to see aspects of Marty's character that were unsavory and self-serving. Why hadn't I seen this before? It would be interesting to see which pissed him off more when he learned the truth. Would he be more upset about the loss of all the free business advice I doled out to him daily, or simply sad that I was no longer in his life?

I had a bad feeling about that one.

There were many other smaller but still important details to wrap up: severance pay for my employees, contract terminations, new lawyers, new banks and bankers. Everything I'd spent years establishing needed to be changed.

It was worth it, I told myself: at last I'd have a life in place of my own choosing, on my own terms. If I planned carefully, nothing—no one—could stand in my way.

And so it was that I walked into my office on Monday morning, and Marty immediately knew something was up.

"Hey."

"Hey," I said. Smile, smile, smile.

"What the hell are you smiling about?" Marty wanted to know. "Glad the Lear didn't crash?"

"There's always that."

"Pretty big smile." He looked doubtful. "The ice maiden have a temporary thaw?"

"Hmmm."

"Do lunch?"

"Can't today."

"Why not?" He began using his penetrating technique, taking off his glasses and wiping them while maintaining eye contact. Very little gets by Marty.

"I'm going shopping," I told him. Lies are best, I've found, when you stick as close to the truth as possible.

"Shopping?"

"Clothes shopping."

"A little early for fall suits," he said, more skeptical by the minute.

"Tommy Bahamas."

"Say what?"

"I've chartered a sailboat, an eighty-footer. Going on a cruise for a few weeks. I need a change." Certainly the latter was the truth. "Let's have a sit-down later about my schedule."

"*Do lunch,*" he insisted.

"Can't." Marty will take a hint eventually, if it hits him on the back of the head like a jibing mainsail.

"Tomorrow then," he said, and finally left me alone.

I walked into my suite of offices, and Elaine said good morning.

"You're looking very...happy," she said, finding the word after a short search.

"Thank you," I said.

This gave her pause, but only temporarily. "How was your flight back? No more incidents?"

"Oh, that. Fine, perfect. A little oil pressure problem—no big deal."

She seemed to accept this as it was presented: a glitch that was fixed. "Eric is a marvel," she said, then, "You've got a ten o'clock with the analysts."

"Alright."

"And a one o'clock with the dentist."

"Skip the dentist."

"Mr. Darlington, I made this appointment for you a month ago. I'm afraid if you cancel it you'll have to wait a month to get another one." Sometimes Elaine likes to pretend she's my mother; sometimes I let her.

"Oh, I'll be back by then," I said. Nonchalance was my new middle name.

"Back?"

"I'm going sailing next week."

"Oh!" She automatically consulted her calendar. "The doctor from Caracas is coming next Tuesday, Mr. Kahn made the arrangements. And there's the geologist from Montana on Wednesday about the gold mines. I see here that Mr. Kahn will not be in New York on that day. He has booked the Lear for Wednesday and Thursday. Shall I reserve the jet for you on Friday, sir?"

"No. I'll probably fly commercial to Miami on Monday. I'll be gone about two weeks, so you'll have to cancel what's pending. I'll meet with Marty and Milton later to discuss this with them." Over the weekend, I'd already made a list of business pending and found there was very little that couldn't be picked up by either of my partners. There was never a shortage of money-making opportunities in our offices. Having ducked the worst of the e-bubbly nineties, the only things we seemed to lack where money was concerned was the time and energy to accumulate more of it.

I'd finally realized that the hourglass of my life had trickled away for years in its pursuit. What was left of those tiny grains was too precious to waste, and being back in the office—the treadmill of making yet more money—only confirmed it for me. I couldn't wait for the day I'd walk out of here and not come back. The thought was evisceral, and thrilling.

I went through the motions of the morning, meeting with the analysts, seeing the rest of the staff, but now I was seeing everything in a new light. It wasn't an unhappy group; the whole venture capital business, financing new ventures and reinvesting the profits, was much more exciting and diverse than most office jobs, or straight brokerage. But it struck me that we'd all been on parallel gerbil wheels: More money meant more comforts, faster cars, better schools for our children, bigger vacations. But where did it end? I had seen so many people, including my father, work his heart out for 38 years, and then drop dead of a heart attack a few weeks after his retirement. What was the point?

At one, I had Raymond drop me in the shopping district, then walked a few blocks trying to find a pay phone. I had bigger fish to fry than a few tropical shirts and some Maui Jims. I had a real estate deal pending, and couldn't wait one more minute to hear the voice behind it.

The phone rang and rang and I remembered Big Jim's warning about the phone system in Hubba Hubba. I waited patiently and on the eighth ring the phone was answered by the secretary, then her boss was on the line, the voice honeyed and deep.

"Veronica?" I asked. I suddenly felt as shy as a fifteen-year old.

She said: "The money is here." Sounding surprised. "Our lawyers in Concepción confirmed receipt this morning."

"Great." At least she couldn't accuse me of dragging my feet. "I'd like to close as soon as possible, if that's alright with you. I'll draw up a power of attorney." I gave her the name and contact details for the Concepción lawyer McVey had told me about.

"Of course," she said, and although her tone wasn't sweet, it had mellowed. Maybe she'd decided I wasn't a money-laundering thug, after all. Maybe she decided her family could find some pretty good uses for a million dollars.

I said, "When I come down, I hope you'll let me take you and your family to dinner."

There was a sustained paused on the line, and I wondered if I'd lost her.

"Black Jack will want to come."

"Black Jack?"

"My husband," she said. "He says he'd like to meet you, too."

6.

The week ahead proved to me, yet again, that I was making the right decision. It kept coming at me in a hundred small ways that I was meant to follow my gut, move to Hubba Hubba, and start on the path to becoming human again. What amazed me back in New York was how stuck everyone seemed, how determined *not* to change. Most people worked at one job, while secretly wishing they were doing something else. Many were in relationships with people they didn't even like, and this didn't just include spouses, but friends, co-workers, family members, and business partners. This was my own story, too.

What was everybody so afraid of? Why had *I* been so afraid?

I wasn't sure what the answer was. I only knew I was living on a leviathan ship that was sinking from a cargo of too much denial. I had to jump while there was still time.

***

Few people know that Hubba Hubba means "land of the big coconuts" which is how the World War II expression for a bosomy, sexy woman was born. Despite a history that included the decimation of the coconut business in the early part of the 20th century, Hubba Hubbans resigned themselves to the fact, and either went to church, picked up rum drinking full time, or left.

Seven and a half decades later, after some people from Boston discovered that banana grew exceptionally well in the area, the Hubba Hubbans were employed once more. Now the banana boat came daily to the island to pick everyone up and returned them to the dock at 4 p.m. The Hubba Hubbans could now afford shoes for their childrens' feet, and could take their wives to the Boom Boom Room on Saturday night. Other than that, not a lot changed.

Hubba Hubbans simply woke up, fed their kids and went to work when they had to, but inaction was not construed as laziness, or sluggish passivity. Hubba Hubbans, it seemed, had all the time in the world, and never rushed through life. "Whappin?" was the same greeting everyone received whether they'd last met ten minutes or ten years ago. Ask a Hubba Hubban how they were and you'd receive an enigmatic: "Right here." Problems were as often confronted by a laugh and a "Don't fret," as by any attempt to find a solution.

In my world, problems were identified and solved, rapid-fire. There was no dilly-dallying, no procrastinating, no room for failure, and no patience. Everyone seemed to be in a perpetual state of struggle toward some goal, but weren't satisfied when they reached it. People who had to wait rammed bumpers, cursed, and sometimes shot each other on the way home from work.

I had no illusions about Hubba Hubba. (I did actually, but those particular perceptions come later on.) In fact, I was concerned about such mundane things as where I would live while I built a place of my own. The Boatel? I wondered about telecommunications, Hillary finding out about my plans before I was ready, and how I would maintain a relationship with Elizabeth after the fact.

Meanwhile, I contacted Jarald McVey and made more provisions for my money, which included a complex array of trusts, donations, offshore corporations, a new will, a substantial payment to the IRS, and some cash that would be sitting in the Banco de Concepción upon my arrival. I gave instructions to my bank for an ample deposit to be credited in one month into Hillary's account, covering my annual share of our joint expenses for Foxglove Hollow, and all of Elizabeth's college expenses. I found a new attorney not affiliated with anyone I knew, and arranged my no-fault divorce proposal to Hillary. I wrote a post-dated letter to Marty as well. I organized generous bonuses and termination-of-contract papers for Raymond my driver, Jason my personal trainer, and also for Daniel the chef in case he didn't want to stay on. God knew, Hillary hardly needed a personal chef. And Daniel was another one: secretly wanting to open his own restaurant in Portland, Oregon. Maybe this would be the impetus he needed.

I gathered together all the brochures David Felder had sent me on *Nemesis*, left one on my own desk and gave one to Hillary. I asked her to go with me, of course, knowing her joining me was about as likely as the President flying commercial.

That handled, we sat down to have drinks in the conservatory at the back of the house. Silver droplets from the sprinkler cast a sheen on the deep green lawn and the shadows from the big maples alternated with strips of golden light in the twilight to light up our faces like actors on a stage, which of course, we were—in a manner of speaking.

"Two weeks is a long time," my wife said. Was she having a pang of guilt in deciding to stay home with her lover instead of coming with me? "I remember father took mother and me to Virgin Gorda when I was young. There were these immense boulders—the Baths, I think they're called—I tried hiking on them but the water rushing underneath frightened me and I turned back."

"You were fourteen or thereabouts," I said, the dutiful husband with the keen memory.

"Yes, and it was horrible in any case. I hated it. I missed my friends and was desperate to get home." She took a sip of her drink, a wine spritzer. "I would still hate it."

I didn't respond to this; what more was there to say? I was starting to see Hillary as living in a bubble, a very large, secure bubble that no one could pop. Either you lived inside the bubble with her, as Depaulier was now doing, or you were outside looking in.

I said, "I'd like to talk about Elizabeth, if you don't mind,"

"Why should I mind?"

"Her dating this Pierre fellow. How long has this been going on?"Always the indefatigable father, the answer, I knew, would also be a clue about how long she and Depaulier had been going at it, information I might, or might not, require later when I was trying to end our marriage.

"Oh...eight months, or so, I guess." *How many more had there been before the Frenchman, I wondered?*

"I see. And he is going to Holyoke, just down the street from Elizabeth at Smith? Is that correct?" I thought how convenient it might be for all parties. Michel could plead justifiable visits to his nephew, Hillary to our daughter. If they bumped into each other in western Massachusetts, who would find it odd?

Hillary said, "Well, it *is* convenient. Elizabeth will have a friend close by." I felt that she wanted me to accept this *fait accompli*, and wondered why, when so many of my other opinions didn't seem to matter to her, this one did.

"I want Elizabeth to make as many of her own choices as she can. I think we've been overprotective of her," I said.

"Overprotective?" Hillary's voice arched. "Of a beautiful, young woman who has a large personal fortune? I think not."

I said, "I'd like to meet Pierre, if you don't object. Say Friday? Just the four of us?"

Daniel came forth at this juncture and gave us crudités with a yogurty dip and offered to freshen our drinks. My wife took the smallest baby carrot, no dip, and nibbled at it like a cautious rabbit.

"I'll be gone on Monday. Elizabeth will be doing her freshman indoctrination soon after. I'd like to meet him sooner, rather than later."

"Of course, Friday will be fine," my wife told me. But I had the distinct feeling I was impeding upon other plans.

I sat and sipped my drink as I looked past the lawn towards the woods in back and wondered if any animals did live out there, other than squirrels and the occasional fox. We'd been warned about coyotes coming into the area but there was too much control here. Wild animals would never be tolerated, which is why when I'd read Melanie's books about bears just a few days before, I identified with the protagonists whose only desire was to leave the Gold Coast without getting shot.

7.

I finally had my lunch with Marty on Thursday, the same day I bought my Harley Davidson V-Rod, to be shipped from the Port of Miami to Concepción. Don't laugh. I also bought the leather pants and jacket. Maybe this was why I didn't like Marty anymore. He didn't want to play my new game: buy a V-Rod and a set of leathers and retire.

Still, there were lots of details to work out, transport being only one of them. Elaine reserved and paid my first-class round-trip ticket to Miami, half of which I planned to use, and also prepaid my cruise on *Nemesis*, which I did not.

The rest was up to me; I made most of the arrangements on a cell phone bought for this purpose, which I planned to discard as soon as it had served its use.

Hillary, I knew, would want to retaliate when she found out I'd left for good. *Father, I thought you should know: Richard has abandoned me.*

Harry "If-you-ever-hurt-my-little-girl-I'll-kill-you" Goodman would probably leave no stone unturned in trying to find me, if only to nail me financially. *I,* therefore, planned to leave no stone unturned in keeping my whereabouts a secret.

My future plans did not include becoming Harry Goodman's prey, nor spending years being dragged through a minefield of divorce litigation by his eager-beaver lawyers.

I'd use my new Concepción lawyer for correspondence with McVey and an anonymous email address for the rest. I needed to buy some time before anyone knew where I was; everyone needed to get used to the idea of my absence before reacting.

Also, the idea of sharing Hubba Hubba was anathema to me. I'd found this little anachronistic hideaway and wanted to keep it that way. I had an almost pathological desire to keep the place a secret. I'd spent a lifetime living up to other peoples' expectations of me, and wanted to ensure that my new life would have no such impediments. The little part of the world I was about to inhabit could have a big No Trespassing sign hung around it as far as I was concerned—that is after Yours Truly had set up camp.

With these notions and many others subconsciously notching my belt, I joined Marty for lunch at India House. We'd already had our meetings about him and Milton covering my commitments while I was gone; this was to be a pleasurable lunch, a little send-off before my "vacation," which was scheduled to begin the following Monday.

I knew Marty was going to be angry with me when he found out about my real intent; how angry, it would be interesting to see. We'd always maintained our autonomy in the business; our funds weren't commingled. On the business side, my leaving would be a sustainable loss, nothing he couldn't get over.

On the emotional/friendship side, I'd begun to feel I didn't really like Marty much anymore. I could just imagine his reaction to Hubba Hubba: flagrant snobbery. Marty had no trouble detaching from those who disagreed with him: his father, his ex-wife, even Hillary being some of the examples that sprung to mind. He could be ruthless, selfish and dogmatic, and I saw that I'd always forgiven him that, stood by him when the chips were down and the sympathy vote was in short supply.

He had implored me to follow my heart about Hillary, but that was easy for him. He hated Hillary, or at least he *seemed* to have a big pot of antipathy for her always bubbling away on the back burner. If I really followed my heart, as I was about to do, I guessed he'd have a whole different reaction.

And that is how we started our lunch, Marty verbalizing his view about what was "best" for me, and me watching him and waiting.

"Let's have a drink, shall we?" He ordered for both of us, didn't even look my way.

"God, I'm sick of chicken," he said, scanning the menu. "Mel is on this chicken craze: eggs in the morning, chicken at lunch, chicken at dinner. I'm going to have a nice steak. What about you?"

"I'll have the chicken," I said. "And no scotch for me," I told the waiter. "I'll have a beer—that new microbrew?"

"You're drinking beer?" Marty asked. "At lunch?"

"Looks like it," I said, rimming my glass with a wet fingertip and after a while it began to vibrate and make a nice piercing sound. A few tables of suits looked our way.

"Stop that," Marty said. "What's the matter with you?"

"With me?"

"You're acting weird."

I said, "Maybe I'm acting like myself for a change," and looked back at him.

"And maybe you *need* a change. Like a vacation."

"That's where I'm headed. Vacation."

"Well," Marty said, trying to get back on familiar ground. "Tell me about it. Where are you going? Is Hillary really not going with you?" He raised an eyebrow.

"I'm going alone, yes. First stop Cuba, then the BVI."

"That's a travel writer for you. Includes all the lush details."

Our drinks came and I guzzled mine out of the bottle. Move over Peter Fonda.

"Thirsty, too."

"Why don't you shut the fuck up?" I said, very calmly. I never knew I could be so calm. Marty looked at me, his mouth opened like a small cave. "You've always got a comment about everything, you know that? It's a lousy habit."

I put my empty bottle on the table and the waiter practically ran to get me another one. He must've thought I was a dissatisfied customer.

"You're deeply pissed," Marty said. His lips looked like they were being stretched on a rack.

"I guess I am." I drank my second beer like I'd drunk my first and the carbonation made me belch. Marty started to comment on this, then thought better of it.

"Try and calm down," he said.

"Give me one good reason I should." I was still very angry.

"So you can think," he said reasonably.

"What I *think* is that I'm a big boy who doesn't need anyone to run his life."

"You think *I'm* running your life?"

"Mine and everyone else's. Jesus, Marty. Can't you see what a control freak you are?"

Our food arrived, and Marty looked at his steak and said nothing. "No," he said finally. "I can't."

I had no retort to that and ate my chicken. I had nothing more to say to Marty, did not want to press him further. If someone can't see something, they can't see it. Denial is a very large, muddy river.

Marty might be brooding now but I knew how quickly he'd bounce back. I also realized something else about Marty that day, something that took me back and saddened me. Marty Kahn—old renegade hipster, my best friend for more years than I could count—was a selfish son-of-a-bitch. Marty no longer just joked about elitism, class, money and power struggles. Marty believed that if he played the game the right way, he could come out on top. Marty Kahn was for Marty Kahn. It had never been clearer to me. Everyone except Marty was in his peripheral vision. Even me.

I realized Marty was going to be another casualty in my new life. There'd be no motorcycle leathers in Marty's future, and no change of scenery, either.

I could not imagine a stranger scenario than Marty wedged between Big Jim and Daddy Joe at the bar at the Wreck Deck drinking Mi Abuela.

I'd go to Miami as further cover for my ruse and to meet David Felder about my yacht charter on *Nemesis*. I'd get my V-Rod shipped and start studying Spanish. I'd fly down to Concepción via Mexico and begin laying the groundwork for my new life in Hubba Hubba.

How hard could it be?

8.

I left the office early that day; in fact I didn't return at all after my lunch with Marty. Why bother?

I still had to pick up the road maps and some books I'd ordered and arrange shipment of the Harley. I needed to buy a good quality rucksack and some basic clothing items: T-shirts; jeans, which I could cut off later if I got too hot; and some boots that would serve double duty on the bike, then during construction at Coco Beach.

I also wanted to find something special for Elizabeth. She'd already had her graduation gift from her mother and me. I wanted to find her something that was personal, something that would convey both my love for her and also serve as a reminder of what I deemed some of life's important messages. I wandered into the philosophy department of the bookstore, was surprised to see some of those old boomer favorites: *Zen and the Art of Motorcycle Maintenance*, (now *there* was a timely little tome); Kahlil Gibran's *Siddhartha*. *Be Here Now*, by Ram Dass, was now cheek-to-cheek with the Dalai Lama, indicating I'm not sure what.

At last I found what I was looking for: a small paperback that had impacted me most as I tried to find my true self at her age, though unfortunately I'd discarded much of what it contained.

I went to the gardening section next and found a book on tropical plants for Veronica, as a peace offering. I made inscriptions in both books and had them gift-wrapped.

I left and began walking out of the financial district, something I hadn't done in many years. I began noticing the people I passed too, which was a disquieting exercise. Most people I saw looked well dressed and fit, in N.Y. black. Everyone also seemed on a tight-lipped mission, even the tourists, who continually looked up frowning, clicking and snapping.

I walked through Chinatown and Little Italy—same thing—toward the Lower East Side. God knows why. I guess I was beginning to feel like a man on a mission, trying to find a happy face, even a contented one.

Everyone piled into the streets at five o'clock and I finally saw something that gave me hope: a group of four young women—office girls, I guessed—unselfconsciously laughing and jostling each other as they walked with purpose down the street. I followed to see what was entertaining them, and could hear them talking about a man called John, then words like "pervert," "scuzball," "dickhead" began floating back to me. Did they all have this one boss they hated? I imagined some middle manager, a big-bellied, bully making their daily lives a living hell.

Then they all turned in through a red padded door and I looked up and saw a sign overhead: COLLEGE GIRLS! MORE DANCING! MORE SKIN! MORE FUN!!!!

More fun. Apparently many young women earned money to pay tuitions this way. Wanda Lust a.k.a. Wanda Petrowski had done it, and though she was definitely a little loopy, her psyche seemed to be in fine shape. Who was I to judge? Thank God Elizabeth was financially independent.

I used my new cell to call Raymond and have him pick me up. The red padded door was the end of the line for me; it was time to head back to more reality on the North Shore.

***

Hillary was not at home that night, she had a meeting of some kind. *Yeah right, my mind said, a voice like Big Jim's. A meeting. Har har har.* No matter. Daniel and I had the whole of Foxglove Hollow to ourselves, and so we brought several bottles of wine up from the cellar, and began to drink them while I watched him make us a big, spicy pasta with squid and clams and smash the garlic for garlic bread. Along about bottle one and a half, he admitted he had a lover in Portland. Why had he never told me this before? I listened and encouraged him to go back there before it was too late, which he must've thought was weird.

After dinner, I got out a stepladder, brought it to my bedroom, and began unhooking all the drapes from the windows. Daniel caught them as they fell, rolling them competently into big balls with his arms saying it was better this way, that the gilt paint wouldn't crack if the fabric was rolled. Better than folding. Much better.

It was thus that Hillary found us, about eleven or so. Rolling up silk draperies in my room.

She said nothing, just crossed her arms, sighed deeply and left. And so we just kept unhooking and rolling, like we were on an assembly line. Then Daniel began singing:

Oh Danny boy, the pipes, the pipes are callin'
Oh Danny boy, the pipes are callin' me...

Friday morning dawned; I knew it was dawn, because the sunlight was coming in through the window piercing my brain.

I had a hell of a hangover, but I walked to the window anyway to appreciate my new view: the dewy grass, the *flick flick flick* of the sprinklers, the lone coyote....no kidding, there was a coyote standing in the middle of the lawn. He was looking around, knowing he was in enemy territory, but not caring so much that he'd stayed in the woods. I watched him: a lone gray animal standing in the early morning sunshine, probably looking for food. He didn't seem frightened; wary perhaps, but not intimidated. I tapped on the window at him, and instead of running, he just looked up at me. And it was probably my imagination, but I swear to God I saw that animal smile. His tongue lolling half out, his incisors in plain view, he looked right at me as if to say: Fuck you. I live here, too. He then turned with leisure, and walked away.

I wondered if it was a sign.

If it was a sign, I wondered what the hell it meant.

I then went in and had a very cold shower.

Friday night and I'd already drunk a gallon of mineral water, had a nap, packed my rucksack. I sat on my bed, and began scribbling some notes to Hillary and Marty, then realized this was over the top. I'd never normally write notes like this before going on vacation, and I wasn't committing suicide, for God's sake. Let them eat cake.

I decided to burn them, along with some old correspondence I found in my desk. For some reason, this tickled me. I was letting the ashes fall into a metal wastebasket I'd propped between my legs and giggling, when Hillary came into the room unannounced for the second time in twenty-four hours.

"What are you doing?" she asked.

"Having a small fire." Trying not to laugh.

"What's so funny?"

"Marie Antoinette."

"Oh yes...Marie Antoinette. How could one not find her amusing?"

I asked my wife, "Why do you refer to yourself as 'one'? Why not say, 'How could *I* not find her amusing?'"

Hillary ignored this. "I hope you'll be fit for this evening."

"You mean for dinner in our own home with Elizabeth and her French boyfriend?"

"Yes," Hillary said. I could see I was beginning to get to her. "Drinks at seven," she said, and left the room.

I never expected to like Pierre, but I did. He was not as handsome as his uncle, my wife's paramour. He was taller, more gaunt but not as debonair as Depaulier. I could see that Elizabeth was besotted by him; her eyes barely left his face.

And she looked better; love agreed with her, I guess. She'd lost weight, her face had lost some of its chubbiness and her complexion, one of her best features, seemed even more radiant than usual.

We had drinks and hors d'oeuvres and when Hillary left the room to check the table arrangements, I asked Pierre a little about himself.

"My wife tells me you're going to Holyoke in the fall."

"Yes, sir. I found Holyoke to have an excellent curriculum in international business."

"Is that your area of interest? International business?"

"I hope to do my undergraduate degree in this, yes," Pierre told me in slightly accented English. "Then I want to be a lawyer." He grinned. Poor kid. Probably thought it was just what I wanted to hear.

"Well, that's very.... admirable, Pierre. Close to Smith, too." My daughter gave me a warning look.

"Yes, sir," said Pierre. He was trying hard, but I couldn't get a reading about how he felt about my daughter. I asked Elizabeth if she would mind checking on her mother, and she gave me a truly evil look as she pulled herself out of the chair and left the room. She was even beginning to sigh like her mother—not a promising sign.

"Are you intimate with my daughter, Pierre?" I asked him when the young woman in question was out of earshot. I took a pull of my club soda and tried not to look too hard at him. Casual.

"I...."

"I won't hold it against you." Looking at him now. "Just give me a straight answer. I'd like to know the truth."

"Well, I..."

Of course the Grand Interloper chose that moment to reenter, Elizabeth close on her heels, like a puppy.

"Dinner is nearly ready," the lady of the house said, giving me the hairy eyeball. "Shall we go in?"

We all sat down. Hillary at one end of the table, me at the other. Fortunately, we had a smaller dining room table for intimate meals like this, not the formal one where we'd need intercoms to converse.

"So..." I began, as Daniel brought out shrimp cocktail and dispensed them. "Where were we?" Pierre took a gulp of water. He was strung as tight as catgut on a violin. I was sharply brought back to sitting at Harry Goodman's table and feeling exactly the same way.

I picked up my cocktail fork, and after the slightest hesitation he did the same.

"I saw a coyote on the lawn today," I said.

"Never!" said my wife.

"I've seen it, too," said my daughter.

"This morning it was. Bold as could be." I shrugged, and bit into a plump, pink, shrimp that had probably been bobbing around in the Gulf of Mexico last night. "Do you have coyotes?" I asked Pierre. "In France, I mean."

Of all the subjects he'd prepped for this evening, I was sure coyotes was not among them. "Aren't they dangerous, sir? I mean wolves are…."

"Life is dangerous, Pierre, if we fear it enough. At least, that's my opinion. I think this coyote was merely hungry."

"Richard is being facetious," interjected my wife. "Of *course*, coyotes are dangerous…I will have Raymond contact the warden tomorrow."

I winked at my daughter's boyfriend. "No wild animals allowed in *these* parts, Pierre. Hope you keep that in mind."

"Mother," Elizabeth began to protest and Hillary gave me one of her withering looks, the one custom-made for me.

"I think you're right, sir," Pierre bravely said. "'Fear is but a pale flame against my burning passion.'"

"Napoleon?"

"Benjamin Franklin."

"We could use a few statesmen of his caliber these days."

"Yes, sir," said Pierre, trying not to looked too pleased at his victory. He would do all right, I thought. More than all right if he didn't keep pretending he was from a wealthy family.

Daniel cleared away our first course. Since Cecilia's demise, he was doing double duty as cook, server and washer-upper. I hoped he'd be going to Portland soon. The strain was starting to show.

The rest of the meal went smoothly enough. I tried not to behave in an aberrant way and embarrass my daughter. I remembered at her age how blown up in scale everything seemed. This was the first young man she'd ever invited home; the potential for upset was staggering.

We talked about the weather. I told them about my upcoming trip.

"Your freshman orientation is almost here," I said to my daughter. "I'm afraid I'm going to miss it."

"Mother is bringing me," Elizabeth said, making me feel cast out. "They're having a mother/daughter luncheon two days prior."

"And do they have father/son luncheons at Holyoke?" I asked Pierre, and realized my *faux pas* as the words passed my lips.

"My father is deceased," Pierre said, eyes on mine. "My uncle will take me up, get me settled."

"Ah...your uncle. The famous French poet?" I asked. Now I *was* being facetious.

"Yes. He is incredible." *Eencredible.* "In France he is considered to have great talent."

"I don't doubt it." I looked at Hillary who was totally absorbed by her sole *meuniere.* "That should work out well. Michel can escort you all in my absence."

My wife looked at me—I thought she looked frightened; but the look quickly vanished, leaving me to wonder a minute later if I'd only imagined it.

"I have a little something for you," I told my daughter later that evening, having followed her to her room. I gave her the package, wrapped in dull, gold paper. "Something that meant a great deal to me at your age."

She looked at me and smiled, her eyes alight under long, dark lashes. "Thank you." She unwrapped it slowly, with ceremony.

"Think on These Things?" she asked, making the title a question.

"By an irreverent man named Krishnamurti."

She was—as they say—clueless. "What's it about?"

"Not toeing the line," I said, because that was what the book had meant to me.

"Thank you," she said again, and gave me a long look. "Are you alright?"

"Better than alright. I'm happy."

"Mother says you're behaving strangely."

"Darling, I realize your mother is someone very close and dear to you. Perhaps I am behaving...a little differently. I just want you to know that I love you, too. Never doubt that. I will *always* be there for you if you need me. Understood?"

"Yes." She had grown pensive.

"I think Pierre is a nice young man, by the way. Not that I *know* him very well."

She smiled at this, but something seemed to be tugging on her, something she wasn't ready to tell me.

I looked at her, and held out my arms, and she came to me for a good-night hug.

"Good night, sweet pea," I said, using my childhood endearment for her.

"Good night, daddy long legs," she answered with long-overdue affection.

All we needed now was a bedtime story with a happy ending.

ESCAPE

1.

My departure from Foxglove Hollow was nothing if not anticlimactic.

On Monday morning Hillary and I had breakfast together, read the papers together. Said very little to one another, as had become our habit. I then rose, came to her end of the table, and kissed her on the cheek.

"I'll be in touch," I told her. "My flight is at noon. I need to be at JFK two hours before."

"You're flying commercial?" This seemed a surprise.

"Marty needed the Lear."

Elizabeth came down. I didn't want to overdo it. I kissed her on the cheek too and resisted the temptation to give her a hug, smell her silky, dark hair, carry her right out of there.

"Don't let them indoctrinate you too much at Smith," I said, smiling.

"I won't."

"You're only having black coffee?" The breakfast that Daniel had prepared, some fruit and toast, was pushed aside.

She smiled her mysterious smile. Foiled again.

"I guess I'll be going." I don't know what I expected: a cymbal crash, a teary good-bye, a pat on the back? Instead I had two women watching me over the rims of their coffee cups, looking like they wished I'd just go so they could get on with their plans.

I got into the back of the Town Car and Raymond and I headed up the long, sealed driveway out of Foxglove Hollow. Like a foreign correspondent who'd been on assignment too long, my leaving was bittersweet. I'd done my best for a woman I'd been committed to and thought I loved. But it was time to leap for the last helicopter before my mission destroyed me.

Dressed as a business-class passenger flying off for vacation, my rucksack and boots were hidden inside my normal traveling luggage. Raymond—last name Strezlecki—the dedicated driver and fix-it man who'd worked for me for more than a decade, suddenly decided to have his first heart-to-heart talk with me. His wife Marta, a domestic, had recently run off with the Nicaraguan gardener who worked on the same estate as she did, but the gardener had beat her several times. She wanted to come back to him now. What should he do?

"What do you *want* to do?" I asked him. This was a whole new world for both of us.

"She very young, sir. I think it was too much care, three children so quick. She doesn't speak English very well." I don't think Raymond had strung more than three sentences together in addressing me in all the years I'd known him. His demeanor had been impeccably professional: he'd taken care of the cars, overseen general maintenance of most mechanical aspects of Foxglove Hollow, been a reliable handyman and a closed-mouthed, diligent employee. I barely knew him.

"Do you still love her?" I asked. He gave me a long, sad look in the rear-view mirror and shrugged.

I was beginning to wonder if unhappiness about love was a contagion.

Raymond parked at the curb, rushed to find a Sky Cap who'd take good care of me, relinquished my bags when he was satisfied that I'd be well looked after on the next fifty yards of my journey.

Of course, I knew that it would be a long time before I saw Raymond again—if ever—so I grasped his forearm as I shook his hand and gave him a meaningful good-bye. He was due his vacation and would be hearing from my attorney in a month or so. I imagined his reaction when he received his bonus: ten thousand dollars for each of the ten years he'd been in my employ, plus full ownership of the classic Daimler I kept in the garage. He could start his own company with it—as a private chauffeur—if he liked.

Inside the terminal, a woman was screaming her lungs out.

"No, no, no," she cried. She was pointing at a well-dressed man in a turban and Punjabi suit standing in line. Security guards had come running to where she stood and began trying to assess if the woman's hysteria was legitimate.

"He has a bomb in there—in his, his...turban. I know it. I'm not getting on a plane with HIM. NO WAY." The woman was also well dressed. On the face of it, a fortyish, professional woman with a slim briefcase and nice jewelry. Except for the screaming, she looked quite normal. Around her, New Yorkers of all ilks looked variously disgusted, scared, amused, put out and looked around for others who would support their view.

Luckily, I had a prepaid, electronic ticket, as did the Indian, and we went through a short line to check our bags, then to security where I relinquished my shoes temporarily, had my wine opener and nail scissors removed from my carry-on permanently. The Indian had to pass through a thorough going-over with metal detectors that passed over him without a blip.

We boarded the plane and I was relieved to not see the screamer anywhere in sight.

The Indian man came on though, just after I did. He looked at me with liquid brown eyes, smiled and sat beside me.

I thought: Now here it comes, a spiritual explanation of the ugly scene we'd confronted at the airport.

Instead, he ordered a double Johnny Walker from the stewardess, took out a pulp paperback and ignored me completely.

I ate my lunch, and dozed all the way to Miami.

2.

Miami Airport was the usual hustle: long concourses streaming with people, kiosks loaded with bestsellers and tourist junk. I cued up for a Cuban coffee, then hailed a cab for Ft. Lauderdale.

The traffic was thick at rush hour, even with five lanes of heat-soaked tarmac, but I made it to the office of David Felder, yacht broker, across the underpass from Pier 66 in under an hour, which he seemed to think was some kind of record.

David was a big, Jewish wise guy wearing a gold Star of David that was large enough to clobber somebody. He was drinking what looked like grapefruit juice, but then he wheeled back in his chair, pulled out a bottle of Smirnoff and offered me a Salty Dog, too.

Maybe I was missing Marty, at least the old Marty and the old me, because David Felder just got to me. He had a laugh that could stop traffic: big and brazen, followed by the long wind-sucking wheeze of a dedicated smoker.

I liked him immediately, sensed that he was a self-made man who'd made it big. I asked him about himself, and he said he had two daughters, Thevi and Marisa, and lived in a big house he called The Ponderosa over in Las Olas.

"So, Dick. You ready for a little *Nemesis?*" Haw, haw, haw, wheeze.

"Actually," I said, "that's something we need to discuss."

He stopped mid-wheeze, scrutinized me with narrowed eyes. "The money's not refundable ya know. They're all provisioned and ready to sail you to Havana tomorrow. The whole crew is rarin' to go." He took a big gulp of his drink and pressed the intercom. "Sheila! Where's the effin ice?" He looked at me some more. "You wanna back out?"

"No," I said. "But I'm not going. You can keep the money; you can take the cruise yourself with your wife and kids. I only have one condition."

I could see David Felder was a man used to having conditions thrown at him. He grew very calm and focused, reminding me of a panther, only paler. "So what's the deal?"

"You can't tell anyone I *didn't* go onboard if they ask."

"That's it?"

"That's it."

"You on the lam?" Sheila came in with the ice, and he loaded his glass, poured it half full of vodka, added the juice, then poked his finger in it and bobbed the ice around.

"Not from the law, no," I said, after Sheila left. "I'm making some changes though, and don't want anyone to find out where I've gone."

"So you booked this yacht at a cost of five large a day for two weeks, as a *smoke screen*?"

"Yep." I was beginning to feel quite pleased with myself.

"Jesus."

"What's the matter?"

"And what if they send the Coast Guard? What if they call the Ernest Hemingway Marina and you're not there? What if your wife makes a little Satcom call to the yacht, and you're nowhere to be found?"

"The crew has to lie, too."

"Captain Bob is gonna hate that shit," said David Felder. He leaned back in his chair and smiled. "Staying at the Pier tonight?"

"Thought I would."

"Okay. Let's do dinner at Burt and Jack's. Say eightish in the bar?"

It was an invitation I couldn't refuse. Life gets lonely sometimes when you're living undercover—just ask James Bond.

Burt and Jack's will always be a favorite of mine because of the memorable night that I spent there with David Felder. I had a three-pound baked stuffed lobster, at his insistence, and he had the surf n'turf, which was a 16-ounce steak done rare *plus* the lobster.

David told me some senior citizens came in here and what they took home in doggie bags could feed them for a week. "And let the dog go fuck himself!" Haw, haw, haw.

"So, what about the wife?" he asked between bites of steak rare enough to wiggle. "I hate to be the one to break it to you, Dick, but most people go on cruises with *other* people."

"My wife doesn't like to sail...or fly commercial."

"Oooo," said David, rolling his eyes. "Flying commercial really sucks."

"Actually, I'm leaving my wife," I said.

"But you decided not to tell her this little fact?" He'd started on the lobster now. Big juicy chunks that he plunged into melted butter and then swirled around. "There could be big lawyer pow-wow on that one."

"I'm betting on it." I pushed my plate back and ordered coffee. David ordered Death by Chocolate and a Grand Marnier.

"You got a plan."

"More or less."

"I presume you're not staying in the good ole U.S. of A."

"You got it."

"Let me see," David said, leaning back. "I see an offshore hideaway. The Bahamas?"

"Nope."

"The Caymans."

"Uh-uh."

"Am I getting warm?"

"It *is* warm. It's in the Caribbean. I really don't want to say more than that."

"Shit, yeah. I bet I know...the D.R., right?"

"David, I'm not going to tell you—OK?"

"Ha! I knew it! You're gonna hunker down in one of those Oscar de la Renta bungalows, play golf by day, get laid by night. Ho, ho. But hey, if you think the D.R. is hot, you oughta try Hong Kong."

"Hong Kong?"

"Yeah, I got a boat builder over there—Ling Yachts? Got an exclusive to sell the line in the States. So I go over every two months, do some business, have some r and r, buy Linda some of those Bulgari knock-offs she loves. Not as cheap as it used to be, but still a hot city. Dim sum, Peking Duck. I love Chinese, but you gotta watch 'em."

I didn't know if he was talking about the food or the people.

"I got a good life," he said, but I wondered if he was really happy, or just playing with money as a substitute. I liked David; liked his humor, his no-bullshit directness. If I was staying in south Florida, we might've been friends.

Instead, I was leaving on the morning flight to Mexico City, and then to Concepción.

On the drive back to Pier 66 he told me he'd decided to use the cruise I'd bequeathed him, at least a week of it. "Give a week to Sheila, give one to Al; he's the office manager. Keep 'em sweet, ya know?"

I had the feeling under all the smarminess, David Felder was a big softie. In fact he *looked* like a big plush cushion, a testimonial to a lifetime of excess.

We pulled into the hotel entrance, and three valets rushed over.

"Hey, Mr. Felder. How are you tonight, sir?"

"Park it for you, sir?" It seemed like there might be a struggle for the keys.

"Hi, guys," said Felder. "Not tonight. Take good care of my friend here, will ya?"

He gave me a big pat on the shoulder, looked me in the eye.

"Tip 'em big," he leaned over and whispered across the front seat of his gold Rolls. "A lot of guys think big, tip small. Which type are you?"

"I was always a twenty-percent man."

David Felder shook his head and laughed. "The more you spread it around, the more fun you have. Guaranteed."

"I'm learning," I said, thinking of the ways I planned to use my fortune in the future. I was sure David was right; spending all the money I'd managed, hoarded, entrusted, protected, capitalized, and previously paid to the Feds, was definitely going to be fun. No doubt about it.

3.

I took a flight to Mexico City. Fun it was not. Too much turbulence reminded me of jet engines shutting down. I could live without a repeat, even though the incident had changed my life, hopefully for the better.

I was glad to touch down in Mexico City, though its size has always baffled me. Marty and I once had a call from one of the tequila companies who wanted us to fund some new agave plantations for them, but in the end we didn't take it on. There were too many risks. Mexico was a labyrinth of contrasts: old powerful families and young drug lords; reform-minded politicians and ancient, corrupt government. Caught in a maze of bureaucratic maneuverings, reliable information was often hard to pin down, bad for due diligence, but the perfect place to disappear, or change flights.

My flight to Concepción was in three hours, so I spent the time reading *501 Spanish Verbs* in the first-class lounge.

My overall impression of the Mexican culture, at least at the airport, was that it was very much like the States—a trend I'd noticed more in my travels. The Americanization of the world.

The Hubba Hubbans, on the other hand, seemed unaware of what they were "missing." Either that, or they just didn't give a damn. They were surrounded by incredible natural beauty but had apparently never considered tourism as a possible source of revenue. It was "da company," or nothing.

Problems—trabells—were a laughable concept. Hubba Hubbans seemed to have a deep acceptance that things would work out. And like a bunch of hard-partying Buddhists, they lived fully in the moment, trusting that there was nothing so serious a couple of belts of Mi Abuela or a visit to the padre wouldn't cure them.

I thought I'd get along fine.

I also realized I was thinking more and more about seeing Veronica again. Little clips of her kept popping into my mind. When I thought about Hubba Hubba, I thought of her, too. She was a standout with her western education, someone who most certainly did not go with the flow as the others did. Maybe I wasn't as ready for the counter-culture as I thought.

I got on the plane to Concepción and thought about her some more. I sketched some plans of my future bedroom on a cocktail napkin, an open room with a platform bed in the middle, mosquito netting billowing around it. Hmmm.

I closed my eyes. Saw Veronica lying on the bed with all her clothes off, a come-hither look on her face. Funny, but her faceless husband was nowhere to be seen.

It was nighttime when I arrived in Concepción, my first visit to the capital with the same name as the country. Did people address their mail Concepción, Concepción, like New York, New York? How efficient was the mail system anyway? Questions like this, mundane things that I hadn't considered before, began carving little paths to my brain.

I cleared customs and immigration with scant attention, found an English-speaking driver, and we zipped along into the city via the Corridor Norte in a late model Toyota upholstered with red fur, and the temperature of a meat-locker. Was the fur supposed to keep you warm in the frosty air?

In my zeal to leave, I hadn't made a hotel booking and asked for suggestions, which perked up the driver who sized me up and suggested the Intercontinental. That was fine by me. Nothing like a whole new life to make you want to pull some fresh linen over your head.

The hotel's lobby was a Western, five-star invention of marble floors, damask drapes, with a distinctly Latin display of orchids center stage. Ah—civilization.

My driver strode to the reception desk and began speaking earnestly to two handsome young men in dark suits, probably about his commission. I held back to give him a chance to do the deed, but after less than a minute he shrugged, and came back my way.

"Fool."

"What?"

"They fool. *Convencion de religiosos.*"

I wasn't following, so went to reception myself, smiling with confidence. "I'd like a room, please. Just for one night."

"We are fool, sir," the young man with Aristides on his pocket told me politely.

"Come, come," I said. "You must have one single room for a weary traveler like me." Aristides looked at his accomplice, I mean his fellow receptionist. This one was called Dominic. Dominic shrugged too, and gave me a dazzling smile.

Behind them a giant aquarium filled with yellow and blue fish and black and white coral made everything seem surreal. God, I was tired.

They finally had an exchange in rapid Spanish and bent to their respective keyboards—and miracle of miracles, found a room for me. But it wasn't clean.

"Oh."

"But it weel be," said Dominic. "Very soon. We have a convention for two nights, somebody check-et out."

"Lucky," said Aristides. He was smiling now, too. "Take a seat, sir. We will fix it up."

An hour and two *Hola!* magazines later, I got into my room— *gracias a Dios!*—as they say in the phrase book. A bed, a hot shower, a minibar; what more could a man want?

Beyond the gauze curtains was a balcony. Beyond the balcony, the Bay of Concepción and the twinkling lights from the old quarter looked magical. The tide was out, unfortunately; Concepción and its seven hundred thousand residents didn't have a sewage treatment plant yet. But I was undeterred. I took out a little bottle of Chivas, filled a glass with ice and went out for a nightcap on the balcony, being careful not to breathe through my nose.

I had arrived in my newly adopted country, so it was hard not to feel optimistic.

Tomorrow the tide would be in, I'd get my Harley out of customs and discover a little more of what Concepción, the capital, had to offer. I'd also lay my hands on some of the money I'd wired down to start my new adventure. Easy peasy.

4.

I woke up to find a young maid standing at the end of my bed. She smiled fetchingly, then left. How long had she been standing there, I wondered? I grabbed the sheet around my bare nakedness and rolled up to a sitting position, then smiled. If a young woman wanted to ogle me while I slept, who was I to complain? The new Richard Darlington was not going to be such a tight-ass snob. No sirree.

I went into the bathroom where I practiced my suave look, the one where I raise my right eyebrow up and down. I flexed my arms to each side, and grinned. When you're traveling alone you have to do something to entertain yourself.

I ordered coffee—delicious. It came with a flaky croissant and three little pots of English jam. Not bad. I ate out on the balcony looking down fourteen floors to the sun-sparkled sea, relieved the tide was in. Concepción was an anomaly. To my right, the old quarter jutted out on its own peninsula looking from a distance like a fortress, which it had been, according to the pamphlet in my room, whose 16th-century brick dungeons and stone buildings now housed museums, embassies, chic restaurants, and the Presidential Palace. On my left, another peninsula, this one crammed with high-rise buildings of glinting glass, reminding me of Miami.

I found a customs agent in the Yellow Pages, after much searching, under *Aduanas, Corredores de*. J.J.'s advert was partially in English, the only one that was. For the hell of it, I skipped past the A's to *Bancos* and began counting. When I reached a hundred, I gave up. Concepción's reputation as an international offshore banking center was secure.

Jarald McVey would have effected the wire the previous week, and assured me I'd be able to access my money by merely showing my passport at the Banco de Concepción. I showered and put on a fresh shirt, feeling bouncy as a cheerleader, but without the pom-poms.

The heat hit me like a blast furnace as I left the hotel lobby, but the force was with me, and an air-conditioned cab was right at hand. I jumped in and we sped off toward the Via España, me trying to strap myself in. Latin machismo, I was finding out, was never at a greater zenith than behind the wheel of a car, and as there were over nine thousand cabs in the city, it made for an interesting ride. Normal-looking men swerved violently, inserted their vehicles into intersections to cut each other off, gave each other the finger, honked, braked hard, and swore. They also gave a little toot-toot to any woman in a skirt, and did not discriminate between young, old, fat or thin. All women in skirts were apparently beautiful to a Concepcionisto male, or Tisto. It was the noisiest traffic I'd ever been in; a tableau that was half romantic comedy, half thriller.

I found myself, finally, in the sanctuary of the main branch of the Banco de Concepción, passed through security, smiled happily as I went up the stairs to meet the officer in charge of new accounts who would give me the already printed checks in the name of a Concepción corporation set up for me in advance by Jarald McVey.

This is what really happened: No one spoke English, at least in the immediate vicinity, so someone had to be found. That person was on a break, but would be back soon, at least that's what I gathered from the sign language. I picked up the bank's annual statement, in Spanish, sunk deep into a spongy orange chair and began thumbing through it.

A half hour later, a pretty black woman of about twenty-one in a dark blue suit approached me and smiled. She said something that sounded like "follow me" and so I did. We went down a line of desks. She finally pointed to a chair in front of one of them, then sat down and began typing away at a keyboard and looking at the screen, ignoring me. Three feet away from us was another desk where a similar scene was playing itself out. The lack of privacy was unnerving, but Damaris—thank God for nametags—hadn't even asked me who I was, or what I wanted.

At last she looked at me. "Name?"

"Richard Darlington."

"Meester Reechard Darling-town," she repeated. Tap, tap, tap. "Paspor?"

"Right here." I was getting good at these approximations of English. Maybe I could find work as a professional translator.

Damaris scrutinized my photo and each stamp in my passport page by page, looking up at me at regular intervals. Finally, she seemed satisfied by a review of all the places I'd traveled in the past five years or so, and opened back to the passport number, and typed that in, too.

Then we waited. "Is slow." She said, folding her arms and looking at the screen, serene as a cat. Then something must have popped up on the screen that alarmed her, because she got up with my passport in hand and hurried away without looking back.

Several minutes later I was greeted by a committee: the bank manager, an assistant manager and two security guards. I knew who they were because of the nametags in the first instance, and the guns and badges in the second. Behind this entourage was Damaris, looking like a whistle-blower.

"Come with me, please," the manager said in perfect Tisto-accented English.

We walked as a group to his office. Everyone we passed stared at me as if I was an escaped convict. We arrived at a door with PRIVADO written on it in bold letters. Whatever the manager had to say would not be heard by every other bank official and client on the floor. I was feeling luckier by the minute.

He indicated a seat, the assistant took the one next to mine. The two security guards stood outside the door. Their guns were not drawn, however.

"Meester Darlingtown." His eyes looked like poached eggs behind thick glasses; his skin was tough and pocked, like a lizard's. "Perhaps you know—but maybe you don't—here in Concepción we have very streek rules about money."

"Yes," I agreed. "Most banks are the same."

Mr. Lizard ignored this. "That is why when someone comes to us and wants to put more than a meel-i-un dollars in cash into a corporate checking account, we have to ask a lot of questions." The assistant nodded sagely at this. "I hope you understan'."

He took a deep breath, as if the whole subject was painful to contemplate. "Our government, in cooperation with other nations, such as the Uni-ed Stays, want to stop the drug trafficking problem. Money in large dee…that is to say quantities, is often linked to thees problem."

"I am not a drug dealer, but a businessman," I said in my defense. Thanks a lot McVey, I was thinking. Thanks a whole fucking bunch.

"I am shor this is true," he said in an exaggerated way, as if I was learning English, not Spanish. His eyes twinkled in encouragement though, reminding me of Hubba Hubba's Mayor Fernando. He didn't want to *lose* the sale, just cover his ass.

"What can I do to facili..I mean, make it easier for you to open the account?" I smiled, trying to keep it simple: the obedient client who couldn't wait to make a substantial deposit and earn this institution twice the interest it was going to pay me.

"We need three references from Concepionistos. Do you know of three of our citizens who could give you a personal recommendation?"

"Well, yes. But they're not in the city."

"Ah…where are they then?" He steepled his fingers, tapping them together. He still looked hopeful, smiling his lizard smile.

"Hubba Hubba."

"Hubba Hubba?" he repeated, trying to hide his dismay. "A bit of a *fantasia*, no? Ees beautiful, but…" he shook his head. "I'm not so sure…."

"But Hubba Hubba *is* part of Concepción, is it not?"

"Si, si, certainly. Do you have some names for me? I will also need *los numeros de identidad*. Let's try."

What a helpful man. What a wonderful, sincere individual. "That shouldn't be a problem. May I borrow your phone?"

"Of course." I took out my wallet and called Veronica's number. The connection was clear, the phone rang and rang. Nobody home. Next I tried The Boatel.

"Dick? Back already?" Big Jim's voice sounded just like I remembered it: a foghorn in the mist. I explained the situation, asked if he could help. His reply: "Whada buncha fuckin' pencil grinders. Sorry, buddy. I ain't got an ID. WANDA!"

Wanda came on the line, but I didn't know it, because she didn't say anything. After a few seconds of silence, she finally coughed politely.

"Wanda? It's Richard."

"Oh hi."

"Wanda I need three references for a bank application. Do you have any ideas?"

"Well, sure." The phone went clunk as it hit the counter. A few minutes later she was back. "I got my references from Julie, who got them from somebody in her family. She says they're official."

"*Official* bank references?" The bank manager, sitting across from me, got a smile on his face indicating I was on the right track, either that, or he was passing gas. "Thank you, Wanda. Would you mind sharing them with me?" She gave me three names of people I'd never heard of, and their identity numbers. I dutifully noted them down.

"Are you coming back soon?" she asked me. "Everybody's getting pretty antsy."

"They are?"

"Well, yeah."

"People are missing me?" Trying to get the drift of Wanda's meaning was like trying to read seaweed on the beach at low tide.

"Sort of."

"I'll be up there in a few days."

"That's good. Are you going shopping, by any chance?"

"Hopefully, yes," I said, smiling at the bank manager.

"Pick me up some hair color?"

"Sure thing." She gave me the details. "Also if you find any chocolate chips? I'm also out of Jell-O, the red one." The bank manager watched interestedly as I made my notes.

"You comin' in on the ferry from Rambala?"

I hadn't thought about it. "Isn't there a ferry from Platanillo?"

"Yep, but no road connects the city to Platanillo. You gotta come in from Rambala, which takes you to Hubba Hubba direct."

"Right. See you in a few days, then." Which I hoped was true, but looking at the sheaf of papers the bank manager was laying out, I wasn't sure.

5.

I left the bank with assurances from the manager that my funds would be cleared by morning and my new checkbook ready and walked into blinding sunlight. It was time to pay a visit to the English-speaking customs agent I'd contacted, a man with the unlikely name of Jesus—pronounced Hay-zeus—Jones, who was going to help me clear my Harley.

I entered the fray of Concepción traffic: blaring horns, multi-colored buses, darting pedestrians and fruit vendors to arrive at Jesus's office intact. I took a guess about which button to press—none had any indicator of its occupant—and felt lucky to find him on the third buzzer I tried. "Come up, Mister Darlington."

Having left the international banking world behind, I felt buoyant and confident. Of course, life in a new culture would have its glitches, but soon I'd be on my V-Rod riding through the Concepción countryside to Hubba Hubba.

And then I met Jesus: a big, wet-looking man with a bright, red face and a jolly manner and had my doubts. His desk was piled high with files, and his office had a stale, musty smell as if the air conditioning filter hadn't been changed in a few decades.

"'Allo," he greeted me in a favorite Latin perversion of the English language greeting.

I introduced myself, and took his big sweaty paw in mine. I sat in front of his massive wooden desk, and he sat down behind it in an ancient gray office chair that protested loudly when he put his weight on it.

I pulled out all my documentation, the name of the shipper, the pro forma invoice. "It would have arrived yesterday," I told him.

"Mm-hmm," he said studying everything very professionally. At last he looked up and smiled. "A Harley-Davidson, hmmm?"

"Yes."

"A car, no?"

"No...a Harley-Davidson is a motorcycle." Jesus. I mean Hayzeus. Had the man been living on another planet? How could anyone think a Harley-Davidson was a car?

"Jesus, I wonder if..."

"You can call me J.J.—all my friends call me this."

Thank Christ for small favors, I wanted to say, but didn't know how Jesus might take my using the Lord's name in vain.

After half a dozen phone calls, defying any logic that I could follow, J.J. located the Harley. It was in a storage area near the airport, and so we went down the stairs and out to his car, which I was shocked to see was a big, white, immaculate SUV with enough shiny chrome to blind an army. We climbed in and he got the A/C started in the knick of time. Sweat poured off his red face, but once we got going, he seemed to adjust, weaving in and out of traffic Tisto-style, winning through intimidation.

I got to know him better on the half-hour ride, and decided, in spite of his musty office, love of freezing air, and lack of organization, J.J. was a decent guy.

He gave me a thumbnail tour of the city as we drove to the airport through an amalgamation of neighborhoods that switched back and forth between residential and commercial areas in several eye blinks. High-end, million-dollar-type residences sat close to the city center, while slummy low rises clung to overpasses and everywhere there were street vendors, students, business people and pedestrians hawking, shopping or just striding along.

We whizzed through the banking district, past the Miami-style skyline of Punta Pargo's high-rise condominiums, and out to an area called El Silverado, which was just one big shopping district from end to end. The big fast food chains were all in evidence, as were some U.S. retailers. When I told J.J. of my plans to build my beachcomber's dream house, he began pointing out the big hardware and home improvement chains, as well as furniture and appliance warehouses.

Leaving the world of drive-in dry cleaning behind didn't mean I wanted to do my laundry down at the old mill stream, or sit on logs bare-assed. Roughing it had its limits as far as I was concerned. Simplifying my life didn't mean I wanted to be without comfort. Still, in the beginning, I wanted to see what I really needed rather than have old assumptions follow me around like a full set of Waterford crystal.

Except for the Harley, the money I'd transferred to the Banco de Concepción and a new type of credit card, which held some of my assets in digitized gold, I'd arrived empty-handed in Concepción. It'd be interesting to see what I'd want to purchase, what I deemed as essential to my new life. It would be interesting to see what kind of "asset protection" Jarald McVey would be able to put into place for me in the weeks ahead—before my divorce hit the pages of the *New York Times*.

At last we pulled into the parking lot of a large, modern building, and J.J. led the way with purpose and authority. Inside, a group of beige uniforms sat around drinking coffee and looking bored until J.J. showed them the pro forma, and like a bunch of kids at Christmas, they couldn't wait to follow me into the customs warehouse and watch me uncrate the Harley and roll it into full view.

A Harley V-Rod is one of those things that just seems to have a certain impact on people—both male and female. Especially when it's all new brushed chrome with no road dirt and not a scratch on it. I took the key out of my jeans, swung my leg over, started it up, and every man around me just broke into a big grin to hear its controlled roar.

I then gave everyone rides around the parking lot, even the *jefe*. He said he needed to test it too, according to J.J.'s translation. Whatever. I was getting a lot of bang for my buck giving a bunch of Concepciónisto customs guys, whom I'd just met, a free ride around the building where they went to work everyday.

Afterwards, we liquidated by certified check my one and only tangible Tisto asset.

We were then free to go, and I followed J.J. back into the city center along long stretches of park-like green on well-paved roads where the Yankees had once had a big military base. It was a breeze.

We arrived back to the hotel unscathed, and had a couple of beers.

"The highway to Hubba Hubba, is it in good condition?" I asked him.

"Is *that* where you're going?" He seemed to find this funny.

"I've bought some property up there."

"For a hotel?" He was still smiling.

"No, no. I'm going to…well, I don't know exactly what I'm going to do yet. I have some ideas, though."

"Ah, Hubba Hubba," he said, getting a dreamy look. "*El paraiso de la republica.*"

"Huh?"

"A paradise, that's what Tistos call Hubba Hubba. But nobody goes there."

"Why is that?" I was beginning to find this mild amusement about my new adopted island a bit annoying.

"Too far to travel and Tistos don't like to travel too far." He thought about it some more, and sighed. "The Hubba Hubbans. Them are different."

"They seem quite happy, if you ask me," I said, feeling defensive.

"*Exactamente,*" J.J. latched on to this. "They *too* happy!"

I snorted.

"Blue Monday, Ruby Tuesday. They got a reason to have a party every day of the week."

"Blue Monday?" I'd not heard about this.

"Oh, ho, ho. You'll see. You remember what J.J. say: Them people's different." He seemed not to want to say more, and frankly I found his opinion limiting.

"And the road?"

"Ah, *si*. The road is *excelente*."

I felt some relief at this. At least my tax dollars were paying off with constructive results somewhere in the world through the U.S. Army Corp of Engineers.

"Gonna drive to Rambala?"

"Yep."

"Lots of *transitos*...but the road? *Es perfecto*."

"Will you get the plates tomorrow?" I only had the customs papers, which gave me forty-eight hours to get the registration sorted out.

"Tomorrow? Of course. *Mañana*, I will finish everything."

It was my turn to smile now. *"Perfecto,"* I said, though shortly I would have a whole new definition of the word.

6.

If I've learned anything about living in a Spanish-speaking country, it's that certain words have vastly different meanings and pronunciations in the field than in any classroom or dictionary. Take the pronunciation of my name, for instance: Reechard Darlingtown. Need I say more?

The word *mañana* is a perfect case in point. The English translation of *mañana* is "tomorrow", and so if today is Monday, for instance, tomorrow would be Tuesday. In Concepción, though, *mañana* means *some tomorrow in the future*, not necessarily the next day, and usually *not* the next day. It can also mean "never." This creates all kinds of stress until you figure out that *mañana* really means: not now. It's a way to put something off without outright refusal. You see? Nothing to *mañana*, once you get the hang of it; I've even started to use it myself to wriggle out of things on occasion.

Another word used often in Concepción is: *Como. Como* is another one of those words whose actual translation simply does not wash. *Como*, in the dictionary, means "how" or "why," as in the handy phrase: *Como esta Usted?* But the *real* use of the word used on its own as an exaggerated interrogative is Latin drama brought to its pinnacle. *COMO? is* really a stalling technique. It basically signals that the speaker has been: A. Caught in a lie and wants to change the subject; or B. Pig-headedly refuses to understand what you've just said in either Spanish or English. *Como* is indeed a showstopper of the highest caliber, but with judicious use can be used by the recent arrival, for example, to react to an excessive bill.

Perfecto, is of course, Latin mendaciousness brought to its height. There is absolutely nothing perfect about *perfecto*. Trust me. *Perfecto* most closely resembles the word "whew" in English, and is used broadly here to get someone off your back. For example, you could walk into one of the local municipal offices, give a long discourse of your grievances, complete with all your files, stamped receipts, official affidavits from other municipal offices and indicate your extreme displeasure with all of the contradictory rules, regulations, laws and customs being interpreted willy-nilly throughout the republic. And you could point out that even within the same *building* the varying policies, interpretations, and mishandling of documents, fees, reports and permissions by elected and appointed officials, inspectors, engineers, secretaries and accountants, were so mind-boggling and ambiguous that you were considering an immediate return to your home country....and all that you would get in response would be a series of nods, a lot of eye contact, and of course, at the end, that word so fitting, so well...perfectly suited to the Latin character: *Perfecto. Perfecto* means, in this context, I've listened to everything you have to say and there's absolutely nothing I'm going to do about it, so would you please just leave? In other words, *perfecto* is an acknowledgement that life is actually very imperfect, and more subliminally is an accusation. Why would anyone expect life to be perfect, except for some displaced, uptight gringo? Just tell 'em what they wanna hear.

So it was that the day after I had my promise from J.J.— *mañana*, in other words—I would learn firsthand the true meaning of the word. By the time I hit the road three days later, I'd feel the unbridled glee of someone who has wrestled a bureaucratic juggernaut to the ground and come out on top. I've also learned that there are no true victories in this culture, only temporary wins, many setbacks, and lots of frustration in between.

In my new "simpler" life, I'd had to wait another forty-eight hours for my funds to be released and get my checkbook in hand; the same amount of time to get my papers for the Harley in order and finally be able to drive the damn thing away. I'd had my room at the Intercontinental changed once, been propositioned twice, and eaten some iffy seafood that left me running to the john during one notable sleepless night.

I tried to call Elizabeth on her cell phone the next morning but her voice mail picked up. I felt anxious about her reaction once she found out my intention to divorce her mother, and wanted to stay in close touch with her. I assured her voice mail that my trip was going well but that it was extremely difficult to reach me, so just thought I'd check in, etc., etc. I promised to call again soon, but meanwhile gave her my new Yahoo email address so she could stay in touch with me. I asked her to please give me an update. How had the indoctrination gone? Did she like her new roommate? How was Pierre?

I wondered how Hillary was managing and remembered the fearful look in her eye when I mentioned Depaulier's name that night at dinner. Was she afraid I was going to find out? Maybe she was planning to divorce *me* and have a permanent relationship with the Frenchman. Now wouldn't that twist old Harry's guts around! Meanwhile, they were probably enjoying their freedom with me gone for a few weeks. Maybe they'd holed up at the Sturbridge Inn, or found a quaint little B&B up in Vermont.

I realized I couldn't care less. As long as Elizabeth wasn't adversely affected, Hillary could do as she pleased.

Meanwhile, I had my own conundrums to solve: getting from Point A to Point B on my new imported motorcycle, for example; sounded simple on the face of it.

In reality, getting to Hubba Hubba turned out to be anything but simple though, and reminded me of being back in Mr. Litchfield's Driver's Ed class. A believer in the Reality School of Driver Education, Litch loved to dress up like a cop and give us fake traffic tickets so we could "get the feel of what it's like to break the law." Unfortunately, all Litch's classes were in English, not Spanish.

My new Rules of The Road look like this:

Lesson One. The speed limit is completely arbitrary and yes, the road, part of the Inter-American Highway system, is practically seamless, built as it was with good old Yankee know-how, millions of U.S. dollars, and the hard work of thousands of determined Concepcionistos working shirtless under a broiling sun. The varying speed zones, I'm convinced, are whimsical and unmarked to provide fodder for a cash-strapped economy.

The first *transito* who stopped me, like the others that came after, had on a crisp beige uniform, no hat, a serious, invasive look in his eyes, and a gun. He told me in broken English that I had exceeded the speed limit and asked to see my papers. He went through my Harley documents—all ten of them—one by one, and kept giving me a penetrating look, as if any minute I'd finally admit to my sins, try and escape, and he could wrestle me to the ground, pistol whip me, and throw me in a dark, urine-soaked prison from which I'd never emerge alive. Instead, he took all my documents, walked slowly back to his car, and didn't come back for twenty minutes.

When he came over again, he seemed friendlier. "Okay," he said, and showed me a large white sheet with a long list of numbered infractions. He pointed at number five: *Velocidad exceso*. He had checked another box which had the numeral 80, against where he had written "60". It didn't take a graduate degree in Spanish to figure out that I was being accused of going 80 kph in a 60-kph zone, but when had the signs changed? As far as I could see, the countryside here looked exactly like it had a few miles back; there weren't more houses, more pedestrians, nor even a school.

He pointed at the amount of the fine, conveniently spelled out as $75 U.S. dollars. "You pay now, is cheaper," he said, smiling.

Ah ha.

"Recibo?" I asked. Maybe asking for a receipt would put an end to the charade.

"Perfecto," he said, taking out a carbon-copy tablet and carefully filling it in.

He tore it off and gave it to me, and to my untrained eyes it looked like an official receipt, and so I handed him the money—fifty bucks—and he cheerfully folded the bills, put them in his pocket and told me to have a nice day in Spanish.

Lesson Two. Even though it feels like a shakedown, the government actually does have a policy of discounting traffic violations on the spot, as it avoids unnecessary paperwork back at

Transito Central. Not a bad idea when you think about it, though disconcerting for the newcomer.

The second *transito* who stopped me had a different reason for fining me, but otherwise was a near clone of Transito One. He looked like he'd barely started shaving, had the same starched uniform, the same probing eye contact as those grizzly Turkish customs officials in the movie about the hash smuggler in *Midnight Express*. Having already been chased by a police vehicle with a siren and flashing red light in the middle of nowhere, I was now vigilant about my speed. What I had not yet learned was: my beautiful new V-Rod that I'd ordered in Miami and paid to import, wasn't really mine at all.

For the uninitiated, if you're driving a vehicle which is titled in the name of your Concepción corporation, you need a special *letter* from the company directors, in other words, associates of your lawyer whom you've never met, that gives you permission—the President of said corporation—to use the vehicle in question. Otherwise, they treat you as if you may have *stolen* the vehicle, and this creates a lot of stress for a serious young *transito* who wants to do the law-abiding thing and get his fines paid off on the spot and get his Transito Brownie-Point Quota for the day.

Luckily, I'd purchased a cell phone before leaving the city, and would've loved to use it to call my attorney so he could explain everything, but I was now out of cell phone range, and had to be escorted back to the nearest town where I could contact my lawyer, Licenciado Martinez. After that, the letter had to be written, signed and faxed to the nearest *transito* station from whence the confirmation eventually came that I had permission to ride my own motorcycle. Cheerfully, the *transito* discounted my fine, shook my hand, and I was once again on my way.

I'm ashamed to admit it, but yes, I still hoped that by keeping within the speed limit, with official permission to ride my Harley in hand, I could reach the ferry before ten p.m. and be pulling up to the Boatel in Hubba Hubba by midnight.

Lesson Three? There is no right-on-red option at stop lights. Red means stop, OK? No exceptions, especially in Concepción.

7.

The ferry ride to Hubba Hubba from Rambala was pleasurable by default: it was the first time I'd spoken English in twenty-four hours, and there were no *transitos* onboard.

I awoke from a dream where I was clinging like *The Fugitive* to the underside of a bridge while freezing white water lapped at my feet. I woke up to numb feet from the air conditioner, and heard the rumble of diesel engines outside my window that meant the morning ferry was loading up. I dressed fast, got a nice low-cholesterol breakfast of fried dough and creamy coffee to go, and headed down to the pier while a big group of locals—mostly fishermen—gathered to watch me and my new motorcycle get onto the ferry, jostling each other like school boys.

The ferry, a big steel platform with a pilot's bridge, had brawny wheels of rusty chain and high freeboards, felt sturdy enough, but shuddered violently as each successive truck pulled onboard. I parked the bike—and myself—as close to the bow and upwind of the diesel fumes as possible.

The bike secure, I leapt onto a small platform next to the chain for a better view. The lucid waters looked like chipped glass; on the horizon was a little green speck. Hubba Hubba?

I felt a tap on my shoulder and turned to find a short, handsome man with a wide smile and square, white teeth standing next to me. "Hey, man."

"Hey," I said.

"You no stand here. Chain comes here." On his T-shirt was the word "Marinero."

"Thanks for telling me." We hopped back onto the deck, and I extended my hand. "I'm Richard."

"Si, si," the man said, laughing and taking my hand. "I know who you is. The gringo."

I wondered about this, but didn't comment, fixated as I was on the sight of the wet anchor chain being pulled up mechanically through a rusty hole next to where I'd just been standing, and coiling itself around a spinning drum in big, clanging loops. "Are you from Hubba Hubba?"

"Si, si. I am cousin to Onassis. He tell me you come back."

"Ah, Onassis." I thought: Could this be a coincidence? "How is he?"

"Oh—*bien*. Y Blanquita. She want to see you *mucho*." He laughed and slapped his thighs. Women who lust after you, he seemed to say. What are you going to do?

"Blanquita?" I'd nearly had a mental lapse about Onassis, never mind his underage sister. "How did you know it was me? There it was again: western logic pointlessly geared into consciousness.

"Oh, he tell me it was you," said the guy, confident he had the right guy, and that reasoning was superfluous. "Marinero" still hadn't told me his name, so I would forever associate him with his T-shirt, which I later found out means "seaman" or "sailor", but could've meant "psychic" for all I knew.

"Aren't there other gringos around here?"

"They's some other gringos—shor," he continued. "They's Big Jim and Wanda, Daddy Joe and Sister Patrice, they lives on Little Conch. Down Isla Esmeralda way, they's Dune and his woman...ah. I forgit." Marinero turned and jumped back next to the windlass, heaved a big lever down next to the chain-encircled drum, and gave a quick hand signal to the tower. We lurched off the dock. He planted his sea legs, crossed his arms, and looked confidently over the prow: a good-looking Latino proud of his role as Keeper of the Chain.

I was next visited by a Latin man with a huge, rolling gut collecting the fares. Price for one motorcycle and passenger? Five bucks. Andres introduced himself and told me in Spanglish this was the main transport by which goods and services arrived in Hubba Hubba.

166

"Ten trock, three times a week. Hubba Hubba starve widout da ferry."

I inquired about prices and he gave me some incredibly reasonable rates and the names of a few truckers who worked the route from the city. Soon, I explained, I'd be bringing materials up from the city to build my house. This seemed to amuse him.

"Good luck, man," he said with a smile, and went on about his job.

I leaned over the rail, watched the water hitting the prow and felt a little thrill that I'd gotten this far. So far, my trip was going more or less according to plan. No one knew where I was; no one would find me unless I wanted them to. An atavistic feeling overtook me. I was free! I was happy!

We steamed past little mangrove islets, speckled reefs and sugary beaches; I saw pelicans, dolphins and Hubba Hubba itself, a shimmering dot growing ever closer on the horizon. It was all as beautiful as I'd remembered it.

I watched the island's approach, and then the ferry dock, and had an inspiration. My purchase of Coco Beach had been successful, so why not enlist Veronica's help to buy up some more? We'd create a magnificent green zone that I'd put into an environmental trust that my daughter would manage one day. It was perfect. Or *perfecto*, as my Spanish-speaking friends would say.

8.

I rolled off the ferry on my Harley, a big smile on my face. Wanda came running up looking teary, and threw her arms around my neck. Marinero winked and nodded at me; I was obviously in that secret fraternity of men who were irresistible to women—just like he was.

"Jim's had a stroke," she said. "Let's go quick. I left him alone." She jumped onto the seat in back of me, and we headed up the Calle Principal as people stopped and stared.

We pulled up in front of the Boatel; my heart was pounding. How bad was it?

At street level, Mayor Fernando was waiting for us, his dimples drilled into place like matching screw holes. Behind him were half a dozen musicians from the fire department.

"That rotten son of a bitch—" Wanda whispered in my ear. "He's the reason Jim got sick."

"Welcome Meester Reechard," the mayor said, moving closer to me as Wanda scampered up the ladder. "Welcome back to Hubba Hubba!" At this cue, the firemen began blasting out a welcoming *murga*.

"Well." I said when they had finished. "What a surprise."

"Wanda told us you were coming. We know how much you enjoy the island music," the mayor told me. His smile looked like it had been branded onto his face.

"Thank you," I said to the firemen. Enough of this. I wanted to get onto the Boatel and find out what the hell had happened to Jim.

"Ees nothing," the Mayor told me, spreading his arms like a bandmaster. "You are very welcome, Meester Reechard. Very welcome to Hubba Hubba."

"I need to go." I started toward the ladder, and he stepped in front of me.

"Nice mah-chine," he said, pointing at the Harley with his chin. "You take me for a ride some day—no?"

I didn't answer.

His dimples had grown shallower, like chips in plaster. "So you buy Coco Beach," he said, coming to the point at last.

"Yes."

"Ah...well," he said. "I guess George di'n't tell you about the little problem, then?"

"What problem might that be?"

"Oh, ees nothing, probably we can fix it. Just an old *servidumbre*." He shrugged.

"A servi—what?"

"Oh, dat George," said the Mayor, my new confidant. "I *knew* George di'n't tell you." He smiled at me again, and I felt his eyes on me, and wondered why I hadn't noticed it before. Mayor Fernando wasn't just making a play for my money, he was flirting with me because he was gay.

"If there's a problem, I'm sure we can resolve it," I said. "I'll speak to Veronica." Hopefully, she'd give me some legal protection from this avaricious little fucker if I needed her to.

"Oh—Veronica! She ees not happy with her daddy." He laughed lightly. "Veronica can no fix thees problem. She no got the power." He folded his arms across his chest.

"Really?" I said. I wondered what Mayor Fernando would look like without his set of perfect white teeth.

"I have to go see Jim now." I pushed past him to get up the ladder.

The dimples disappeared. "Veronica knows all about it. Black Jack, he owns it." He had a sudden desperate air.

I started up the Boatel's ladder.

"That a pretty motociclo—muy pretty. You better come see me about a permit to drive it in Hubba Hubba, Meester Darling-town." But he was talking to my back.

The sea breeze came directly at the Boatel's starboard side and I felt its freshness wash over me. Being with the mayor always made me feel as if I'd just rolled in a swamp.

On the Boatel's deck, I was reminded again of Big Jim's luck in having run aground at this particular spot—directly on top of a reef with a continual north breeze. As a tropical hotel site it was sublime, a fact that had not been overlooked, I was sure, by Hubba Hubba's pragmatic Mayor Fernando.

Down below decks, it was quiet; I found Wanda upside down under the galley table.

"Wanda?"

"Gotta lock these guns up," she told me, "before someone gets hurt." I was looking directly at her tiny denim-covered bottom.

"Where's Jim?" I asked, and finally her little pixie face came around and looked at me.

She gave a big sigh. "He's in the cabin. But be careful. He's got a shotgun."

"Terrific," I said, and walked forward to the master cabin. "Jim?" I heard a gurgle in reply. And then I saw him: Big Jim Flynn who had seemed so invincible and full of life now had a half-melted face, drool on his chin, and a shotgun across his knees.

When he saw me, he picked it up and tried pointing it. "Give me that fucking thing," I said, lunging for the weapon, "before somebody gets hurt."

There was a brief struggle. His grip was incredibly strong. But then he let go, as two big tears fell out of his left eye and coursed down his cheek.

"Farghhh," he said. "Whaa...nice."

I unloaded the gun and went to find Wanda.

"What the hell happened?" I asked her. She sat at the galley table with a rusty padlock in front of her. Her normally luminous gray eyes were red-rimmed and as large as teacups. She wasn't looking at me but at Shakey, who'd appeared on the top step of the companionway heading down into the galley.

"He had a fight wid da Municipal Council three day aback," Shakey explained. "They want to take da Boatel."

"And...?"

"And Big Jim, he blow a gasket," Shakey explained.

Wanda nodded at this. "The Mayor said we could pay him ten thousand dollars to extend the lease, or leave. And that's when Jim got out the gun." She pointed at a place just above her where two rough-edged holes had appeared.

"He aimed for his *head*?" I asked.

"Yep," Shakey said. "But he missed." Now there was a philosophical tidbit to chomp on.

"And he didn't go to jail?" I asked.

"The mayor had a gun, too. The police said it was self-defense. See?" Wanda said. I turned and found two more bullet holes in the bulkhead behind me. I was more incredulous by the minute. Citizens who took aim at public officials and got away with it? What had ever happened to due process?

"The jail, she fool," Shakey clarified.

"Besides, they can't make us move," Wanda said, thrusting a paper into my hands. I could tell she was getting impatient with the whole conversation. "We have a contract with Mayor Fernando. It's good for five more years, at least." I looked at the well-worn document in Spanish, a scrawled signature and what appeared to be a notary's stamp.

"It looks official," I said, completely clueless.

"Yep," agreed Shakey. "That's the notary, all right." He didn't seem happy.

"So?"

"He forgit da *testigos*, man."

"Witnesses," Wanda translated. "We got the contract and got it notarized, but forgot you need two witnesses to make it legal."

"I'm sure something can be worked out." In my old world there were rational, legal solutions to every problem.

Shakey snorted at this. "Huh! Next time dey'll take out Cabino and make da space fo' Big Jim, no fret. Cabino—ha! Mayor takes him out when he needs him. Dey put Big Jim in his cell next time."

"Who's Cabino?"

From the other cabin, I heard Jim repeat in a loud voice: "WHAA...NICE!"

"What's nice?" I asked Wanda.

"He wants an Ice," Wanda said, and leaned into the cooler to get him one. "You take it." She passed it to me. "Every time he sees me he tries to get me in a head lock."

I walked into the cabin with Jim's Ice, but didn't give it to him. His speech and motor skills were impaired but from the light coming back at me I was pretty sure he knew what was going on.

I squatted down in front of him. "You want this?" I asked, waggling the beer just out of his reach.

He leaned forward and almost fell out of his wheelchair. "Not so quick. I'm going to find Veronica and see what she can work out. This needs to be sorted out legally, Jim, not like Clint Eastwood in a bad western."

Jim shook his head back and forth. No way.

"Veronica needs to get a restraining order, for a start. You need to get everything into Wanda's name and then we'll apply for a new license for the Boatel. What's the mayor going to do? Hire a tractor and pull this leviathan out of here? No way. We will deal with this sanely and sensibly. I want you to agree, and then I will give you this beer." Richard Darlington, I thought, high-level diplomat.

He finally nodded, and I gave him his Ice, and then went back out to the galley.

"I'm going to go see Veronica, try and get this sorted out," I told Wanda and Shakey.

"Huh!" Shakey said, shaking his head as if I were light a few billion brain cells. "She married to Black Jack, man. He da president of da Municipal Council."

Undeterred, I went in to have a shower. When I came out I found my Harley chained to a palm tree. Next to it sat a man the size of a small house with a big, wild head of hair and a ragged, greasy T-shirt.

Cabino?

9.

He stood up and I saw he was huge: at least six four and over two fifty. His eyes were black and bored into me like twin coal lasers. His hair stuck out all over his head in thick, long, Rastafarian locks.

"Hi," I said, and tried smiling. "You must be Cabino."

He grunted, and passed me an envelope with my name typed on it, and a blue stamp that said Alcalde.

I opened the envelope. Inside was a list, also typed, from Mayor Fernando. It read:

Improper parking of motor veehicle: $10

No local permit: $50

Wrong side street: $20

No seat belt: $10

Light, she break: $10

Total: $100

I walked to the front of the Harley, and sure enough, my headlight was cracked. It looked like someone had used a big rock and worked on it for a while.

"I wish you hadn't done that," I told Cabino.

I went back up the Boatel's ladder into the Boatel, and asked Wanda. "You have a hacksaw? The mayor has chained up my bike and someone smashed my headlight."

"Holy shit!"

Shakey sucked his upper teeth with his tongue. "That sombitch."

Wanda went down under the table again and came up with a big chain cutter from the gun locker. "Will this work?"

I went back out, and Cabino was there, waiting. I started to cut the chain off, and he just clenched and unclenched his hands, watching me. I don't think the mayor had prepped him for this outcome. He'd probably had a 100% expectation, in fact, that Cabino's only job would be to escort me to the palacio so I could pay my fine and get the key to the padlock and unchain my Harley.

I threw the chain into his hands; mounted the bike and started it up. "See ya!" I said, and roared up the street just like Steve McQueen would've done.

Three blocks along, I parked the bike where I could keep an eye on it and went inside.

Veronica's receptionist smiled when she saw me and tapped the inner door, then went in. Veronica came out and extended her hand. She was dressed impeccably in a navy and white suit, and though she wasn't as cold as before, she was still distant and business-like. What was with me and haughty, uptight women? Was it a special gene I had?

We went into her office and sat down.

"Big Jim tried to kill the mayor," I said, getting right to the point.

"I know," she said. Her eyes still looked sad, then she glanced down and tried not to smile.

"We need to do something other than pay a ten-thousand dollar bribe to the mayor. Do you have any ideas?" I leaned forward and saw that my fly was unzipped. *Perfecto.*

"Um..." she turned discreetly away to get a file.

"I thought we could put everything in Wanda's name and get a new lease." I suavely tried to zip myself up while twisting away, wondering if in Veronica's presence I could ever get things right.

"That's a good idea," she said, ignoring the activity around my crotch. "Then she can pay the new lease payment into the treasury, instead of into the mayor's pocket."

"Great," I said, finished at last. "Can you draw up the paperwork?"

"The Mayor is a *cabron*. Just remember, he is a *cabron* with no conscience." Her tone called to mind sociopaths who ripped the wings off butterflies for fun. "He won't just quit."

"Jim needs a lawyer," I repeated.

"Yes, I will help Mr. Jim. The Mayor wants the Boatel for himself, of course."

I waited for the rest.

"It is the only hotel on the island. He wants to add on to it and make it into a casino."

"A casino? In Hubba Hubba?" I was incredulous.

"Of course."

"Did anyone ever consider the ecological damage to the surrounding area? The Boatel is going to rust itself into oblivion on that reef, eventually. But to make it permanent, string it with lights and put in a half dozen flush toilets...?" I could just imagine what a casino á la Fernando would look like.

Veronica snorted like her mother. "Hubba Hubba has its own rules, Mister Darlington."

"Please call me Richard." This obsequious use by Hubba Hubbans of the Mister-word, as in Meester Reechard, was starting to make me feel like Rhett Butler reincarnated.

"The thing is this, the Mayor doesn't care. Purely, he has no care for the people here. None. His office? It's like a bank. People come and go. The people with money, they go to the front of the line. It's one long *fila*, and he's the cashier at the head of it." She dispensed this information like Tic Tacs. There was no emotion in her words. *Resigned.*

"Why doesn't someone stop him?" I was becoming indignant. This was a democracy for Christ's sake!

"The Mayor is elected," Veronica told me with a calm that was beginning to get on my nerves. "No one can take him out until the next election, or until *fiscal* decides to prosecute. If someone can prove his criminal actions, then they can get him out but it's a long investigation. Time they figure it out, it's time for somebody new."

She crossed the tips of her long elegant fingers and looked at me.

177

"I see," I said, though I didn't at all. As far as local representation was concerned, it wasn't looking too hopeful for the citizens of Hubba Hubba. But they had voted for him by a majority. I wondered why.

"The Mayor also told me today there was some conflict over the land I bought." Now that I was dangling my feet in the pool, why not go for full immersion? "A servi-something. Do you know about this?"

"A *servidumbre*?" she asked. Her voice had a note of fear.

"Yes, what is a *servidumbre*, exactly?"

"It's a right of way," she said, clearing her throat. "The piece of land *behind* your farm belongs to the municipality. People have the right to reach the beach through that side of the property, this is in the title deed. I'm surprised your attorney didn't mention it." She had brought the fear under control, but I could still feel it, like a beating heart, in the room.

"No one told me about it," I said. In response, she began studying a file on her desk, trying to dismiss me.

The silence in the room began to grow exponentially.

"The mayor said your husband Black Jack owns it."

"You want the money back?" she asked, finally looking at me with those beautiful, moist eyes.

"I'd like to see where it is, Veronica. I want everything clear."

"I think you will find hardly anyone uses it," she said, the closest she'd ever come to trying to assuage me. So why did I feel—not feel, *know*—she was keeping something else from me? This triggered the old visceral reaction; a need to control with a good dollop of anger mixed in.

"You're not telling me everything, Veronica. What is it?"

She looked at me with a set jaw. "I have nothing to hide, Mister Darlington."

"We'll see about that, won't we?"

"I never wanted you to buy the farm," she said, stung and suddenly she looked her age, about thirty-five, or so. "I tried to prevent it. Please remember this."

"Oh I will," I told her, getting up. *Don't fuck with me.* "Let me know when Jim's leases are ready. I'll be paying his legal fees. And let me know when someone can come out to Playa Coco and explain to me what the hell is going on with the servi-whatever."

She said nothing and I strode out into the sunlight where I found Cabino sitting on my bike.

He pointed at the palacio building two blocks away. "Don't fuck wid me, mahn." This was no gentle giant but an intimidating enforcer for an elected official.

"Get off my bike and we'll go to see the mayor." Surely even Cabino wouldn't strangle me right on the Calle Principal in front of all the park's pedestrian traffic.

"I watchin' choo," said Cabino, as I got on the bike and cruised slowly up the street. In a few giant steps Cabino was behind me and followed me in through the main entrance.

A sign over one of the doors said *Alcalde* in curly black script, and I walked into the reception area where a motley group of people lounged against ancient, scarred wooden desks—the Municipal Thugs? A bleach-blond Latina with a tight-fitting dress had me sign a book, and then tapped at the inner door while everyone watched her and said nothing.

Mayor Fernando opened the door himself, looking as pleased as if he were having a party and I was the guest of honor. He and I then went into the inner office, while everyone else stayed outside. The air-conditioner was on high, with the temperature hovering somewhere around central Antarctica.

"So, Meester Darling-town. You come to pay your fine, no?"

"No," I said. "This is not a fine, it is a bribe, and I refuse to pay it."

"Oh," he looked surprised at this. I guess successful shakedowns were a regular, acceptable occurrence in Hubba Hubba.

"My lawyers in the city will be informed of this, and I assure you, Mayor Fernando, if you ever touch my private property again, or break anything that belongs to me, you will have bigger problems than a lousy fucking hundred bucks."

That made him smile. "Profanity cuesta ten doll-ar." Did this guy *ever* give up?

"We'll call it even then. As I need to replace the headlight you smashed." I stood up. "If your goon comes near me again, I'll have a restraining order put on him."

I walked out the door, and the municipal thugs were all busy looking at their fingernails.

Cabino was nowhere to be seen.

10.

In the street the light pounded down out of a blue sky like shards of glass and I wheeled the Harley under a big shade tree next to the park. Maybe a snow cone with sweet syrup would help chill me out.

Mayor Fernando, I'd decided, was a small-time hood with a limited power base; an official bully with curly eyelashes, and dimples. It was good to get my position established with him right in the beginning, I assured myself.

My thoughts went back to my meeting with Veronica. I'd been hoping to make a fresh start with her, become someone charming and affable in her eyes. *Or at least a lovable, irresistible forty-nine year old stud.* Instead I'd nearly gotten my dick caught in my fly, and hurt her feelings yet again.

Like the syrup on the snow cone, I then nearly collided with her husband. Of course, I didn't know it was Black Jack on sight. What I saw was a powerful-looking black man with a shaved head and a gold chain glinting from fifty feet away, leave a side door of the palacio building and head with great determination through the park. Without looking up.

As he drew closer, I realized he wasn't as imposing as he first seemed, and that he wore fine-rimmed glasses. The air seemed to separate as he moved through it, and I was just getting ready to stand aside, wondering how short-sighted he might be, when he stopped short in front of me.

"Ah..." he said, looking me over and extending his hand. "Reechard Darling-town, is it not?"

"Yes." His smile was penetrating, his body relaxed, like a jaguar that had just had a good meal. I put out my hand. "How are you?"

"Very fine, very fine. And you? How do you like sweet Hubba Hubba thus far?"

"Very fine," I parroted. *Except for elected officialdom,* I wanted to add. He laughed at this, showing me a front tooth capped in gold, like a Christmas package.

"And you are?"

"Jack Murillo. I believe you know my wife, Veronica." Curiously formal.

"Ah...Jack." Black Jack in the flesh. Had he just received a briefing from the mayor?

"Veronica tells me you have bought the family farm." *For a million dollars* was left hanging in the air, unspoken. "The *coco* farm," he added, a little derogatorily, I thought.

"Yes, coconuts are my favorite. I love to hear them hitting the ground with that big, dull thud." I smiled.

"A coco *farmer* then." Baiting me.

"Perhaps."

"Not much money in coco nowadays."

"Profit was not my motive for buying Coco Beach," I told him, simply. Was he going to admit owning the servidumbre? I thought I'd wait and see.

"Ah...we have a saying here: A man who needs no profit, profits none. We all have our moti*vation,* though, as you say, and our trabells too." Island *patois* aside, this was no island boy, I thought.

"Now trouble...that is something I wish to avoid. We have a saying in New York: 'Trouble follows where weak hearts lead'."

"Interesting," said Black Jack, thinking about it, though a look of mild surprise passed over his face. This was a man, I thought, used to dominating most conversations.

"Orange or strawberry?" I asked, as the vendor of snow cones and multi-colored syrups neared us.

"Not today," he told me, "but thank you. My wife just called and asked to see me."

Jack, honey? I've just had that annoying Mister Darlingtown in my office—the one who bought the farm? I think he's headed through the park right now. Maybe you should go and meet him face to face.

"Don't let me keep you," I said pleasantly. Was Black Jack, with his thug's nickname, a lucky gambler or merely good with instruments of torture?

Actually, Jack was much more charming than I'd imagined; a handsome, educated man who, by the way, looked like he'd have no trouble acquitting his conjugal duties. In fact—I hate to admit this—but Jack and Veronica suddenly seemed in my mind's eye like the kind of couple for whom the term "twin flames" was invented, the kind of flames that would generate enough heat to incinerate a New England farmhouse in the middle of winter.

How had I ever deduced, from one meeting no less, that Veronica was unhappy in her relationship with him? What a genius! I said goodbye to Jack, sat on a park bench for awhile watching my Veronica fantasy waver like a mirage, and melt, like my orange snow cone, in the hot, Caribbean air.

I went back to the Boatel to tell Jim, Wanda and Shakey about my meetings with Veronica and the mayor.

"Farghh," said Jim.

Shakey sat at the galley table listening, and shaking his head.

Wanda was making notes. I said, "So, the idea is that Veronica will draw up a new lease in Wanda's name and the money will be paid directly into the town treasury."

Shakey snorted at this. I knew he wanted to give me his input but wanted to keep his energies focused in a new direction. Sitting around the galley table made me realize again how small and cramped the Boatel was with more than two people in it.

"Shakey, I need some help"

"Shor," he said, looking surprised.

"I want to start building a place to live out at the beach. Could you try and line me up a good local builder and we'll meet about it tomorrow morning?"

"At the Dia y Noche," he said, getting up. He looked relieved to be getting out of the Boatel. It seemed there were some undercurrents going on between him and Wanda, but I couldn't peg them.

I told Jim, "I'm going to keep your gun for the time being." No debate on that one. I picked it up from where it lay on the galley table, brought it back to my cabin and unloaded it.

I went down to the Wreck Deck to have a drink. I thought a little bit of My Grandmother was just what I needed at the end of this day.

A man was sitting at the bar with a bandana tied around his graying hair and a T-shirt with a picture of an Absolut vodka bottle with a label that read: Absolution Now.

"Hey," the man said. His smile was wry as he stuck out his hand. "Escaping from the Big Island? Join the crowd."

"The Big Island?" I was unsure what he meant.

"The States. I call it the biggest island on the planet." I smiled and nodded.

We traded some statistics about ourselves. Joe was a former priest, originally from Norfolk, Virginia.

I started by telling him my full name and he paused as if the name rang a bell. "Do you favor Richard, Rich or Dick?" he asked. His eyes were lively gray and clear, as if everything in life was ultimately entertaining.

"In my old life I was always Richard. Now I guess I'm turning into a Dick." We laughed.

The locals called him Daddy Joe, or just plain Daddy, though he hadn't had his sixtieth birthday yet. Daddy Joe had been a fighter pilot in the Vietnam War, he told me, who'd turned priest in the aftermath, then clerical songster. He'd met his current wife, Sister Patrice when he joined the Heavenly Harmonizers, a troupe of singing ecclesiasts who'd had a hit single on the Christian music charts called "Winging It In Heaven."

"Then the Feds came after us. They said we were felons. They don't really have a category for clerical celebrities, so they decided to hit us for tax fraud and make us criminals instead."

They were excommunicated by the Church the following year for making too much money and falling in love. A wayward Jesuit from Amherst, Massachusetts had married them and they'd bought a boat and discovered Hubba Hubba soon after.

"We bought a love shack over on Little Conch Cay." He pointed across the channel at a pink board house with a slight list and a nice 40-foot ketch parked in front. "We call it the Tilton Hilton."

We ordered a couple more drinks and Joe told me the rest: about the neighbors who still favored their over-the-water outhouses ("pooh-pooh fish factories, Patrice calls 'em"). They'd also made a stab at conversing with the locals. "Which has completely decimated my English," Joe said. "Now I say things like 'Make I say' and 'Whappin?'"

The local cantina would sporadically play all night, stop at four a.m., then be habitated by a group of determined Charismatics clapping and crying "Hallelujah" from five am to seven. This sometimes proved too much, even for an ex-communicated priest.

"Some weekends, we just haul anchor til the bruja passes, then come back around Tuesday or so."

"Not Monday?" I inquired. He looked at me as if I were a few peels short of a banana.

"*Blue* Monday?" he asked, and when I continued to look blank, he didn't explain, just made a kind of ho, ho, ho noise deep in his throat.

As we talked, Lovinia, our large smiling barmaid, kept the cold beer coming and as the sun turned an oily violet over the channel, gave us a plate of salty, fried plantain slices.

I asked him if he missed the States.

"Who could miss a place where all the rental cars are red Hyundais, and people consider Nicholas Sparks' books to be a literary tour de force? Nah. We haven't been back in years."

And where was Patrice? "Oh she'll be along. Never misses happy hour after all that communal wine she used to pilfer behind the altar." Daddy Joe was like a mood alchemist. In his company, I began to feel the mellowness of my first visit to Hubba Hubba return, my earlier misgivings dissipate. I felt a spark of hope; maybe I could make a new life here if I had a friend I could talk to.

I threw out a feeler about Black Jack. "The President of the Municipal Council? Oh yeah. Jack Murillo has the power. Just don't ever call him Black Jack to his face. He no like it, so." Joe laughed.

I told him about my purchase of Coco Beach. "So you're the one! We were off cruising when that came down. Nice hit." He looked at me with fresh interest. "Wondered what you was doing here; didn't see a sailboat."

Joe, I suddenly realized, hadn't asked me one direct question about myself up to this point. The old habits of the confessional, I guessed—waiting and listening. It made me want to confide in him, a big change for the Richard Darlington of old.

"So...are we going to be permanent neighbors, or is this a passing fancy?"

I took a breath, preparing to tell this man I'd just met about discovering Hubba Hubba and my still-secret escape from my old life, when a woman driving a small skiff with a 15-hp Yamaha, crashed into the edge of the deck and crawled out on her hands and knees with a line between her teeth.

"Patrice," Joe said, glad to see her. "She doesn't drive very well." She tied the line to a table leg, stood up, brushed her knees off and smiled at us.

"The eagle has landed," she announced. She had on a lime-green T-shirt, was fit and tanned, with damp, multi-colored blond hair, glossy peach lips and sunglasses that rode down on her nose. This was the former *Sister* Patrice?

"This is what happens to repressed youth," Joe said, looking at her. "They turn into sexy nomads." He grabbed her around the waist and kissed her neck.

She giggled, enjoying it. "Hi," she said, extending her hand. "I'm Patrice."

"Dick Darlington," I replied, thinking how weird that sounded.

"Nice to meet you."

"Dick bought Coco Beach," Joe told her.

"Fabulous! Congratulations."

"Thank you. As soon as I get a straw roof over my head and buy some stumps I'll invite you for dinner."

"You're going to need *everything*," Patrice observed.

"That's true."

"Have you thought about a builder yet?" Joe asked.

"Shakey is getting some names for me."

"Yeah? Just be careful. Construction has a new meaning here. You'll find most builders have a specialty: framing, or windows, or laying floors. Some specialize in drinking one week, working the next because they drank their last paycheck."

"There's Desuze," Patrice offered, "but he's from Platanillo."

"Or Ishmael."

They went back and forth, slinging Old Testament names back and forth like a Bible class, and at length reached a tentative consensus that the twins Zachariah and Ezra were probably the best of an unskilled bunch. "But watch the windows," Joe warned me. "They don't really get window placement." It was a warning, I admit, that I neither understood nor would remember.

Joe, Patrice and I had dinner together at the Sum Fun, sharing the crab in hoisin sauce and an assortment of small dishes that cost virtually nothing, passing the evening as easily as old friends. I still hadn't shared my tale of why I'd come to Hubba Hubba, and they hadn't asked. The mood didn't seem right to get into it, and I was enjoying myself too much to do a recap of my former life in New York.

I did ask about the Internet, though. I was hoping to set up a wireless connection for myself as soon as possible but meanwhile needed to communicate with my daughter. Was there an Internet café that I'd missed on the Calle Principal?

Patrice gurgled her unique laugh. "The only choice is Kiss 'n' Tell."

"Sorry?"

"The local phone company? They're really called *Cable y Intel*," she told me. "But the lovely Renata listens in occasionally. She's the worst gossip in Hubba Hubba, so be careful what you say."

"You're joking, right?"

"Kiss n' Tell," Patrice repeated. "On the street it's called *bochinchi*—gossip. In Renata's case, it's more like telephone journalism. Sorta like the CIA."

"Ah...Renata," said Joe, laughing. "She's one of Fernando's favorites, after his wife and boyfriend, of course."

I remembered the tall woman in the caftan on Hubba Hubba Day. How many lovers of both sexes did Mayor Fernando have? "So...she listens in, and then tells the Mayor..."

"Who tells the Municipal Council," Joe added. "So everyone knows what everyone else is doing."

"Just one big happy Hubba Hubba family," Patrice said.

"And the Internet?" Was this for real?

"Just make sure you press the delete button when you're through. Then delete everything in the delete folder," Joe said. Both he and Patrice seemed positively complacent about this invasion of privacy.

"You have to accept it, or drive yourself crazy," Joe told me. "You'll see. There are some things you can work to change..."

"Like pooh-pooh fish," added Patrice.

"...and other things you just have to accept."

"There's always the Land of the Free," I said.

"There's always that," Joe said, and we all grew silent contemplating this option. Was it worth risking your First Amendment rights to live outside the box?

Joe said, "You know the same shit happens in the States—it's just bigger. Like a wide-screen with hundreds of cable channels. In Hubba Hubba there's only one channel and it's in black and white."

Patrice added, "We call it the bouillon cube because everything's so small and intense. You'll see."

I secretly was hoping that I'd be an exception, of course.

That the mayor would forget I existed.

That Black Jack would relinquish the servidumbre on my property.

That Cabino would go back to jail and that Veronica would have a bout of amnesia and forget she was married to Black Jack.

As my father used to say: Hope is only wanting turned into delusion.

I would soon find out just how right he was.

11.

I lay in bed sound asleep when I heard noises up on deck. Heavy footsteps trying to sound light but not succeeding very well.

I got up and went into the galley and checked that I'd locked the door of the companionway that separated inside from out when I came back from dinner. Now someone was moving the brass door handle, testing the lock. I held my breath. Should I get Jim's gun?

The motion suddenly stopped and the intruder walked away as softly as his weight would carry him. When I heard the creak of the ladder going down to street level I knew whoever it was had given up for the time being.

The next morning I told Wanda about the intruder.

"Do you have any idea who it might be?"

"Cabino?" she suggested helpfully.

"Cabino wouldn't let a flimsy lock stop him, would he?" I could hardly imagine Cabino taking a delicate approach to breaking and entering.

"Maybe he didn't want to wake up the whole street," Wanda said. "Maybe…"

Jim threw his toast on the floor and began pounding on the table in a rage.

"SHA….SHA….SHA!" he said. His face had turned bright red and his eyes watered in frustration.

"What's he trying to say?" I asked Wanda.

"Shakey. He thinks it was Shakey up on deck…" She looked horrified. "He thinks Shakey…that Shakey was behind the whole shakedown with the mayor."

"Let me handle this," I said to Wanda. "Just go."

She didn't need a second invitation. Jim's rage was building steam faster than Mount St. Helens.

He swept the table clean of plates and cutlery, toast flying, scalding coffee tipped on its side. I thought he'd have another stroke in a minute if he didn't calm down.

I went behind him, locked his arms with my own and rolled him backwards away from the table. "That's enough!"

He tried to get me in a head lock and nearly succeeded. We struggled for a few minutes and my hands finally found the cord to someone's cell phone. I wrapped it around both his wrists, then anchored it to the arm of his wheelchair.

Some invalid!

I took a deep breath and tried to calm down. I picked up the toast off the floor and threw it in the sink.

"You're nothing but a big hairy pain in the ass, you know that?" I told him.

He mumbled some curses at me under his breath.

"And a gargly old fart," I added. That got his attention. "You better get your act together, Jim, or I'm going to send you down to the city for therapy."

"NARRR....GO."

"Tough shit," I said. "Because you can't do this to Wanda. She looks like she's going to have a stroke herself."

He hung his head at this. I was convinced that Jim knew most of what was going on, but his motor skills were more scrambled than a Spanish omelet.

"Veronica's agreed to help with the Boatel's problem, and I'm going to help with expenses. But I'm going to stop the whole thing unless you straighten up." He still wouldn't look at me. "That means gratitude." I leaned over, into his face. "No more toast on the floor, no more bullshit. And start working with the speech therapist, Jim. If you don't, you're going to be pretty damn lonely down here. I'll make sure of it." He tried to look tough but his lower lip was trembling. I walked up the passageway without looking back, glad his guns were out of reach.

I went to the Dia y Noche to meet Shakey after that, thinking how glad I'd be to have my own place. The drama of living in town was starting to get to me.

Having missed breakfast, I was also starving. At the Dia y Noche you could get everything from island news to liver and onions about 18 hours a day. This morning I settled for the "punkin" bread and coffee and it really wasn't bad, though I was starting to miss Daniel—and I'm sure vice versa, as I'd been the only one to eat a regular meal in the House That Harry Goodman Built.

Shakey came and joined me right after.

"Whassup?" he asked.

"Experiencing punkin for the first time." I lifted my fork on which a quivering bite of gelatinous pumpkin pudding/cake was balanced.

He clicked his teeth, shook his head. "Kids' food." Maybe in time I'd have the liver and onions and prove my manhood to all the Dia y Noche clientele. Meanwhile, "punkin" and its near cousins "banano" and "coco," also jiggling, but in different colors, would be my breakfast of champions.

"How's things?" He was sizing me up but still looked at me with warmth in his eyes. There was no way that Shakey and the mayor were cooking up anything. He cared about both Wanda and Jim the way I did.

"Other than needing a place to live and all the essentials, just fine."

"Zach and Ezra—you know who they be?"

"They're builders, right?"

"Yeah, well. They's available."

"Good man. When can they start?"

"You got the materials? They can start immediate."

I planned to call J.J. later this morning, ask him to be my procurement agent in the city.

So far I wanted a pickup truck, a setup for wireless Internet, satellite TV, and a 500- kw generator so I could plug in my power tools and eventually all my household appliances. I also needed a bed, fridge, freezer and indoor plumbing. Life was rich with possibilities when you were starting from nothing.

"So. You's stayin," Shakey said.

"That's the idea."

He spun his styrofoam cup around, then twisted it into trash. He commented, "Gonna need some hep. I's a driver. Can do most thing. Know the people hereso. Got contacts."

"What would be a fair price for all this?" I asked.

He named a figure, half of what most kids earned making quarter-pounders in the States.

"I'll pay you double what you ask because you're going to earn it. I've got a lot of work to do out there, Shakey, and I'd like it done in a timely matter."

"Quick like."

"Exactly. Also, as my Spanish is limited, to say the least, and I'll need you as a translator."

"Uh-huh."

"So. We can start right now if you want."

"Shor."

"First you can show me where Kiss N' Tell is."

He grinned. "That easy."

Renata was as I remembered: tall, big-boned, with a serious brown face. I'd also remembered Big Jim telling me about her caftan, bought by Mayor Fernando. The mayor, in addition to being a thief, was also an adulterer who was having multiple affairs with partners of both sexes. Whatever way you bounced it, it added up to a lot of spring in the mattress—and a lot of hours in any given day. I wondered how he managed it.

I was also realizing that in Hubba Hubba, sex—the enjoyment, withholding, swapping and competition for it—probably constituted the main form of entertainment. As I didn't plan to be reunited with my wife ever, and had alienated the one married woman I *was* interested in, getting satellite TV was beginning to seem like a high priority.

Renata studied me as if reading my mind and I smiled at her brightly to throw her off the psychic trail.

Shakey said, "Whassup, Reenie?"

"Right here, Shake. Whassup wid you?"

They then began having a rapid-fire Spanish exchange, or maybe it was *guari guari* as some of the words sounded like broken English. At the end of it, Shakey said, "This here be Mistuh Reechard Darling-town."

"How you be?" Reenie asked. Her face remained passive, her smile turned up at the edges, like a frozen fish. Why did I have the distinct feeling this woman didn't like me on sight?

Shakey said, "Mistuh Reech wants to use da compew-tah. He needs to get hisself a international account for his cell, and a sataleet-ay for Coco Beach." Shakey had great recall, I'll give him that, even if his English left a lot to the imagination. Renata understood him perfectly.

She went behind a desk and took out a sheaf of papers and handed them to Shakey. "He gonna need an *abono*, *tres referencias*. Sata-lee-tay no have. Phone card he can buy now. *Cuesta viente.*"

Shakey translated, "She say you can buy a phone card for twenty bucks, rest take time."

"When can I get a sata-lee-tay?" I was starting to feel agitated.

"*No sé*," she shrugged.

"How can I call the U.S?"

"International calls all hereso," Shakey told me, while Renata crossed her arms and regarded me with the sympathy of a well-fed shark.

She said something to Shakey that sounded like gibberish.

He translated, "You gotta go make a deposit, go to da city to get international *servicio* on your mow-bile. Dat's da onliest way."

I shrugged in apparent acceptance, knew I'd get a wireless setup if it meant paying off the President of Kiss 'n' Tell and having one shipped from the States myself. Meanwhile, Renata showed me into a little booth where an ancient Compaq with a barely legible keyboard awaited me. She slammed the mouse onto the desk and the screen sprang to life.

Renata then said in quite passable English, "It take a few minute to warm up so." A sign with the word "PACIENCIA!" glared at me from the wall. Yeah, right!

Once I got logged into my e-mail—eight minutes—I found I had 33 new junk mail messages, plus one from my daughter and one from David Felder.

My daughter's said:

Daddy, Dn't know if u check your ems while traveling, but hope u do. Nd to talk. Mther is weird. Smith ok, but I mis my rm and D's cooking, caf food horrible! Pls call me on my nu cell: 508-555-1604 asap. Luv u, Elizabeth.

Daddy? My daughter called me Dad at a stretch, but rarely Daddy. Hillary had been "mother"—always. "Daddy" just sent alarm bells ringing; it worried me more than the reference to Hillary, whom I already knew to be in full perimenopausal swing, the loss of appetite—which was explainable—or Elizabeth's aversion to grammar.

The second from Felder, dated two days previously, was easier to decipher:

Hey Richard. How's paradise? Thanks again for the free cruise— Linda and the girls loved it. Lucky for you, I was onboard in the Bahamas when your daughter called on the satcom, got the number from my office. I told her you'd gone off fishing for a few days, and would contact her later. Her cell is 508 555 1604. I tried to play it cool. Told her it was hard to get through, etc. She sounds like a nice kid. Shake it easy. David.

I exited the little booth, asked Renata if I could make an international call. She told me, dubiously: *"Cuesta* tree dollar *por minuto* for the Unied Stays". I got out a fifty and she rubbed it between her fingers to make sure the ink wasn't still wet, wrote down the serial number, then went behind a glass partition to place the call.

A thin rivulet of sweat began running down my spine. I'd called Elizabeth from the city to put her mind at ease, and now she wanted me to talk to me less than a week after I'd left. Was anything wrong? I hadn't left any specific information with Hillary about contacting me, and never expected she'd try. Now my daughter was sending me an urgent-sounding email. Was she alright? Her damned voice mail picked up again, and now I was the one who felt like I'd pop a blood vessel.

Didn't anyone answer their phones any more? I left my own cell number, and hoped she'd call me back.

There was nothing more to be done, so after I took a few deep breaths, Shakey and I walked through the park and went to meet Zachariah and Ezra—the two most available carpenters in town.

12.

Zach and Ezra could have been second-line stringers for Miami Heat: tall, dark lean men who wore matching baseball caps and looked at me with quiet attentiveness as I explained about what I envisioned for housing at Coco Beach.

"I need a cabin 'til I build the main house. It can be one big room with a separate bathroom, as long as it's weather tight." Nod, nod. "I want windows on each wall with screens and shutters that can be locked on the inside. I'll also need a dry place to park my bike, and some kind of tool shed." More nods, exactly the same.

I continued, "I'll need a list of materials for these, and a price. I want to get started right away."

Zach finally broke rank and asked, "What wood you want? You got yo laurel, cedro, nispero, zapatero..."

Ezra continued, "Oh yo batello, roble, y criollo—dat man wood."

Zach nodded at his brother, "Manwood best for hard."

Ezra added, "Cedro beta."

Shakey: "Laurel da cheap-es."

Zach: "But soft, man."

Shakey: "Da man no ask-et for da most hex-pensive shit, just a bodega y a roof."

Ezra, the voice of reason, repeated, "Cedro, he da best. The beetches no like it."

"Bitches?" I asked.

Zach explained. "Doze da beetches does eat da wood."

"Bee-*chos*," Shakey the translator said. "Dat be da correct pronunciation."

They all grew silent, contemplating this. I said, "Cedro sounds fine, just tell me how many board feet and whatever other supplies you need, and when we can start."

Zach asked Shakey, "Need a plano, so?"

"Nah. I go see de Alcalde, man. He don't need no plano for a bodega. Shit." Zach and Ezra agreed that this was probably so...by nodding, of course.

Richard Darlington, good citizen and new resident, announced, "If I need a plan, I'll be happy to pay whatever municipal fees are owing..."

They looked at me like I was eight inches short of a floor joist.

Shakey explained vaguely, "You gonna pay, Mistuh Reech, donchoo worry. We gonna pay da municipality fo' a construction permit. No fret."

It was mid-afternoon and one *sancocho de gallina* (chicken soup with some large mystery vegetable chunks) later, I headed out to Coco Beach and left Shakey to sort out the details of my one-room cabin and tool shed with the carpenters and get me a construction permit.

I rode out of town and children ran out to wave at me as I cruised through La Cabaña on my Harley, past the beach where Onassis had taken me to meet his sister, and where an accidental siteseeing trip had changed my life.

I hummed along the coastal road on packed dirt and sand feeling happier than I'd been in years. My deep-felt roots to this island were still a mystery. I could've chosen anywhere in the world to start my new life, but I'd chosen Hubba Hubba. Crash landing near the island of the big coconuts had certainly been a timely event in more ways than one. But sometimes, like now, the unreality of the events that had led me here hit me full force. Had I really chucked in my old life, bought a hundred acres of virgin jungle and beachfront and moved here? I couldn't wait to show Elizabeth this place.

A sea breeze stoked my feeling of freedom. I remembered this kind of high from childhood days, riding my bike, full of anticipation about my next destination. *Da hill,* George had said in a trance-like state on our first meeting, and now I understood why. There was a timelessness and peace here, like entering a living postcard of paradise. This was where I was meant to be, I had no doubt. This was where I belonged.

I parked the bike, bounded toward the crest of the hill to feel the breeze, see the perfect crescent of beach below. Feeling the exhilaration of new ownership...

And then I heard the chopping. I knew it was chopping because it reminded me of Daniel chopping vegetables for one of his Chinese dinners—*thwach, thwack, thwack*—except this was more amplified. Like the vegetables and the knives were bigger.

I topped the hill and looked off into the distance, to the north. Past a grove of coconut palms, I could see there was activity, the shapes of men moving within the boundaries of my property. What the hell were they doing down there?

I went down the other side of the hill, into the grove, and there they were: three Indians swinging machetes. There had been a large swath cleared already, and though no trees seemed to be down, it appeared they were opening up a wide path in the underbrush that began from somewhere behind my property, right through it, then headed for the sea.

"'Allo," I said, and they stopped, looked at me curiously, arms crossed, machetes dangling. I didn't think they spoke English, but thought I'd better make a stab at it.

"Who you are?" I tried.

They looked at me with guarded amusement: Who was this white guy, a foot taller than them? What did he want?

"Who you work for?" I was beginning to understand Joe's lament. Living here turned your English to shit in a hurry. Or was that *sheet*?

One of the Indians, their leader apparently, came forward while the other two giggled behind their hands.

"Who you is?" he asked. This made his two compadres crack up. The words meant nothing, were only being parroted for my sake.

"*Jefe?*" I tried, pulling the word for "boss" from Mrs. Skidmore's sophomore Spanish class.

This created a stir. They spoke rapidly to one another in their native language, yet another new dialect to my ears, and finally agreed to tell me.

"Mista Jack," the leader told me. He was still smiling but more wary now, as if admitting this might get him in trouble.

"Black Jack?" I asked, though I knew they were one and the same. The mayor himself had told me about the existence of a *servidumbre*. Veronica's explanation about a right-of-way had somehow fallen short of the mark. She'd said people had a right to access the beach, not that they'd need a twenty-five-yard-wide path to accomplish it. Was I going to have the whole town trooping through here? It was like a fairway. Would my privacy and the green belt I'd envisioned evaporate?

At my mention of Black Jack's other name they stopped smiling. "No work here," I told them. "This my land." I was beginning to have great sympathy for Tonto. I pointed to my fence boundary some fifty yards away.

They looked at me and shrugged, picked up their machetes, and began slicing through the long grass on their march to the sea, ignoring me.

I needed to speak to George; George could clear up this misunderstanding if his daughter wouldn't.

I went back up to the crest of the hill, the bench where Onassis and I had first sat at sunset, but the sound of the machetes chopping was magnified up here. I wasn't going to rush back into town now at the end of a long, dusty day. They'd be knocking off soon and tomorrow I could find George and solve the problem.

I went back to the bike, took out a couple of still cool beers I'd packed from the Dia y Noche, went down to the beach, took off my shirt and waded in. There was a beautiful natural pool here, a little reef-enclosed Jacuzzi. I could watch the sunset and not listen to the despoiling going on.

When was the last time I'd needed to defend my property from incursion? I remembered the coyote on the back lawn of Foxglove Hollow. The Refugee, I'd called him. Hillary's call to Animal Control had probably sealed his fate in a hurry.

Veronica said the right of way was in my new title deed, but now I knew there was more to this than she had told me. I remembered Jack Murillo's easy self-confidence when we'd met, his almost smug self-assurance. He'd been amused by my purchase of the coconut farm, wondered about my motives. Now I was wondering about his.

The mayor had said Veronica and Jack were well aware of the *servidumbre*, that there was municipal land behind me. It was a "little problem," he'd said, that could be "fixed."

In Mayor Fernando's world, fixing was only about one thing, as I'd already learned first-hand.

In Jack Murillo's view, my new ownership of Coco Beach was probably an inconvenient glitch: a gringo who'd paid serious money for a piece of property that had a right-of-way controlled by him. He would never consider me a real adversary: a guy who'd bought a defunct coconut plantation in the middle of nowhere, who was out of his depth living in an unfamiliar culture and didn't speak the language. Veronica was his wife, George was his father-in-law, the mayor was probably his good buddy, and he was himself president of the municipal council. He seemed to be holding all the cards.

I considered these things as I sat in my reef-made pool, drinking my Ice, watching the sun go down. I'd had, of course, a whole career dealing with adversaries; know-it-all whiz kids, reluctant stockholders, greedy lawyers. Not to mention the greatest challenge of all: the survival skills I'd learned from being thrust into Harry Goodman's world when I'd married his only daughter.

I came to Hubba Hubba to be free of all that, and free I would be. Jack Murillo might not consider me an adversary, or he might have found me amusing. Whatever his take was, it was fine with me.

I dove under the water, opened my eyes. The reef was alive with colorful fish darting in lucid, pale blue water. Whatever problems that existed would be overcome; I knew this with certainty. I'd do whatever it took, within reason, to secure my privacy and live a peaceful life.

I came out of the water and Cabino was there, holding my towel.

13.

You no pay da mayor," he said. He looked regretful about this, took my beach towel, rolled it up and torpedoed it into the water. "He no like."

"Too bad for him," I said, still knee-deep in the water. I wiped my eyes with the palms of my hands.

"I kill you," Cabino told me, as if it were a comment about the weather.

"Now?" Sometimes my sarcasm knows no bounds. I wondered if I could find a weapon of mass destruction on the sandy bottom to defend myself. Behind Cabino, on the hill, the three Indians were watching us.

"When you no think I is, I be, and I do." He turned and strode away, threat delivered. From the back he looked like Ray Lewis, linebacker for the Baltimore Ravens.

I thought about lawyers, guns, private security firms and the power of prayer. Which would I choose?

My towel looked like a big blue soggy fish, and I waded in and got it. God, I hate it when my towel gets wet. Cabino was walking a fine line, in more ways than one. He had to keep up the threats without actually inflicting bodily harm—what good would I be to the mayor if I was dead?

Every time I saw him we had another unfortunate incident like this one.

I'd need to take some defensive action soon—but what?

I cruised back to the Boatel, crusty with salt, and considered my options. I swung myself through the companionway by clinging to the door frame—my latest boyish trick—and nearly kicked Veronica in the face.

Big Jim was sitting in front of her in his wheelchair, some papers and a cold Ice in front of him. Half of his face looked like it was smiling.

"Hi," I said, aware of my sorry state of salt-soaked cut-offs and wet T-shirt. Veronica, on the other hand, was dressed in a pristine lavender suit and violet pumps. She looked at my hair and tried not to smile. Thoughts of Cabino evaporated into the ether.

"I've brought the new lease for Jim and Wanda to sign."

"Thank you." Maybe I could start acting like the civilized man I'd always claimed to be.

Veronica said, "I've explained to Jim about the reef. It is within the municipal environs, but the first twenty-two meters of the coast belong to the nation, which has precedence. If we apply for a concession from the national government, instead of a municipal lease, Jim can keep the Boatel indefinitely." She smiled at giving me this news, and it was the most beautiful smile of perfect white teeth and Hubba Hubba dimples I'd ever seen. In fact, it seemed to activate something primitive in my brain that millions of years ago might have been called animal lust.

I asked, "Does this law apply to my farm, as well?" New information on property ownership was coming at me faster than high tide, and I didn't care. As long as Veronica kept smiling at me like that, I could drown in *servidumbres* and not give a damn.

"Yes, of course. But it's not necessary unless you want to *build* on that first twenty-two meters. You see?" Her pumped foot rode up and down at the end of her long dark thigh.

Now that we'd entered neutral territory, I decided to change the subject. "Would you and your mother and father be free to have dinner with me tonight?"

"Will you take a shower first?"

"Absolutely!" It was the same euphoria I'd felt when Kim LaDue had agreed to go to with me to the junior high dance.

"Actually I was going to invite *you*," Veronica told me. My father came back from the city this morning and I thought we should get together. Talk about the farm."

OK, so it would be a threesome, maybe a foursome if Ella came too. As first dates went it wasn't my ideal, but it was a start. Was her husband coming too?

"Jack went to a convention in Nicaragua this morning, all municipal officials from Concepción were invited to go." Reading my mind.

I told her about finding Jack's Indian workers clearing the swath of land near the boundary line and she didn't look surprised.

"I know. That's why I thought...there are things you need to know..."She smiled shyly at me, and this time I was sure that Veronica was flirting with me. It made my heart soar.

Waiting is not my forte; being on the receiving end, that is. The Deck was just beginning to fill up when I arrived but no sign of Veronica or George. So I got a waterside table, gave Lovinia an order for a bottle of Mi Abuela, ice, tonic, and cokes.

And thought about how much I hated waiting.

Seven thirty came and went, and when I finally saw George's bright yellow *cayuco* heading across the channel from Little Conch Cay I felt my whole body exhale. Finally.

The cayuco bumped to a stop in front of me. Veronica was first up and out, agile in a frilly red blouse and tight jeans, tying off the bow.

"You look lovely," I said. She reminded me of a red hibiscus.

She said, "You combed your hair." Veronica's sense of humor was like a turtle's head poking out when you didn't expect to see it.

Ella gave me her hand, and I pulled her up onto the dock. In return, she hugged me to her broad chest like I was a baby, then gave me a big smack on the cheek.

"Hello, George," I said, and we shook hands.

"Well, well." He looked me over. "Look like Hubba Hubba agreein' with you! You gettin' handsomer by the minute!"

Around us the locals watched us and buzzed; it must've been quite a show. I was the rich guy who'd bought Coco Beach, George and Ella were the locals who'd made good. People smiled and raised their glasses. I wondered what they thought of Jack's absence, my presence next to Veronica.

I poured drinks all around. "Ah…" said George, taking a big swallow. "Dis da life."

"Careful," Ella warned. "Dat's pure sugar."

"I got me a little diabetic condition. Gotta watch it," he told me. He took another drink.

"Mum and Dad went to the city," Veronica said. She seemed anxious to keep her father on track.

George looked at me with his serene brown face and said, "Sent some money to the Unied Stays. Divvy up the money between all my chil'rens, equal shares. T'anks to you." He raised his glass.

"De nada," I said.

I felt happiness brim up inside me.

Veronica said, "Dad, please tell Richard about the *servidumbre*."

"Ooo yeah, well…let me see." George squinted, pulled his nose, and thought about it. He looked out to sea, poked the ice cubes in his glass, took out a terry facecloth and wiped his forehead.

Just when I thought he was going to ignore the question entirely, he said, "You know Veronica here is wid that man, Jack Murillo. Dey's married." Veronica rolled her eyes at this.

"He a big *city* boy," George continued. "Came to Hubba Hubba to find a little pond where he could be a big fish. Oh yeah."

I watched Veronica as I heard her father run down her husband, but she neither interrupted nor disagreed. Merely looked serious, much as she had when we first met.

"When dey married, I promise Jack I'd give him somethin'. Ya know? A little wedding present from Ella and me."

At this, both Ella and Veronica looked out to sea. Whatever George had done had obviously not met with their approval. Still they didn't comment.

"So…one night, afore the wedding, he takes me out. You know…a boy's night. We went to the Boom Boom Room. Dat da local club."

"Oh yeah," Ella said. "Da Boom Boom Room. That's be da glamour spot of Hubba Hubba, for shor."

"Well, we had a fine evenin'. Lots of fun. Wanda be dancin'. Jus' good clean fun." He gave Ella a challenging look. "But I admit it…I made an error in judgment dat night. God strike me down!" He drained the rest of his drink at this pronouncement, and looked sorrowful.

"It was a mistake," said Veronica in a forgiving voice, to which Ella snorted.

I helpfully said, "This has to do with the *servidumbre*?"

"Whappin? That damn Alcalde he brought a paper to da club, say: 'Hey, George. You got dat nice farm up der, plenty o' space. Why donchoo give a little piece to your future son-in-law, nice *servidumbre*? Den he buy da municipal land behind it, build a nice house and den he can reach da beach.' And der's Jack leanin' over me, smilin' wid his eyes at me. He say, 'George it shor would mean a lot to Veronica and me, if we could have a little piece of dat der farm, just a little slice like.'"

"I say, 'So, you gonna buy da municipal piece behind?' And he say, 'Oh shor I is, George. I gonna build me a nice little house wid a sea view, build me a dock and take Veronica and da kids out in a boat'."

I said, "So, of course you agreed. I would've done the same."

"You would?" George clasped my forearm with his brown hand.

"Let him have it," I said. I didn't need to think about it. Jack Murillo, it seemed, had a legitimate right of way. There was no point in belaboring it further. "I'll build a fence."

"You will?" Veronica's relief was obvious.

"Of course."

Ella gave me a motherly look of approval and respect. I was on a roll.

"Just tell me one thing. Did Jack ever build the house?" The stink in Jack Murillo's little pond was starting to rise to the surface.

"No house, no dock," George said. "Sumbitch."

"I'll get a surveyor out there, mark the line so there's no confusion." I didn't want to embarrass Veronica any more. Whatever Black Jack and the mayor were really up to, I'd tackle it in my own way, in my own time.

Lovinia came over, and everyone ordered. There were three choices on the menu: Lobster, fish and octopus, and because I was ravenous after a day of threats, siege, and falling in love, I ordered all three.

14.

Zach and Ezra showed up for work forty minutes late the next morning with a list of supplies and their toolboxes. Shakey had arranged for Onassis to take us all out in his truck and the twins had located some nice dry two-by-fours so they could start on the framing immediately.

We stopped at the Lucky Dragon to buy some bags of concrete for the footings, some four-inch nails, some sheets of zinc. I told Shakey about the *servidumbre* problem and he smiled knowingly.

"Jack tricky," he said. "Shakey take care of that shit, no fret." He showed me my construction permit from the municipality. "See? Not so hard."

We arrived on the property and I showed Zach and Ezra where I wanted the cabin built, and they nodded earnestly. "We'll knock it down later," I told them, and they gave me a curious look. "It's only temporary."

Shakey didn't waste any time, but marched down the hill to confront Jack's Indian workers. I heard raised voices, but a few minutes later the chopping stopped. Was it really going to be as easy as that?

Shakey said, "I tell dem stop that shit—dis here private land."

"They won't come back?"

"Huh!"

At the risk of offending him, I had to know. "What did you do?"

"I got it all work out, Mistuh Rich. You let Shakey take care of that shit."

We spent the morning staking out my new abode, drinking *agua pipa*—coconut water—directly out of green coconuts sliced open at the top by Ezra's machete, and getting the footings in place. It was satisfying work, and I was glad to see that I could keep up my part under the tropical sun. All those years of tennis and workouts were finally paying off.

At one, we knocked off for lunch, but no one had remembered to bring any food. Shakey used my cell phone to call Onassis to bring out lunch from the Dia y Noche, and then we rested under the big palm trees and waited for it to be delivered.

I asked Shakey if he'd heard the news about Veronica's plan for the Boatel, or had any new information about Mayor Fernando's efforts to shake Jim down. In the skewed reality of Hubba Hubba, the Mayor appeared to be both Shakey's adversary—he was friends of Big Jim and Wanda—as well as his ally. He could march in to the Alcalde's office, and get whatever paper he needed. I didn't examine this too closely; I had given Shakey the money for the construction permit. It didn't take a genius to figure out how he'd gotten it so fast.

Shakey was vague. "The mayor, he a sumbitch." Laughter at this from Ezra and Zach. "He don't get no casino der. Huh!" Shakey's air of authority gave me only a short-lived feeling of security.

At ten past two, Onassis showed up with a big grin. He had some greasy brown paper bags filled with cold hamburgers and half a dozen tepid sodas.

"Tomorrow," I told Shakey, "let's try for either hot food or cold drinks. Put a gas fridge on the list for the city." Come hell or high water I planned to be sleeping out here in less than two weeks, even if it was under a zinc roof and mosquito net. The Boatel, with Big Jim in his wheelchair and Wanda looking uncertain and weepy, was becoming too damn small.

We spent the rest of the afternoon pouring cement and laying the footings for my little cabin. I even chose the layout—my first attempt at architectural design without Hillary, who'd meticulously positioned every stick of heirloom furniture in our twenty-six room house completely free of input from me. The bathroom, I decided, would go in the rear right corner, the toilet under the window so I could have a view of the coconut palms while pissing. My crew found the idea both novel and appealing; I had a consensus.

At five we knocked off. At least I'd had the sense to bring some beer and put it under the reef where it would stay cool. We sat under the palms and drank without speaking, just looking out across the green to the gently lapping sea. I felt tired but content. Thoughts of Hillary and Marty fluttered across my consciousness, but I batted them away. I planned to call them both in a couple of days. I wanted a divorce in the first instance and an early retirement in the second. I'd arranged certified letters to be sent after I'd left. They would have had them by now. But I'd already moved around my assets to protect me, and secured Elizabeth's future into the bargain. New York was history.

Meanwhile, I'd started to convince myself that peace had less to do with environment than detaching from the past.

But life is funny. Just when you think you've finally figured it out, reality charges through the door. This time it took the form of a big, sweating brown man who came lumbering up the hill toward us looking like a determined bull.

"Uh-oh," said Shakey.

I cleverly asked, "Who's that?"

"That be da liar."

"Huh?"

"A liaaa-er. You know, does practice de law. *Licenciado.*"

Zach and Ezra looked studiously out to sea at the big man's approach. The atmosphere had changed to summer-storm thick.

I rose to greet my guest as he huffed and puffed the last twenty-five yards. "May I help you?"

"Reechard Darling-town?"

"One and the same." He didn't offer to shake my hand.

"Mistuh Darling-town, I am the legal representative de Sr. Jack Murillo, Licenciado Ballena." He took out a handkerchief and began mopping the copious sweat from his forehead. He never smiled, nor made eye contact, but his air of humorless plodding determination put me off the most.

"Yes?"

"You stop da work heah?"

In response to this, Shakey came over and said something to the lawyer in *guari-guari* that sounded like: "Wat-you-fat-fuck-wanna-come-here-ta-mess-wid-my-brodder-fo'?"

Licenciado Ballena's squinty eyes grew wide at this and he began panting. His brow furrowed; I thought he might start pawing the ground.

He reverted to angry Spanish, reached into his briefcase and withdrew a document which he shoved at Shakey. It was if I'd evaporated into thin air. Licenciado Ballena then turned and began trudging down the hill.

Shakey studied the document, shook his head and began making negative hissing and clucking sounds.

"What is it?"

"Jack Murillo want to put a sequester on yo' property. He say he got a right to make a *servidumbre* and he gonna do it. The Alcalde, he stamp it."

"Hmmm." I looked out to sea; the undulating surface was all soft streaks of gold. On the reef an egret stood as still as alabaster, and waited.

"Maybe it's too perfect," I said to Shakey, Zach and Ezra. "Maybe that's why." Above us green palm fronds danced in the breeze, and suddenly and without warning, a huge hairy coconut landed with a deliberate thump at my feet.

"*Hayzeus!*" cried Shakey, pushing me out of danger after the fact.

"Dat was close," said Ezra.

"Oo yeah," agreed Zach. But nobody moved.

"Looks like there might be trouble in paradise," I finally said, and we all looked out just in time to see the egret catch a nice little mullet and swallow it whole.

15.

The next morning after a solid eight hours, I went into the head and took a long hard look at myself in the mirror. My eyes were blue and clear, my skin was getting brown, I'd lost weight. I was ready to jump in the ring.

I made some notes on the Boatel's galley table, had some coffee and walked out into the bright, fruit-scented air.

The phone company office was open at 8 a.m. and no one else was there. Renata was in position, of course, looking like a forward tackle for the New York Giants but with a different uniform. I smiled at her, and gave her my daughter's number. Elizabeth had still not returned my call.

Luckily, she answered the phone this time sounding sleepy, and I was sharply brought back to the sweet powdery scent of her childhood bedroom. I remember thinking how vulnerable she was then, how strong my urge was to protect her. Some things never changed.

"Hello, darling."

"Dad? Daddy?" The voice was on full alert now.

"Do you want to wake up first, and I'll call you back in a few minutes?"

"No! Noooo! I'm awake. When are you coming home? I talked to David Felder..."

"Where I am right now they don't have very good phone service. I'm sorry, but I'm doing the best I can."

"You're supposed to be home soon, aren't you?"

I sidestepped that one. "If you need me, I'll be there, Elizabeth. Count on it."

"Mom found part of a note in your wastebasket. She doesn't think you're coming back."

Well that was one for the books. Hillary going through my trash?

"Is that why you sent me an email? Why haven't you called me?"

Silence.

"Elizabeth—what is it? Tell me."

"Oh Daddy…" she said.

And suddenly I knew, just from her tone of voice; I knew everything I needed to know and more that I didn't. I flashed on Julie, age sixteen, already showing. "Elizabeth, you and Pierre… you're not….?"

There was a long pause. "I think I might be. The drug store test said positive and I've missed my period. But mother doesn't know, and you mustn't tell her! I don't want her interfering in my decision!"

"Elizabeth…" Shock and fear hit me like clubs, followed by a strange calm and the realization: my almost twenty-year old daughter was no longer my ward but another adult. Outside the window Renata looked at me and tapped her watch as several people milled around outside the booth.

I said, "I'm calling you from a public pay phone and there's a line of people waiting…" I gave her my cell phone number again and told her to call me back immediately.

She did, and we talked. And talked. Me sitting on a pale blue bench in Hubba Hubba's park; Elizabeth, presumably, sitting on her dorm bed and missing her morning classes.

She told me things that amazed me with their acuity (of course I know about Michel and Mom, Dad—duh! He's Pierre's uncle, remember?) and I realized that my twenty-year old daughter— pregnant or not—really was much more of an adult than I'd ever given her credit for. She'd been well educated and had traveled extensively. She could program a computer, ride a horse in dressage, play bridge, speak French, and knew the difference between dozens of financial instruments. Whatever decision she made, I'd stand by her.

She said about my trip, "Mother was expecting this. When you said you were going to take a two-week cruise by yourself, she knew something was up."

"Well, I don't want to involve you in this, Elizabeth. I just want to make sure you and I still have a relationship whatever happens between your mother and me."

"Of course," she told me, sounding insulted. "I'm not a child, Dad."

Hillary, I knew, would be horrified by the thought of an adult Elizabeth. Children, in Hillary's world, were to be molded—as she had been—relentlessly and long into their adult years. Tenet one: Young society women did not get pregnant before they were married and always took precautions. Elizabeth had. If the precautions failed, it was time for The Solution, which usually meant a short trip to Europe. The fact that Pierre had gotten Elizabeth pregnant was enough for him to be immediately black listed—no matter who his family was. Pierre would now be considered too careless and too selfish to ever be acceptable husband material.

"So, you're not coming back?" I could hear the uncertainty and fear in her voice. Guessed that Hillary had chosen not to tell her about the certified letter.

"If you need me to come, I'll be there in a heartbeat."

"I'll let you, know, Daddy Long Legs."

"Keep me posted, sweet pea. You've got my number. I love you." I hung up and looked up into the big leafy tree remembering George's words. It was my job to protect my daughter but there were dynamics in her life now beyond my control. It was my job to be supportive, help guide her in making her own highest choices—not decide what was best for her, as had been done to me.

Back at the Kiss 'n' Tell the customers had all disappeared and Renata and I went through our ritual again: I gave her a fifty, she held it up to the light, gave me the clipboard, I wrote the number, she dialed it through, and I went into the sticky little booth and waited for Hillary to pick up on her private line.

This was a good time: before her daily meeting with the tennis pro, before the engine was fully revved up, while she was still in bed sipping her Earl Grey tea, almost docile.

This is how it went:

Hillary: "Hillary Goodman speaking."

Me: "Hello, Hillary."

"Richard?"

"Yes."

"Where are you?" Demanding.

"Did you get my letter?" There was absolutely no need for Hillary to know my whereabouts.

"It arrived yesterday. Is it true you want a divorce? If so, I feel it would have been much more civilized if—"

"Cut the crap, Hillary. Will you? And can we please talk about this like real people, instead of Shakespearean actors."

"So it's true then."

"Yes, Hillary. It's true. I want a divorce."

"May I ask on what grounds?"

"Why don't you ask Depaulier next time you're lounging around the Strawberry Bankes Motel?"

There was silence for a moment, then, "Michel has returned to France."

"I see."

"Richard. We've had our problems, God knows. But maybe if you'd seen fit to stay, instead of leaving…"

Life is full of surprises. Of all the potential reactions I'd imagined Hillary having, suggesting our marriage was salvageable was not one of them. I'd heard the fear in her voice though, and it clicked. The fabric of her life—at least in public—was comprised of a neat hierarchy of other married couples. If Michel didn't step up to bat after a quick non-contested divorce from me, she might well be alone for a while. Hillary Goodman-Darlington: single, white, female?

"Hillary…" I knew this wasn't the moment to push her. Hillary—a gorgeous, fit, wealthy woman—was still Harry

Goodman's daughter, a spoiled little girl used to having her way in all things. If I wanted to get *my* way i.e., a non-contested divorce, I needed to assuage her and give her an out.

"We owe it to ourselves to find a better way," I said.

"I see," she said after a pause. Either she was plotting my imminent assassination or really missed me. It was hard to say.

"I've spoken to Elizabeth." Talking about our daughter, whom we both loved, had always been safe territory.

"Yes, she seems to be adapting well at Smith," she said. *If only you knew.*

"I've left Marty written instructions regarding her trust."

"Yes, both of your letters arrived. My father also called..."

"For moral support...."

She reacted to this with that special snotty tone I loved so much. "It's always about my father, isn't it? You've always resented him, haven't you, Richard? Well, perhaps if you'd been more like him...if you'd been from my background, you would've understood him better..."

"I married you, not your father, Hillary." Now there was a bit of profundity to chomp on.

"He thinks you're a terrible coward, you know. He said..."

"Hillary, I don't honestly care one whit what your father thinks of me, and haven't for years."

"He wants..."

"Hillary, this is between us. We've had a reasonably amicable marriage and now we should have an amicable divorce—don't you agree?"

Cold silence. Hillary always hated to be interrupted.

"Hillary?" I said. I did not plan to come back to Renata's pay phone soon. I planned to return to New York never.

"I can see now my father was right," said Hillary, as composed as an egret, and just as focused on the kill. I could picture her in her bedroom, surrounded by the Impressionists she loved, sipping her tea in utter civility. "Marrying you was a dreadful mistake."

"In that case your father should be pleased it's over." Sometimes life hands you a tidbit and you don't even have to dive for it.

"*Touché*, Richard. Yes, he does seem pleased at the prospect."

"Good, then. Let's move forward."

"My God, Richard...all those years," said my wife, sounding sorrowful.

"We don't need to be enemies," I said, but when she didn't say anything, I knew she'd already hung up.

16.

I headed for the Dia y Noche for lunch feeling stronger than I'd felt since I arrived. Maybe it was time for the liver and onions at last.

Shakey was meeting me to review my list for the city and I needed to fax it to J.J. Shakey suggested that he could go down, load everything into the pickup I was buying, and drive it back himself. We could save on transport, but more importantly, get everything back without the hassle of using a trucking company. I called J.J. and promised a transfer later that morning to his account.

Shakey was pumped up about going to the city.

"I'll get all da cosas for da casa, boss. Don't fret."

Zach, Ezra and I would continue with the construction. Shakey had found a surveyor, and we were going to mark my new boundary with a fence and get rid of the Black Jack *servidumbre* problem once and for all. We headed over to the bank and went to see what Lucky had in stock. After that I had my own plans: a little fact-finding mission I'd be conducting all by myself.

Lucky—whom I'd met through Shakey at the beginning of my project—was at his place by the door at the Lucky Dragon Almacen, the world's most chaotic hardware store. He was a big, moon-faced Chinese man who loved to work crossword puzzles, listen to the radio, smile at everyone who entered, then ignore them.

Today he looked at me and apropos of nothing asked, "You from No Fuck?"

"Excuse me?"

He laughed lustily, his eyes disappearing into the fleshy folds on his face. "Joe, he from Nofuck, Virginia. Ha ha ha. Thought you from there, too."

"No, I'm from New York."

"New Yak? Big place."

"Yes. I like Hubba Hubba, though."

"You like this place? How come?"

"It's very beautiful…"

"Beauty skin deep!" Lucky declared. "The women nice, though." He smiled at me slyly.

"Yes, there's that…"

"What you want with this black boy?" Lucky asked me, nodding in Shakey's direction. I wasn't sure if he was kidding.

I looked at Shakey, saw him grin. "You old, yellow devil! Look who callin' who color?" Their eyes glinted at each other

Lucky turned to me. "What you want, Mistuh New Yak?"

"I need a fence, materials for a half mile of fence."

His eyes opened wide at this, and laughed. "You fencin' Coco Beach and buyin' from me? Guess this gonna be my lucky day!"

Shakey left on the afternoon ferry for the city and I went down to the town pier and found a *cayuco* and driver for hire that looked about right for the job. The local boys all wanted a piece of the action and jostled each other to help me into the boat with my rucksack, camera equipment and water jug. When I gave them all two "quatas" enough for a snow cone each, they took off, flip-flops flying.

I directed the Indian, a non-English speaking local, to seaward and off we went. When we were about a mile out, I pointed north and we changed course.

We cruised along the coast like tourists, past La Cabaña beach, and about two miles further came to Coco Beach. I took out my camera, began shooting pictures, then got out my zoom, and took some more. The view of the property from this perspective was magnificent: a big, velvety green hill ringed by rolling surf and topped with palm trees. I could make out the tall stick figures of Zach and Ezra and faintly heard them pounding nails.

A little further on we came to Jack Murillo's right-of-way where it wended its way from behind my property to the sea. The Indians were swinging their machetes again by order of the mayor, and I took some pictures of this with my zoom lens, then pointed behind them where far up in the tree line I saw a glint of zinc.

I'd seen enough. Jack, in contradiction of what George told me, had indeed constructed some kind of building back there. I wondered what he used it for.

I carried on. North of my farm there were miles of deep golden sand beaches—completely empty. The surf here was pounding big, with heavy currents. Not a place to land, or possibly even swim, but probably the most pristine Caribbean beach I'd ever seen.

The circumnavigation of Hubba Hubba continued. We went past Drago Point and around a little green atoll strung with vines where birds with long white tailfeathers and bright red beaks swooped through the air like dancers—Bird Island.

We rounded the point and headed back toward town. The mangrove was thick on this part of the coast. Indian houses made of poles and thatch were built over the water. Naked children waved and smiled at us as we motored past. Now we were "insi" where the west coast of Hubba Hubba was almost fully protected from the prevailing northerlies; the light chop made a little slap against the hull, lulling me.

I fell into a reverie about Veronica, my favorite new pasttime. She was a mystery: her marriage to a man like Jack Murillo, the lack of children. I thought of her some more. Her caramel skin, long legs; she was really starting to get to me. I thought of Marty falling in love with Melanie, remembered thinking how dramatic and silly it seemed. For the first time, I truly began to understand how Marty felt.

I seriously doubted if he'd understand me though, let alone forgive me. It was time to call him and find out.

17.

When he came on the line, I thought it was someone else. Yelling or screaming, I expected. Bashing and berating, I anticipated. Instead I got this deadly calm.

"Well, well Richard. You're still alive, then?"

"And you, too," I said.

"I don't suppose you're going to tell me *where* you are?"

"That's not why I called." It would take more trust than I currently felt about him, before I gave him the keys to my freedom and anonymity.

"Of course not. Your letter…well. It was very clear on that point."

I waited.

"So, what is this, Richard? A master game of hide and seek? I guess I don't have to tell you how devastated my father is. Your departure has done shit for office morale too, let me tell you." He couldn't have cared less how I was.

This was the Marty I was glad I'd left behind: the blaming, shaming, scared shitless Marty. Now his worst nightmare had come to pass: he was going to be in the driver's seat, making decisions I'd always made for him.

I said, "Milton has certainly been through it with the two of us, I agree. But if your decision to divorce Marlene didn't kill him, I don't think my leaving the office will."

"That's a low fucking blow."

"Milton knows exactly how it is for me, Marty. Believe it. He made me over in his image. He and Harry together."

"That's bloody unfair."

"It's the truth. And while we're on the subject, why don't you give the staff a bonus from me, Marty, and cheer them up? I mean— that's why everybody's there, isn't it? That's why *you're* there."

"You're a real prick, you know that?" said my former best friend. "Since when is making money such a horrible crime? You used to like it…."

"After the first hundred million or so, it begins to lose a bit of its shine, Marty, don't you think?"

He drew a sharp breath at this. I had desecrated his most sacred cow. "Jesus. You really have gone over the edge."

"Not over the edge, Marty. Just out of the game."

"And Hillary?"

"Christ, Marty! Do you think I'm going to run back there? Keep up the whole fucking charade? Give me a break."

"Well, she deserves better," he said, coldly. "She called me. So did Harry." *How the worm does turn!*

"Bully for them."

"And Elizabeth?" He was trying to hook me.

"I'm in contact with Elizabeth. In fact, that's the reason I'm calling. To make sure we're clear about Elizabeth's future."

"Elizabeth, schmizabeth! I'm so sick of hearing everyone talk about her best interests. As if she's a poor little waif…"

"I thought you always had her best interests at heart, Marty. That's why I gave you the general power." The statement was as laden with innuendo as the branch of a ripe breadfruit tree.

He tried another tack. "You realize this liquidation is going to cost you millions, Richard. The Feds will skin you alive…"

"All proceeds into Elizabeth's trust, then?" He was mad as a snake.

"Just like I said." I was sure he was recording our conversation. "Just certify that the proceeds came from me personally. I'll undoubtedly have to prove it later."

"Undoubtedly….?"

"Good luck, Marty. I wish you well."

I put down the receiver, standing in the Kiss 'n' Tell with a pounding heart.

Marty Kahn was who he was, and would stay that way.

I'd chosen to change.

But for the first time, I saw that in changing I'd forced him to change too, when all he wanted was for everything to stay exactly the same.

I felt a tap on my shoulder and turned. Renata was there, with my change.

I headed to the Wreck Deck later that night, irrationally hoping I might catch a glimpse of Veronica, whom I hadn't seen in days, and could forget all about Hillary Goodman and Marty Kahn.

Lovinia made me a big plate of lobster in garlic sauce, and it was very quiet. I ordered another beer, and looked across the dark water of the channel wiggling with light to Little Conch Cay. Was Veronica over there in her nightie cuddled up with her husband?

Around nine o'clock an old man named Mango showed up from Isla Esmeralda. He had on a bright yellow hat, a blue shirt, white shoes, and carried an old banged-up guitar which he kept twirling around. After awhile he settled down and started playing old Creole tunes, which he didn't sing as much as speak in *guari guari*.

Around ten, Joe and Patrice showed up while Mango talked/sang about bananas and Yellow Fever and lovemaking in odd places. He was soon joined by the Swinging Dicks, and a bunch of other musicians I'd never seen before. They all started jamming together.

The place started to get packed, the floorboards vibrated.

"What's all this about?" I asked Joe.

"Blue Monday," he said. "We can't sleep with all the racket so we come over here until they're finished."

Joe ordered us another round and as it grew late, more of the locals began to appear. I saw Julie, Shakey's "cuzin," and Coralia, his aunt. Julie looked even rounder now, which reminded me of Elizabeth. I commented to Patrice about it.

"You ever notice how many shoes are lyin' around here?" she asked me.

"You mean..."

"I mean on the beach, in the woods. You always find a single shoe, or a sandal or sneaker, never a pair. Big ones, little ones. You'll start seeing 'em too. I call this place 'Land of the Lost Shoes.' Guy past you on the playa collects 'em in a big old freezer, hopin' to get a match one day, I guess." She sipped her drink and looked thoughtful.

"Lots of 'behind the barn' here." Joe added.

"Or anywhere there's a flat place." Patrice smiled. Had she *really* been a nun?

Speaking of flat places....I was dog tired. I said good night to my new friends, and slipped away to the Boatel; all was quiet. I took a cool shower and lay on top of the sheets. I felt the sea breeze wash over me and went to sleep.

The clock showed 3:12 in glowing green when I woke up and heard footsteps on the deck right above my head. I remembered that I'd forgotten to lock the companionway door. Shit.

A moment later, I heard the stealthy turn of the little brass handle, the muffled footfalls of an intruder.

I jumped up, stuffed the pillows back under the sheet, and grabbed Jim's shotgun from underneath the bunk—too late to do more. I scampered into the head and looked back at my bunk where the log of pillows looked like a skinny-ass version of me.

Just in the nick of time.

When I saw the back of Cabino's head, I hesitated. I watched him lean over the form in the bed and wondered what he'd do. Was his intent to strangle me where I lay, or would he have a pang of conscience for a completely unarmed, sleeping man?

Had the mayor really given the order to have me snuffed?

Cabino lifted a big machete over his head and with both hands, brought it down into the pillows where my head had lain a few seconds before.

It was then I remembered that the gun I was holding wasn't loaded. And so I did the only thing I could do. I whacked the back of his head with the butt-end of the gun with all my might. Cabino fell slowly at first, like the first stage of a demolition. He didn't fall so much as slide downward in slow motion, and after what seemed like an eternity, finally keeled forward into an unconscious heap on top of my bunk.

Thank you, Dios! I didn't waste any time, but tied him in multiple knots, arms and legs both, with the bed sheets.

Then I went to find the police.

18.

Moses Castillo was the Chief of Police in Hubba Hubba and he looked like Hugo Chávez's older, grumpier brother. He lit a big cigar and nodded as I told him about Cabino's attempt to kill me, and how he was now tied up in the Boatel.

Finally, after about a five-minute explanation from me, he grunted and pulled the cigar out of his mouth. "No speaky English," he said.

COMO?! I went to find Lucky to help me translate. He lived just behind his store near the Boatel. He came to the door in a thin nightshirt that fell to his knees.

"What now, New Yak?"

Eventually the three of us made our way to the Boatel, up the ladder and down the passageway leading to my cabin. In front of us sat Cabino, still tied up but wide awake now, his coal black eyes drilling into me with cold, murderous intent.

Wanda and Jim still hadn't stirred.

"This man tried to kill me in bed," I said to Moses. "He used this machete," I said, picking it up. "And sliced through this pillow where my head was supposed to be." I picked up the two halves of the foam pillow. Exhibits number one and two.

Lucky translated: *"Es un matador, jefe. Todos saben esto."*

Moses took his unlit cigar and moved it to the other corner of his mouth while regarding Cabino. No one said anything so I kept up the patter for all of us.

"Ever since I refused to pay the mayor a hundred-dollar bribe, this man has been stalking me...."

"You Yanqui?" asked Moses, just when I'd begun to think he was a deaf mute.

"Yes, I am."

He smiled. *"Me gustan los Yanquis."* God bless America, I thought.

Moses said, "Me seester...*le gustan los Yanquis, tambien."* He laughed then, laughed and laughed. I laughed too so he'd get this murderous psychopath out of my cabin and put him behind bars.

"Actually, I *like* being single," I was on a roll, now. "It's fun."

"Foon?" Moses asked.

"Es divertido," provided Lucky.

"Ah, yah," said the big man who relit his cigar and stuck it back in his mouth. "Foon. *Me gusto* foon, *tambien."* We continued to have a good male laugh at this, all except Cabino.

Moses Castillo still made me uneasy. It must have been the Chávez thing.

"No worry," Lucky said, as if reading my mind. "He's a good man. Do right thing."

Moses looked down at Cabino finally and made up his mind. *"Vamos,"* he said. He undid the knots around Cabino's ankles.

Cabino stood, towering above us, his rastalocks sticking out from his head like unraveled cigars. He ducked his way out of the Boatel and down the ladder to the street where two policemen waited. They shackled him, and they all walked in a group over to the jail, Moses's cigar smoke trailing behind.

I followed Lucky back to his shop. "Won't there be a trial?"

"Huh! Be a trial, sure. But not for years. Don't fret." I thanked him for his translation.

"De nada, New Yak," he said, smiling at me, and winked. "Lucky makes you lucky day!"

I went back into the Boatel. It was sunrise now, and Wanda was in her little pink kimono.

"Coffee?" she asked. She and Jim had remained eerily asleep through the whole Cabino ordeal. "Heard some noise last night—couldn't sleep?" I didn't see the sense of telling her all the sordid details of the Cabino break-in. She was already stressed out enough.

"Cabino paid us a visit last night," I said, playing it down, "but he's in jail now."

'That's good," she said, looking thoroughly distracted. Her little pink kimono wafted around her slight form. Her big gray eyes looked haunted and full of worry, even at this early hour.

Jim wheeled himself out, all dressed, wet hair combed back and ready for his speech therapist.

"Heard voi...ces last night," he managed.

"Yes," I said cheerily. "Cabino came by. But it's all sorted out now." I tried a reassuring smile. No sense aggravating an already unhappy situation.

Call it claustrophobia but the Boatel was beginning to feel like a coffin with the lid nailed shut.

"I'll grab some breakfast at the Dia," I said. I'd make sure there was a much heftier lock installed on the companionway door later today. I said a cheery good-bye to Wanda and Jim, jumped on the Harley and after my fried dough and coffee, sped out to Coco Beach. I needed to get a new roof over my head pronto.

Zach and Ezra had made good progress over three days, even if the windows were all of different sizes and heights. The floor of my cabin was in, the walls were sided, the zinc roof on.

I mentioned the windows and Zach became thickly silent. I decided not to pursue it. I was learning, slowly, to go with the flow of this culture that was light years from the one I knew. So instead of threats, cajoling or insisting, I went for a swim.

In a day or two, if all went according to plan, Shakey would be back with my consignment from the city.

Meanwhile, he'd arranged for the fence to go up by hiring the same Indians who'd done the cutting of Jack's right-of-way. Shakey pointed out, with perfect Hubba Hubba logic, that these men knew the boundaries already and were therefore ideal for the job.

Who was I to argue?

I was learning fast that where personal opinions were concerned, be they about window placement, opening a hole for a fence post, or theories about why the coconut business had failed, Hubba Hubbans could become stubborn and unflinching. Likewise, criticism was simply not accepted, but tossed to the next person like a hot potato, with excuses piled thickly on top like sour cream.

Since my presence seemed to stir up this kind of unease at the moment, I decided to have an afternoon walk through my property. I had about fifty acres of coconut trees, twenty-five or thirty of secondary growth forest, and the rest clear pasture where the hill was. I walked through the old coconut plantation, careful not to stand directly under the clumps of fruit. These fuzzy brown coconuts were enormous and could kill a person with one ill-timed drop. As far as I could see, the trees and fruit looked healthy; I made a mental note to speak to George about the disease that had affected the coconut business. Maybe the library would have some historical information; I decided to check it out.

What was it that Black Jack had built back here way past my back boundary, and well out of sight?

I walked on through an old overgrown path and finally saw the glint of zinc among the jungle vegetation.

I moved forward slowly and saw that the roof was attached to an elevated cabin of about fifteen by fifteen feet; a long palm trunk had been notched out to create a makeshift ladder up to the cabin's floor.

Someone was inside. I could hear low voices, then watched as the whole structure began to gently wobble. A man's laugh was followed by a slap, and then a young girl's sobbing complaint.

The next thing I knew, Blanquita was scurrying down the palm ladder, dress askew. She never looked back, just began running at top speed through the underbrush, back toward the road. Was this the municipal love nest?

I waited until the man himself came down the ladder, then I came out from behind the tree and greeted him.

"Mr. Murillo," I said. "Why am I not surprised?"

Jack Murillo looked like a jungle animal in this landscape: a strong, self-possessed black man filled with macho power. If he was surprised, he didn't show it.

"Ah, Mr. Darlington. Your presence is becoming...how shall I say it? A bit of an inconvenience." He smiled, and I saw how easily he could become violent.

I said, "So, that's what you do back here? Rape under-aged girls?'

Jack Murillo's eyes bored into mine, reminding me of Cabino. "Come, come, Mr. Darling-town. A willing girl is not a victim."

"I think the police chief might have a different opinion."

This made him laugh out loud. "You're making a nice fence, Mr. Darling-town, and this is not your property. You're trespassing."

"I guess I'll have to confirm the facts about municipal holdings with Veronica so we don't have any more misunderstandings."

He laughed at the mild threat. "My wife is *beeuti-full*, eh *Mistuh* Darling-town?"

"Only a fool wouldn't notice." I'd never had such a strong urge to inflict harm on another human being.

"Only a fool, or a white man, would come to a place where he doesn't belong." His anger was like a slap, one minute it wasn't there, the next it was all you could feel.

I said, "I'm sorry you feel that way." What I felt was that Jack Murillo was a bigot with a violent streak that went all the way to his bone marrow.

"In these parts, a wife's first obli-*gay*-tion is to serve her husband and family, then her people. This is not America, Mistuh Darling-town." The strong island accent was back. But any way you sliced it, Jack Murillo was a misogynistic, criminal son-of-a-bitch.

I said, "You seem like a busy man...I mean, husband."

"That is none of your business, so stay out of it." He was starting to lose his cool.

"Will do," I said, and turned to leave. A small part of me was glad I didn't have Jim's gun, otherwise, I might've developed a violent streak of my own.

Back on the hill and within cell phone range, I called Joe. "Will the confessional be open later?"

He said, "What about the place at Sugar Beach ? I'll give Patrice the night off."

"Funny you should mention going to Blanquita's..."

"Gotta dash. See you around seven? I've got a kid in a kayak trying to sell me fifteen pounds of lobster..."

"No problem." I hung up.

At sunset, I drove Zack and Ezra back into town, caught a quick shower at the Boatel then headed back to Blanquita's. The simple beach shack belonging to Onassis's family sat on a white sand beach and in the evening light the foam glowed brightly, making the water come alive.

Blanquita came over and took my order looking as she always did. I could see no psychic scars, no bangs or bruises. She seemed the same as always shy, coquettish, and sad.

I ordered a beer and some *pulpo ajillo*. I wanted to express my concern about what I'd seen, ask her more. Was she going to press charges? And how did you say "press charges" in Spanish?

I wondered about Veronica. Were she and Jack still a conjugal couple? The thought sickened me. In addition to all the other abuse, was my cherished one going to get a nice fat case of viral herpes as an early Christmas present thanks to her husband's indiscretions?

Ten minutes later Blanquita was back with my *pulpo*, another beer, and a proposition. "Me you like?" she asked.

Jesus. "No, Blanquita."

"Como?" she asked, blinking at me ingenuously.

"No, Blanquita," I said, more firmly.

"She coming on to you?" Joe, my itinerant savior, pulled up a stump as Blanquita stood by.

"I think so. But a few hours ago, I thought she was being raped by Jack Murillo."

Joe made a motion like drinking from a bottle, and Blanquita went to get him a beer. "So Black Jack's at it again. He already hit the lottery with Julie."

"He got Julie pregnant?"

Joe raised an eyebrow at me as if I'd been living under a rock. "How did you happen to see him with Blanquita?"

I told him about finding Jack Murillo's municipal hideaway.

Joe said, "I draw the line at incest or child beatings. Otherwise I try not to get involved. The culture here is so different. Monogamy is almost non-existent. Most Hubba Hubbans never marry, just move in together, have a bunch of kids. After about five years, everyone changes partners."

"Musical..."

"You got it. In Blanquita's case, she already has a boyfriend slash husband and is probably trying to make him jealous by getting it on with Black Jack."

"How old do you think she is?"

"Eighteen or nineteen. Older than she looks. She already has two kids."

"*Dios.*" I forked a piece of *pulpo* and looked at it.

"Lost your appetite?" Joe asked, sensing my mood like a blip on a radar screen. "What's up?"

I took a deep breath. "I talked to my daughter a few days ago. She thinks she might be pregnant. She's just gone into her first semester at Smith."

"That's a tough one."

"What should I tell her?"

"If she's asking for advice, she's probably too young to be a mother."

"She didn't ask my opinion. Do you think I should fly back?"

"Did she ask you to?"

"No."

"What about her mother?"

"I don't know." I stirred the *pulpo* around on my plate, thinking of Hillary. "I don't think Hillary knows."

In the darkness surrounding us, the white foam ruffled toward us like lacy edges of a woman's slip.

"Getting a divorce?" Joe sipped his beer.

"Yes."

"Any particular reason?"

"I need to save my sanity!"

"That's a good reason," Joe said, taking a swig from his beer.

"That's not to say I'm not assailed by doubt," I added.

Joe laughed. "And what would the doubt be?"

"That I'd find a woman to love. Someone to share my life with. My marriage—though it needed to end—was a twenty-year partnership. I'm good at partnerships."

"Anybody in mind?"

"As a matter of fact...."

Joe smiled back at me. "She's beautiful and smart, can't say I blame you. Just watch your back."

I said, "I feel like I'm clinging to a parasail. I have no idea if Veronica has any feelings for me, or if I'm just going to have to keep floating and hoping."

"Give her time," said the former Father Joe. "I imagine she's getting ready to make a move. She's no dope."

"Wonder what Black Jack will have to say about that?"

"Veronica's from a big, old Hubba Hubba family. He wouldn't try anything stupid. Or let's say this: he wouldn't try anything stupid that could land his ass in jail."

We drank our beers and thought about this.

Joe said, "Black Jack used to be a big partier. Then he stopped drinking, converted himself into a holier-than-thou politician and claimed his goal was to save Hubba Hubba from economic ruin. Now he's supposedly converted to the Muslim faith and will only eat meat he kills himself. He also has big personal plans for the island."

"*This* island?"

"Rumor has it he's got some links to the big cruise ship lines."

"Holy God." I thought of my goal of preserving some of Hubba Hubba's virgin jungles and defunct farms by buying them up and putting them into an eco-trust. I'd been so busy trying to stay alive though my vision had taken a detour.

"He and his cronies want to nip off about five hundred hectares on the north end of Hubba Hubba and turn it into a little port-of-call paradise like they did in the Bahamas? Install a village of shops, buy a few thousand chaises, put in some bars with cutesy names, and voila!"

"Jet skis and parasailing?"

"Sure," said Joe. "And lock down the action in advance. Get all the contracts for everything. The permits to dock, the dockage fees, the rum."

"The jet skis…."

"Everything."

"How close to reality is this?" Now I had another reason why Veronica had tried to prevent me from buying Coco Beach.

"Not very, I wouldn't have thought. He has some big map in his office with an artistic rendering of the whole project. I think he's just trying to get some financing lined up."

"He doesn't think small," I said.

"Neither should you," Joe said, as if he'd read my mind.

"I guess we'd better order," I said, getting the feeling of what I needed to do.

"What're you having?"

"My usual—everything on the menu."

"Maybe you've got parasites," Joe said.

"One parasite is too many for me." I smiled

"I hear ya," he said, and raised his hand at Blanquita to order more food.

19.

The ferry was going to be two hours late, as usual, so I decided to kill some time and find out about the coconut business. I headed to the library.

The municipal library, like much else in Hubba Hubba, didn't have a sign, but I found it anyway by the ask-and-point method, and walked into the squat, milk-green building and immediately saw Veronica. She was faced away from me, bent forward over a book next to a boy of about eight. I knew it was her before she even turned around; the canary yellow dress was a dead giveaway.

Seeing her always had the same effect on me: I began to get a seventeen-year old body rush, which I covered up by being affably, enthusiastically mature. She, on the other hand, always seemed guarded and slightly amused in my presence, as if she found me funny, but was too polite to laugh in my face.

"Well, hello!" I said.

"Hello Richard." She was the only one in Hubba Hubba who seemed to be able to pronounce my name correctly.

"It was great seeing you the other night—I really enjoyed it!"

"Yes, it was very nice. Thank you," Veronica's perfect, white teeth lit up her smile.

"Did George get to bed okay?" Ho, ho, ho. Did you get to bed ok? No, I didn't say that, just kept grinning at her like someone who needed a frontal lobotomy.

"Yes, he had too much to drink, I'm sorry."

"No! Not at all! That's what family's are for..." Did I really *say* that?

"And how is *your* family?"

"My family?"

Now where did that come from?

"I heard you talked to your daughter."

"Oh, my daughter! Yes, oh yes." Maybe I could bury Renata in a shallow grave behind Black Jack's love cottage and make it look like his fault. "My daughter is in her first year at Smith College."

"How wonderful!" said Veronica. "You and your wife must be very proud of her." *Fishing?*

"Oh, we are. We are." Then, almost offhand: "I'm hoping our divorce will be finalized very soon."

"What? Oh. A divorce? I'm sorry to hear that." She turned ninety-degrees away from me, and looked down at the text book while the young boy she was tutoring continued to watch me with big brown eyes.

"Anyway..." I tried for a more cheery subject. "Looks like the library could use an infusion of funds. Some computers and air-conditioners. Hey! Maybe even some new books!" She smiled at this, but still wouldn't turn back to face me.

I felt a surge of impatience. "What this library needs is a new building with a sign!" That was good. Now I sounded angry.

She finally looked at me. "You're right."

Was it the right moment to tell her what else I was thinking?

Maybe partially. I blurted, "Veronica, I've been wanting to ask your help with some projects I want to set up. I'd also like to set up a charitable trust for some of the needs of this town. I also want to buy some more property to put into a conservation trust. Would you help me?"

She thought about it, propped her head on the back of her hand, and gazed past me with those velvet eyes. "I don't know," she said finally.

"Fair enough."

"No, I mean I'm not sure *how* to handle it best. Should the charitable venture be handled through a corporation, a beneficial trust or a foundation?"

"I'll leave it up to you." I felt the adrenaline rush, again. I had a vision of Veronica and I working side by side, a physical crescendo building between us. "Could we meet soon and discuss the details?"

"I'll let you know." Which I hoped didn't mean she had to discuss it with her husband first.

I gave her my cell phone number and told her I was moving to the farm. She wished me luck but in typical Veronica style turned back to her student and became engrossed in the task at hand.

I went out into the glare of the midday sun with a big smile on my face, my coconut research forgotten.

I walked to the other end of town just in time to see the ferry pulling in. Shakey was in my new pickup with all my household stuff stacked high in the truck's bed and covered with a new tarp like a gypsy made good.

The locals weren't missing any of it, and Shakey, who loved to show off, grinned and kept tooting the horn: a one-man parade coming back from the city. I jumped in beside him and off we went. I couldn't wait to get to the farm and get it all set up.

We passed the Boatel heading out of town and Wanda flagged us down. She still looked sad and preoccupied but put on a brave face. Shakey, seeing her, began making those hissing, clicking noises and shaking his head, and I wondered what was up.

"Going out to George's to set up house. Want to help us out?" She nodded, and squeezed in beside me. I'd only been spending my sleeping hours at the Boatel, so it was hard for me to say. But I found myself wondering: Just how bad was it living with Jim these days?

We drove out on the lumpy road slowly, and made it out to my new home in just under half an hour.

With help from Zach, Ezra and the Indians who'd finished installing the cyclone fence, we were unloaded in less than an hour. The generator was started; the gas fridge hummed to life; we did some quick jury-rigging with the batteries to get a few lights working. Ezra screwed the toilet into the floor and the Indians began connecting the pipes to the septic tank I'd bought from Lucky.

Wanda took over the task of decorating and moved my bed into the center of the room directly in front of the door and the breeze. She took a spare set of sheets and artfully draped them over the windows to make some curtains. She made my bed, arranged the mosquito net around it, then went out and came back with huge armloads of wild ginger and heliconia that probably would've cost two hundred bucks for the bunch back in New York.

We'd set up a gravity feed for the water that was connected to the town supply, but needed a pump to get it up the hill. Zach tackled this, and by four p.m. I had running water, a stove, fridge, lights, a bed and a toilet that almost flushed. If Hillary could only see me now.

"Go get a couple of cold cases of soda and beer," I directed Shakey and gave him the keys; Wanda simply followed him. I watched them get in the truck, Wanda sitting closer to Shakey than necessary, he looking out the window seeming thoroughly pissed off.

I walked out to my porch with its palm frond roof, and realized I'd forgotten to buy a table or chairs. Zach and Ezra, seeing my dilemma, took the Indians and went into the bush at the back of the hill, tools in hand. The chain saw went on, I heard a crash and in about twenty minutes I had six stumps—no table till mañana, though.

Shakey got back—no Wanda—and this time *he* looked red-eyed. Shit. Everyone grabbed a beer, or soda, and I went in to try my shower. Cold water had never felt so good. The tropical sun brought everything to the simplest denominator: cold drinks, cold water, a breeze. All these counted for something now, and I appreciated them.

Which made me wonder what they hell had mattered to me before.

Shakey and I went back to town after that. I'd planned to have my farewell dinner with Wanda and Jim in the Boatel, and invited Shakey to join us.

He replied, "Huh! No, t'anks. I got udder plans."

I bought a sack of lobsters off the pier and found a dusty bottle of Moet & Chandon at one of the little supermarkets in town. I picked up some small blocks of ice from someone who made them in old margarine tubs in their kitchen freezer, got some other supplies, and headed to the Boatel. This would be my last night with Big Jim and Wanda and I wanted to make it special.

Big Jim's speech had greatly improved, though he was still as full of vinegar as ever. Though he was in his wheelchair most of the time, he seemed determined to improve. Veronica was making progress with the concession for the Boatel, and that seemed to be a turning point. The mayor, at least for the moment, seemed vanquished.

We popped a couple of beers, and Wanda put the water on to boil for the lobsters. A few minutes later I heard the strains of music coming from her cabin. It wasn't Ravel, but Debussy. *Afternoon of a Fawn.* Uh-oh.

"Wanda ok?" I asked Jim while I sautéed akee and onions in a frying pan for appetizers.

"She's...fi...fine. Git me another Ice." I gave him his second beer and he guzzled it just like the first. I passed him a plate with the akee and some bread, and waited.

"Moody as sh..sh..shit," he said.

"Not much to do in Hubba Hubba for a young woman," I commented. I was thinking that taking care of Jim seemed to be a full time job, and not a particularly rewarding one.

"Met her in a....hoor...hoor house, ya know. Work...in girl." He drank his beer with gusto and smacked his lips. He looked at me with that old devilish glint. "Don't suppose you know about *that* kinda life....fan...cy pants." He gurgled at the thought.

I told him, "Last time you saw me, I went back to my home in New York and found my wife was fucking a French poet on a billiard table in the basement."

Jim's eyes opened wide at this. "Yer shittin' me."

"Our home—the whole English pub, including the billiard table—were bought by her father, Harry B. Goodman."

"The Tire King?"

"Yep." I opened an Ice myself.

"You married the Tire King's daughter?"

I nodded.

"Yer shittin' me," repeated Jim, but I knew he didn't doubt it.

"So you see. Slumming is not reserved for poor white girls from Manchester, New Hampshire." I took a swig of beer and belched for effect.

"Married a silver spoon."

"Look like it." We both laughed.

Which brought Wanda out of hiding. "Hungry?" I asked

"Yes," said Wanda, getting the butter out and melting it in a saucepan. She seemed more cheerful.

When the lobsters were cooked, we sat and ate a few each in the Boatel galley, while a fresh breeze charged down the companionway and swirled around us and made me forget that the champagne was corked from age, and that I'd almost been killed by Cabino a few feet away.

I wondered what was going on with Wanda and Shakey. But I knew I'd find out soon enough. In Hubba Hubba, I was learning, nothing stayed a secret for long.

20.

My first night at the farm wasn't the most restful I've ever had. I listened to the geckos, nocturnal lizards that prefer making love and eating in the dark, waves crashing on the reef, and toward dawn, a flock of green parrots squawked by like a bunch of airborne phobics—which set off the howler monkeys.

Then the phone rang.

"Good morning," Veronica said.

"Good morning." I was too sleepy for the full adrenaline blast.

"Have a good night?"

I told her about living in the middle of a menagerie. "It's a jungle out here."

She laughed. "That's true."

"Think about my offer?"

"I think it's a wonderful idea to fund these projects."

"I love to spend my money, too." We laughed together easily. "We'll have some other projects to take on," I said as hulking cruise ships loomed in my mind's eye. "We'll need a Concepción corporation with nominated directors. Can you handle that?"

"Of course!" She sounded offended.

"We'll also need..."

"A bank account, a power of attorney and a trustee."

"Um...yes."

"Perfect," she said, crisply. Did she realize it was only eight a.m.?

"Could you bring out the paperwork later?" *And I'll show you my hammock?*

"I'll have to go to the bank, get these documents drawn up. I've got my tutoring session at three. About four-thirty?"

"Great," I said. My heart, awake now, began to thrum in anticipation.

I made coffee by the drip method—that is to say, put coffee in a little linen sack and poured boiling water over it. Yet another high-tech gem from Lucky Dragon Almacen that gave me pause about the Italian espresso maker I'd left behind. I happily poured the rich, dark liquid into a mug, and the phone rang again.

"Dad?" My daughter's voice sent a five-alarm charge through my system.

"Elizabeth?"

"Well....it's over," she said, snuffling.

"Oh, my darling...what happened?" I had a vision of her in her dorm room, alone.

"I had another test, and it came out negative. Then...I got my period."

Thank God. "I guess it wasn't meant to be," I said, hating myself for handing her such a timeworn cliché. I wanted to just touch her shiny hair, hold her in my arms.

"It's just so sad...Pierre and I were planning to go and live in France." Did escaping from New York run in the family?

"Maybe you can come and visit me here one day. It's not France, but..."

"I don't think so Dad. When would I be able to get away?" *Ouch.*

"Well, I hope you're going to go see that gynecologist. What's his name, Nicholas..."

"Tannenbaum."

"That's the one. Should I fly back?"

"To take me to a doctor's appointment? No way!" I was beginning to feel there was a big role reversal going on between my daughter and me.

"Elizabeth, your health is *numero uno.*"

"You're speaking Spanish, Dad?" She let out a small laugh.

"*Por supuesto,*" I said with more heartiness than I felt.

"Mother will take me."

"Your mother knows what happened?"

"Dad...of course not," my daughter the grown up told me. "Do you think I'm suicidal?"

To top off the morning, the mayor was waiting for me at the bottom of the hill, a taxi idling a few feet away, when I walked down to get into my truck to drive to town.

"Meester Reechard!" he said, with his usual bullshit bravado. *"Como estas?"*

"You'll have to excuse me, Fernando. I have an important errand to run."

"Ah, ah." He turned his hands over in a conciliatory gesture. "I only came to talk to you about the electricity..." He pulled his face into mock dismay, as though he hated to bring the subject up.

"What about it?"

"You want, no?"

"Yes, I'd like to have electricity out here. I've offered to pay for all the costs to have it installed. The company is studying my proposal now."

"Too bad," the mayor said. "I can do it for cheap. The manager. He my friend."

"Good for you," I said.

"I get you big discount. Very big. You pay me a fee, and I get it. No problem."

"How much?" I was curious to know the depth of his greed.

"For you? Only fifty thousand." He smiled at me, and batted his eyelashes.

"Fifty thousand *dollars*?" The whole cost of project, according to the electrical engineer I'd consulted, was going to run about $35,000 at the top end.

"Yes!" He clapped his hands together in delight.

"Fuck you," I said, and started to get in my truck.

"Como? Did you say...oh! No, no, no. This is not allowed here. This kind of profane language. I must give you a fine now." He wagged his finger back and forth. "This is not permitted, so. Swearing to a public official."

"You're a total asshole, Fernando, you know that? And if you come out here again, or attempt to shake me down or put out a contract on my life, I will make sure you land in prison. If it costs me everything I have."

"No, no," he kept saying. "You can't…"

But I rolled up the window and turned on the air-conditioning so I couldn't hear him and backed out onto the road.

21.

I went over to Lucky's after that, my favorite new hangout after the Dia y Noche, and leaned on the glass counter gazing in at the collection of artifacts. Flashlights, patchwork oven mitts, screwdrivers, ketchup dispensers, water filters. If Lucky didn't have it, you probably could live without it, was my new motto. The problem was identifying what you needed inside the glass cases, where everything was thrown in on top of everything else. I was mulling over today's options: a choice between galvanized nails, in lieu of stainless steel screws, which he didn't have, and the relative merits of sheetrock over plycem, for a temporary shower wall. As I fumbled with my measuring tape Lucky put down his crossword puzzle, and came over.

"Cabino, he out."

"Out of jail?"

"Uh, huh. They say he break out." He sucked his teeth.

I thought of my earlier conversation with the mayor. He'd probably gone directly to the jail afterwards, and had Cabino released so he could deal with me.

"I'll borrow Jim's gun," I told Lucky, though the only times I'd ever used one—apart from whacking Cabino in the head with the butt end—had been a couple of times in Canada at a hunting lodge with my father when I was in my teens.

"*Cuidado,*" Lucky said.

"Thanks for the heads-up, Lucky." I wondered when the hell Cabino might attack next and what I would do about it when he did.

At the Dia y Noche, I sat and had some *caramañolas* (mashed yuca stuffed with ground meat and then fried) and a cup of coffee. Shakey, who seemed to have a sixth sense about my whereabouts, was not far behind.

"Hey, boss."

"Hey, Shakey. I've got a job for you." I stood up, while the Municipal Thugs watched us from their corner table. "Come with me."

We got in the truck and drove out to la Cabaña. I parked and we sat facing out to sea, watching the waves rolling into shore.

He looked at me quizzically.

I said, "How do you feel about purchasing some property?"

He lit up. "For you?"

"Sort of. But no one is going to know, at least for the time being, that I'm the actual buyer."

"Use sumun else?"

"A corporation, yes."

He thought about this. "You gonna build somethin'?"

"Nope. I want to preserve them. That's the point. I'm going to buy these farms so they can't be developed."

"Uh-huh." He shook his head like I was beyond help. "It's yo' money."

"So it is."

"Veronica in it, too?" He looked at me slyly.

"Not in the way you think."

"She in love wid you." Shakey gave me this fact as cool as a weather report.

"I...."

"Don't say nuthin'. It's da trute. Jack, man, he pissed off." He laughed at this. "Oooo, hoo, hoo. He damn burnin'."

I wanted to laugh, but my throat had seized up.

"And Wanda?" It was out before I'd thought about it.

"What Wanda?" Just as quick as that, I'd made him mad.

"Shakey, if it's obvious to me, it must be obvious to everyone else."

"That white meat bitch." I'd never seen him so angry.

"Jesus! Shakey, that's horrible..."

"Horrible? She kilt my chile wid her. How's dat? Went over to Platanillo whilst I was in da city, and did da deed."

"Jesus, I'm sorry..."

"Dat's how it is." He began zipping and unzipping the compartments of the briefcase I'd bought him. This conversation was over.

"Alright then. Let's get back to business. Start finding me the farms, I'll start buying them."

"Same price you paid George?"

"Yes. Fair market value."

"I'll get you da best deals, jefe. Shakey gonna get da prices real low."

"I knew I could depend on you." Joe had been right: Hubba Hubba maybe only had one channel, but it was all about sex, love and power plays, morning, noon, and night.

Veronica came as scheduled that afternoon, arriving on a new red scooter that I guessed had been bought with some of the proceeds from the sale of her father's farm. As I watched her approach, dressed in tight jeans and a white, frilly blouse, I knew there was only one thing to do, and so I sat her down and gave her a cold drink while the sea breeze whipped dark tendrils into her eyes.

I wanted her to keep sitting there like that forever. It was time to get down to the nitty-gritty.

"I've got a legal problem," I began.

"That's why God made lawyers," she said, a gleam in her eye.

"Cabino tried to kill me with a machete last week, and now he's out of jail again."

There went the gleam. "I know about the machete part."

"Do you?"

"It's a small town."

"If something happens to me, I want you to make sure this property is put into part of the ecological trust I set up. I want to

253

make my daughter the trustee. I want you to draw me up a will that stipulates this."

"Yes, but..."

"Now about your husband," I forged on. "There may well be repercussions to your having me as a client. How do you feel about that?"

"I want to do the work." She looked at me. "Let me take care of Jack."

"Of course, I will." *Easier said than done.*

"You were going to change your mind about using me as your lawyer, weren't you?" She looked at me frankly.

"I thought about it," I told her, "but then a wave of selfishness overcame me."

She smiled. *Enough soul-baring for one day.*

I told her my plan, which was simple: I intended to buy up as many farms as possible along the coast north of my property, including the area where Jack Murillo planned to put his Cruise Ship Village of the Future.

"Did you know what the government has planned up there?" I didn't mention her husband by name.

"The cruise ship thing."

"That's it." She looked at me with that combination of cute and serious that made me feel unstable. "Do we have a conflict of interest?"

"Not on my side. But I think we need to find you a negotiator. Someone who isn't me." I wondered if she felt frightened; I didn't want to undermine her courage by asking.

"Shakey's already agreed."

She said, "You'll be completely in control, because you'll have all the bearer shares, and a general power of attorney." I gave her the contact details for Licenciado Martinez, my lawyer in the city.

I told her about Jarald McVey, and she laughed. "He can't be that bad!"

"Lawyers who are white, fat and red in the face just aren't my type any more."

"Hmmm." She looked at me, considering this.

"Let's talk about the charitable trust for a minute,"

I didn't want to change the subject and tell her all the *other* things I felt. Not yet.

She smiled at me, and nodded. Playing along.

22.

No international cell service meant I had to call my lawyer in the city, have him call McVey and ask McVey to call me.

Twenty minutes later, the man himself was on the line, his usual sucking up behavior on full display.

"Mr. Darlington! How nice to hear from you. And how is the weather today in Concepción? Are you enjoying yourself?"

"Thank you, McVey. All's well here. Look, I'd like you to transfer five million to my offshore account down here. Can you manage it?"

"Oh! Yes, sir. Of course!" His commission would be spent before he hung up the phone. "It will have to come out of the Swiss account first. So it'll be several days."

"That's fine, McVey."

"Business good?" He was fishing.

"Very fine," I said, getting in that nice Caribbean touch.

I gave him Veronica's name and asked him to draw up a power of attorney for her, which seemed to throw him. "A *general* power of attorney...for everything?"

"That's it. Send it down to Martinez by courier after it's been signed by the principals on your end. When I'm ready, I'll go to the city, get it notarized, then send it back to you—alright?"

"Of course, Mr. Darlington."

"A full power of attorney. Don't leave anything out."

"No, sir."

"Good bye, McVey."

"Good bye, sir." It was just as easy as that.

I went to find Shakey. He was at the Boatel and I was quickly putting together a scenario in which Big Jim no longer featured as

Wanda's main man. They were both there, though. Or I should say, all three of them. Jim in his wheelchair, ordering them around, as usual, Wanda looking worn out trying to please him, and Shakey with an ill-disguised look of disgust on his face.

I got an update from Jim on the Alcalde situation. "That rottin' bum fuh..fuh..cker! Came here with some phony document. I tole him to wipe his ass with it." He huffed and puffed.

"Calm down, Jim. Let Veronica do her job." Relieving Big Jim of his independence though would be tantamount to hitting him over the head with an oar, then rolling him over the Boatel's side.

I asked Jim if I could take his shotgun in case of jungle intruders. This had the dual purpose of keeping it away from him in case he suddenly decided to shoot the mayor—or anyone else—again.

"Git my .45," he told Wanda. "And give Dick Old Rel...liable. Not gonna be doin' much deer huntin' down here...."

Shakey came with me out to the truck. He had some farms all lined up, he said, but first I needed to go to the Kiss n' Tell and find out how the hell I could get international access on my phone. Renata gave me her boss's number after a lot of prodding. "You have to go to da city, direct so. Fill out da *solicitud*."

While I was there, I checked my email. I had three new messages, all in the same vein.

The first was from Hillary:

"Richard, I know where you are, and so do my lawyers. Please do as they ask so we might have a civilized settlement in this unfortunate matter. Elizabeth is fine, and adjusting well at Smith. Hillary."

The second from her lawyers:

"Dear Mr. Darlington, This email serves as preliminary notice that we have been retained by your wife, Hillary Goodman Darlington, in the matter of your request for a divorce. We must advise you to return to New York at once. The legal sine qua non *in this case prevents us from going forward with a division of your and Mrs. Darlington's assets until we have specified guarantees from you. Please contact me with your travel arrangements as soon as you have made them, and give me the name and*

contact details of your lawyer of record so we might conclude this business as *quickly as possible. Sincerely, Randall Hawkes, Esq.*

The head honcho for Harry Goodman's lawyers, of course.

The third, straight to the point, was from Harry himself.

"Richard, You always were a fucking slime ball. Harry."

It saddened me that Hillary had decided to involve her father, but I was hardly surprised. He'd been running her life forever, what else was new? I selected all three messages and cheerfully pressed the delete key. Let them eat my gold dust.

Shakey and I went back to Coco Beach and changed vehicles. For our tour of properties north of here we'd need the bike.

He hopped on behind me and we headed up a dirt road one car width wide with lacy greenery forming canopies over our heads as Shakey began his tour.

He pointed to the right. "That be the Correa finca. Thirty-eight hectárea, *mas o menos.*" I did a quick calculation, and got close to a hundred acres. It had ponds, grazing cattle and horses, lots of pasture.

"This side," he pointed left, "is the *hijo*. His son got about sixty hectarea, go down to the sea. He want to sell too."

"Is there more?"

"Huh!" said Shakey. We traversed some old pastures with skinny cows and a few sad-looking coconut palms. We went around old fences, drove around big stands of bamboo, and past one large, blinking, sunbathing iguana.

"Is all the paperwork in order?"

"Seem so."

"Why do these people want to sell?

"No money in cows, no money in bananas or cocos. They like to sell, move on."

"Where would he go? A farmer like Correa?"

"Da kids dey leave. Farmin's hard work." Shakey shrugged. "Maybe he go where da kids be."

We talked about a price that was so low it seemed sinful. "Give them what they ask. Get the contracts from Veronica."

"Meester Reech?"

"Yes, Shakey?"

"You know whachoo doin'?

"Absolutely," I said. "Now let's go see what else lies up this road."

The dirt road led through about five miles of rolling farmland interspersed with primary and secondary jungle. Howler monkeys screamed at us as we passed, the Harley's motor triggered an impending invasion, I guess.

We reached the coast. A thin crescent of sugary sand was rimmed with coconut palms and sea grape. Transparent water was spackled with shades of pale blue and mossy green, and then it dropped right off into the deep blue channel. It was—I could see how Black Jack would think so—an ideal anchorage for cruise ships.

"Wow."

"Purty," agreed Shakey.

There was even a little thatched place that served cold beer and after a couple of these we ordered lunch: whole fried snapper with *patacones* and some slices of tomato. A diesel generator hummed distantly in the background.

The breeze was a nice tropical zephyr that carried a tang of coolness. It was one of those postcard-from-paradise days that gets etched into your mind forever.

"What about all this beachfront?" I asked Shakey.

"She for sale, too, but cain't build on the first twenty-two meters. She public land."

"That's good." Veronica's knowledge had started to rub off.

"You wanna buy dis beach?" Shakey was getting a certain swagger, not that I blamed him.

"Only if the people will stay on."

"You want the peoples them to stay?"

"Shakey, I have a place. I don't want to get into the cattle business, or own a beach bar. I just want to make sure that it's all protected. Later, we'll set up something so the owners and their families can stay here if they want—as long as they don't develop it."

Shakey gave me a long look.

"Don't worry about it, Shakey. Nobody's going to screw me. We'll set up some long-term lease agreements in exchange for maintenance. It'll work out."

We got on the Harley and headed back down the road. We saw sloths, parrots and toucans; the same group of monkeys screamed at us as we rode past in low gear.

"Who owns this road?" I asked over my shoulder.

"The farmers, they do."

"Good." I was hoping this wasn't a municipal road. If it was maintained privately there was a good chance it could stay that way.

The next morning, I found several men clenched together at the bottom of the hill. I waved them up.

One of them, in broken English, explained they were near neighbors of Correa and his son. Did I want to buy their farms, too?

Later that morning, Shakey and I headed up the road behind a very old rack truck with the three farmers inside. Between them, they had about three miles of Caribbean beachfront that they were offering at a bargain price. When I told them they could stay on for at least a year with their cattle, they all thought—I could see it in their eyes—that I'd lost it. Shakey put the deal together right on the hood of the truck, and by sunset, I had Correa's, his son's, and the three other farms all under agreement, contingent only on clear title.

It was a buyer's market, and a seller's market, too, if you looked at it from the farmers' point of view. Veronica, under sudden pressure to get five title searches complete and new title deeds drawn, was a cool-headed professional. I felt like a kid in the snow cone store. No purchase had excited me so much in years.

Over the next few days I talked to Veronica on the phone many times, but only went to town once. I saw Black Jack, but he crossed the street and went into the Dia y Noche with the rest of the municipal bandits. The mayor was strangely absent though, as was Cabino.

Martinez called, and said the power of attorney had arrived from the States. My money was on its way. I needed to get to the city but didn't want to go by road and meet all the *transitos* again. So I asked J.J. to arrange a helicopter—it was only an hour and a half to the city by air.

The crises of the past few weeks finally seemed behind me.

Sweet Hubba Hubba was truly getting sweeter with each passing day.

23.

That evening, I was just sitting out on the porch, enjoying my latest concoction: a can of beef stew with a handful of chopped garlic and some chili sauce stirred in, when I saw a flashlight wobbling over by the *servidumbre*. Was Black Jack smuggling his girlfriends in by sea?

I went inside to slice up two Johnny cakes I'd bought from Jonas, the bicycle bread man, and get myself an Ice, when I heard a thump at the back of the cabin. I didn't really pay attention; I was getting used to the sounds of the jungle now: little love-making lizards, roaring howler monkeys, birds warbling, small mammals skittering through the grass.

I went back out to the porch and ate. No mosquitoes out here; the ecosystem was still functioning. Birds, bats and geckos took care of most of the fly-bys, though I still liked to sleep under a mosquito net at night as a firstline of defense.

The light on the servidumbre was no longer visible, and I thought I'd get a couple of dogs one day. They were a great early warning system out here, and would be good companions. Meanwhile, though, I had Big Jim's shotgun, which I'd put under my bed in case of trouble.

I scraped off my plate, washed it and put it in the dish drainer. All I needed now was a frilly apron.

I packed my bag for the trip to the city tomorrow. It wasn't even nine o'clock, but I was whacked. Since coming to Hubba Hubba, all my days had been equally full and exhausting. Every night I got a solid eight hours sleep and was often awake at dawn.

I closed the shutters, turned on the overhead fan, lit a citronella candle, crawled under the mosquito net and lay on top of the sheet, feeling happy and content with my life. And that's when I felt it: Something was under the sheet and in the bed with me.

I jumped out, and watched it slide out from under the sheet and start to flow onto the floor like a small black river. The snake was long, thick, with a triangular-shaped head, and bold black all over: a full-grown Bushmaster, one of the tropic's deadliest snakes. The locals called them Sleeping Snakes, but this one looked like he'd already had his nap.

He didn't look happy.

Heart pounding, I gave him a wide berth, and went around to where I'd left Big Jim's shotgun, on the floor, near my pillow. Knelt down and looked. The gun was gone.

Perfecto. Someone had planted the snake in my bed *and* taken my gun. It didn't take me long to figure out who.

I grabbed the galley's fire extinguisher, and walked quickly in the dim light to the bathroom, about ten feet away. I then let out a convincing, blood-curdling scream which brought a certain person right through the unlocked door.

"TE MATO! I KILT YOU!" Cabino laughed with the glee of a murderous madman. He was whooping and waving the gun around like an Indian in an old John Wayne movie. Then he saw my empty bed.

"Not so fast, big boy!" I came out of the bathroom, fire extinguisher cocked, and directed the hose of chemicals right into Cabino's face. Cabino tried to protect his eyes, and dropped the gun. Then he tried getting away from me, backing up step by step, stumbling backwards until....you guessed it.

He stepped right on top of You-Know-Who.

Maybe on nature shows they never get enough close-ups, or maybe in person an angry snake seems a whole lot bigger. This snake coiled itself and struck Cabino so fast on his upper chest that it hardly seemed to have happened.

"OWWWWWOOOOO!" Cabino bellowed in pain and horror, as he dropped the gun and ran out into the night.

I grabbed the gun and turned on the lights, just in time to

watch the snake slither neatly out my front door. He'd obviously had
enough of sacks, men, and pastel sheets to last him a lifetime, and
looked anxious to go home to Mrs. Snake after a long, stressful day.
I didn't think he'd be back, either.

I closed and locked the door and bolted the shutters, took a
good medicinal belt of Mi Abuela straight from the bottle, and
waited for the adrenaline in my bloodstream to start to subside.
Then I tried to call the police station. The line was busy, of course.
Shakey had already explained that at night all the on-duty police
took turns calling their girlfriends, so you could never get through.

I lit some extra candles, put the gun next to my bed, then
peeled back all the sheets, and had a good look before getting in it
this time.

Then I called Shakey.

Moses still hadn't lost the cigar, nor look like he'd found his
sense of humor, but he was verily impressed by my semi-finished
homestead.

"Oopah," he said, looking around, before plunking himself
down in my only plastic Adirondack chair. He smoked and puffed.
"Muy lindo."

I told him about the snake, the gun and Cabino. Shakey
translated.

"No kill?" he asked me.

"Me no kill Cabino. Snake." I made a curving motion with my
hand. "Snake kill Cabino."

"Donde esta el cuerpo, entonces?" Moses asked.

"Where's da body at, he say," Shakey explained.

"Me no know. Cabino run into the bush. No come back," I
told him.

"Huh!" said Moses. He threw his cigar onto my lawn, where it
began to smolder.

"Need a body, so," Shakey continued. "See if you kilt him."

"Jesus, Shakey. The snake bit him. He was trying to kill *me*."
Shakey shrugged his don't-shoot-the-messenger shrug.

Moses looked out to sea like he had all the time in the world.

I tried again: "Moses, the *alcalde* wants me dead."

At the mention of the *alcalde*'s name, he perked up. *"El Alcalde estaba aca?"*

"No. The *alcade* wasn't here. He sent Cabino. *Un contrato.*"

That got his attention. Now we had some high-level criminal philandering, not just another boring, attempted murder.

Moses walked off the porch, and over where I'd put the fence to mark my boundary with the *servidumbre*. I followed him like a puppy.

"Que es esto?" he asked about the fence.

"Black Jack," I said. *"Un servidumbre."*

"Ah ha," said Moses, narrowing his eyes.

He gave Shakey a hard look, and rattled off something about *drogas*. Shakey answered him, and he began shaking his head.

We walked along the fence toward the back of the property, and he pointed to a gap close to the ground. *"Aca,"* he said. *"El entró por aca."*

Shakey explained, "Cabino come in from here, he say. Gonna check it out."

"No es drogas," Moses said. He mentioned Black Jack by name.

"He said he watching," Shakey said. "No fret."

"Okay," I said, believing Cabino was dead somewhere in the bush, and Moses wouldn't do anything about it until I showed him the body.

I watched them walk back down the hill, and after that I just sat in the chair staring off into the darkness. Somehow the idea of crawling back into bed had totally lost its appeal. I placed Jim's shotgun across my knees, and must've dozed off as when I woke up, another pink dawn was hitting me right between the eyes.

I went inside to take a shower, moving the now empty fire extinguisher out of the way first. Then I got my backpack and headed for the airport.

On the drive in to town, I wondered: Maybe it hadn't been the mayor, but Black Jack who'd sent Cabino to kill me. Which put a whole new spin on things. And with Cabino dead, what might either of them try next?

Veronica was at the landing strip to see me off. I never wanted to hold a woman so badly in my life.

"Are you alright?" She looked deliciously crisp, and well-rested in a pure, white suit.

"Perfect," I said, running my fingers through my hair.

"Ahem," she said, and glanced down at my fly.

"This is getting to be a bad habit," I said, zipping myself up. What was it that Freud said about accidents?

She smiled at me, while around her a bunch of the local kids giggled, and watched us. "Take care," she said. "I'll...miss you."

Did she really say that? "It's only two days." Maybe I could try kidnapping her if my natural charms didn't pay off.

The prop on the helicopter began to whir, and as I lifted off, our eyes met. Then Veronica turned away, white skirt clinging to her thighs from the propeller's blow back. Around her children rolled in the grass in fear-provoked glee.

24.

J.J. met me at the airport, and we got into his big SUV and charged through the city like an invading army. He brought me up to date on items he'd sourced, the architect he'd lined up. In two days I'd be flying home with the mother lode: a new laptop for wireless access, a generator, enough solar panels to light up Yankee Stadium; an engineer who would follow and assemble my alternate-energy paradise. Mains electricity, I'd decided, could take a big, fat leap, along with Mayor Fernando and his $50,000 "introductory offer."

J.J. dropped me at the Intercontinental; he'd made the reservation himself this time. I saw my old buddies Aristides and Dominic, and was pleased they remembered me.

"Welcome back to the Intercontinental, Mr. Darlington," said Aristides. "Is there anything we can do to make your stay more comfortable?"

"A bottle of single malt scotch…and, oh. The chambermaid I had last time…?"

"Don't worry, sir. Dominic's sister is no longer working at the Intercontinental." I watched Dominic's back as he snuck into the back office.

"Ah," I said, trying not to smile. Sister pushing was either a national pastime, or an epidemic, I couldn't decide which.

I was shown to my suite, and felt relief to be back in luxury. The big soft bed, the quiet hum of central air. I even admired the drapes. I took a long, hot shower, had two drinks sitting on the balcony looking out over the bay of Concepción. Some 50-foot Hatteras Sportfish were just coming back into the harbor. I'd heard there was good fishing on the Pacific side, and many uninhabited islands. Some day I'd go exploring.

That night I ate giant prawns in a bourbon glaze in a former brick dungeon listening to a good jazz quartet; found a cab and left the old city feeling buzzed and content around midnight.

After coffee, around nine the next morning, I was ready to visit my money, and get on with buying the accoutrements of my new life.

J.J. picked me up, and we arrived at the Banco de Concepción on Via España in less than seven minutes, making me feel like I was on a slam-dunk course with destiny. I got out vowing I'd find someone other than J.J. to drive me around. What good would it do if I went to all this trouble, only to die in a car accident?

Damaris looked downright cheery to see me, though as before she indicated the foamy orange chair with pursed lips, then went to find the manager.

I picked up the annual statement, again, wondering how many millions I'd have to deposit to get Damaris to utter the words: "Please have a seat, sir. The manager will be with you shortly", when a familiar baritone voice slapped me back to reality.

"Darlington?"

I looked up, bewildered and then shocked, to behold the specter of Charles Schwabb Hubble, complete in Panama hat and tropical shirt, standing not ten feet away.

"Good God, Charles! What are *you* doing here?" I extricated myself from the orange sponge.

"I thought to ask you the same." He laughed in that phony way of his. A few feet behind him a lovely, young woman with the standard smile and dimples regarded me uncertainly.

"I'm doing some business," I said. "I imagine you're doing the same."

"Yes, business," he burbled happily, darting his eyes at the girl. "Concepción is a great little country. I come down here often as I can."

"Charlie?" asked the woman, tentatively. "I go outside now."

"Alright, Leticia. Go along then." He seemed inclined to pat her on the rump, then thought better of it. He turned back to me. "I heard you and Hillary parted ways. A pity, really. Lots of other fish in the sea, though..." he grinned. He looked as happy as a walrus who'd just had sashimi for dinner.

He took out a silver toothpick, began working it between his long, yellow incisors. "So, what are you doing here, *really?*"

"I'm really doing some banking."

"Come now, Richard. I heard you retired from the business. Living here in the city?"

None of your fucking business. "No," I said.

"In the countryside of Concepción, then?" *With the peasants?*

"Not exactly."

"You're being very mysterious, Richard. Do tell," he said in that irritatingly jocular tone that reminded me of old black and white movies about the British upper class.

I continued to look at him.

"Hiding from the H's?"

"Nice hat," I said, starting to move away. I was wondering if Charles had been the friend whom Helene du Pont had called me about. Had Jarald McVey sent him here, or had he found the place on his own? The world was getting to be a very small place if five thousand miles from home you run into someone you know—and don't like—at the scene of your offshore bank account.

Luckily the manager showed up, and gave me his big iguana smile. "Meester Darlington....right thees way."

"Good-bye, Charles," I said. He proffered a papery hand covered with liver spots large as pennies.

I shook it, and he clung on, suddenly desperate. "Richard...do tell me where you're staying. We can have a drink." From pompous ass to groveler in an eye blink. Not many people knew that Charles Schwabb Hubble, in spite of his pedigree, had not even had a trust fund when he'd married Penelope Astor. He was a groveler, born and bred.

271

"I'm at the Intercontinental," I said, turning away.

"I'll give you a call, we can catch up..."

"Sure, give me a ring." *Give me a ring?* I thought maniacally. What insanity had allowed *those* words to pass my lips?

"*Hasta luego,*" Charlie said with such desperate cheer that being with the lizard was a relief.

In his meat locker office, Carlos Dominguez blinked his puffy eyelids and told me, "With such large deposits, we have many forms to fill out," and took out a sheaf of them. I commented how *inshore* offshore banking had become, which drew a polite laugh from him that sounded more like choking.

I uncapped my pen and signed forms for an hour. What was the money for, where had it come from, etc. etc.

There was a miniscule branch of the Banco de Concepción in Hubba Hubba. The farms I was buying could be purchased up there, checks drawn to the local farmers and credited immediately. No problem. Veronica had wanted to draw the contracts and new title deeds herself; she knew the sellers, and they trusted her. The connection between us was in full view, and Black Jack would not be happy about it. His wife was going directly against him, helping convey farms to me that he himself undoubtedly wanted to have. The local farmers showed up at my door, not the door of Licenciado Martinez who was listed as the president of my corporation. I had negated my own power of attorney, though all the bearer shares were in my possession.

Still, I worried. Would Black Jack become vindictive? And if so, what form would his vengeance take? It also occurred to me that Veronica might use her business with me to even up past scores with her husband. Marriages were funny like that. It was hard to know what kind of power plays were going on unless you were one of the players—just ask me.

I finished my business at the bank, called J.J., and he picked me up to go to the architect's office. Unfortunately, J.J.'s choice was an expert in concrete apartment blocks. But the architect had a friend, a recent graduate whom he thought would fit the bill. I met René later that afternoon, and we clicked immediately. He saw my vision for a tropical house, and sketched it out in front of my eyes. I had my man.

I went to a museum gift shop specializing in pre-Columbian reproductions, and bought Veronica a gold-and-pearl necklace and earring set, knowing I was crossing a line, and not giving a damn.

I went to the phone company to try and meet Renata's boss but he was on vacation. So I took a number and waited for a sales rep who told me, through J.J., that they didn't have wireless service in Hubba Hubba, not yet. I showed him the company's brochure that said they did, and he smiled at me as if I were a few candles short of my tenth birthday. The brochure was a lie; that was the exact translation J.J. gave me. There was no apology for this, just a hint that maybe by the end of the year, the service would be available.

Soon come, as Shakey would say.

Would I like a new cell phone, in the meantime? They had this new model and a package with eight hundred free minutes a month, plus they could give me international access on it. The rep, a young Latino wise ass, was starting to light my wick, but I had no other option. I signed up, gave him a five-hundred dollar deposit, and immediately tried to call my daughter, only to be told that the service wouldn't kick in for twenty-four hours.

The employees of Kiss N' Tell were starting to play a dominant role in my daily life, and I didn't like it. My visits to Renata and the old Compaq would continue for the time being. Coco Beach was too far out of town to warrant phone poles and lines, and who wanted to look at them anyway? I could feel my jaw beginning to ripple like it used to in the old days when something didn't go my way.

Take it light, boss, I could hear Shakey reminding me.

I let it go, always the best option when there's sweet fuck-all you can do about something. We went on buying spree, instead. At the Centro Industrial, I bought a 500-kw generator, a bank of deep cell batteries, enough solar panels to have continuous hot water and lights without the generator, and began to feel in control of my destiny again. We had an early dinner at an Argentine steak house, and then went on to the Casa de Materiales where I bought appliances, tools, a set of overstuffed rattan furniture, some big, plant pots, and a shower curtain.

We went to the Café Dali for a nightcap, even though I was ready for bed. Homemaking was not nearly as easy as it looked, and I felt a tiny twinge of empathy for my wayward wife, whose life-long pursuit of antiques, fabrics, fine art, and household artifacts had engaged her—almost—full time.

"You gonna come back soon?" asked J.J. He was having a Stinger on the rocks.

"I'll have the architect come up, and then I'll give him a list of what I want. I'm not really a city boy, anymore." I was having a no-name cognac that was burning my gut as it went down, and having a strange cooling effect on the rest of me.

J.J. nodded in understanding. With the air-conditioning set at seventy degrees, he'd finally stopped sweating.

We sat back and watched the young ladies; it was ladies night at the Café Dali. Hair swinging, high heels clacking, hips gyrating, they were into full display behavior for a group of older men who sat watching them at the tables closest to the dance floor. Behind them, in second tier at the bar, a group of young men seemed determined to ignore the girls entirely. They drank steadily and defiantly. I thought it was probably time for me to sign up for the old fart's club, if all I could find to do was sit here and watch everybody else and think about home decor.

I said to J.J., "I was thinking maybe I'd get some of those sheer drapes. You know the ones you can see out of...but not really..." and he was nodding politely, when someone tapped me on the shoulder.

"Meester Darling-town?"

I stood up so fast, I nearly knocked over my drink. Jesus. Who was it now? In front of me stood a petite, vaguely familiar woman in a dress that seemed made out of the same fabric I'd just described to J.J.

"I am Leticia, remember me?" I did indeed, and craned my neck to see if I could spot old Charlie lurking behind her. Concepción was getting to be a very small place.

"Charlie, he no come," she said, smiling to reassure me. "I sit down?" And sat.

Euphoric that Charlie was nowhere to be seen, I foolishly asked: "Would you like a drink, Leticia?"

"Oh, *si*! Champagne be nice." She winked at the barman, and he brought an icy bottle of Moet and three glasses to the table so fast I wondered if he had telepathy.

She sipped her drink demurely, and I wondered if she'd swallowed any. I began planning my escape.

"Actually, I was just stopping by for a few minutes. I've got a helluva lot to do tomorrow. Things to buy for my new home..."

"You moving?" Leticia asked.

"Not really. I mean, I'm already settled. Just a few domestic details to wrap up..."

"You no live in da States?"

"Not any more."

"Too bad." She looked genuinely disappointed. "My sister Julie, she wants to go so bad. She pretty."

At once, the resemblance struck me. It was the dimples, I guess.

"She lives in Hubba Hubba," Leticia went on. J.J.raised his bushy eyebrows at me. "But she wants to work in da States. She pretty," she repeated. "Charlie says, lots of peoples them needs somebody to take care of da chil'rens, clean da house..."

"Well, Leticia, it's been nice seeing you again. Take care." I gave J.J. a hundred dollar bill and got up. "I've really got to go."

"Oh..." Her dimples faded.

"Tell Charlie I said hi." J.J. and I had already had the conversation about sealing off my past from my present life. At all costs, I didn't want Charlie Schwabb Hubble to find out about Hubba Hubba or that I was living there.

"See you tomorrow," I said to J.J. as I nearly ran toward the exit.

The next morning I met with Licenciado Martinez to finalize my business with him, and signed the new power of attorney for Veronica, giving her the right to sign my corporate documents both here and in the US. He agreed to notarize both protocols and send one by courier to McVey. I could see his skepticism; I was giving a lot of power to someone I barely knew. On the other hand, he didn't know Harry Goodman, or the depths of his vindictiveness. I needed to bury my assets a level deeper than Jarald McVey, and worried that even Elizabeth's trust might come under scrutiny. As I planned to make her beneficial owner of all the properties I was buying for the conservation trust I was setting up in Hubba Hubba, I couldn't risk even a signature on my own behalf. Poor Randall Hawkes, Esq., would just have to go fuck himself.

I called Veronica later that morning to give her an update, and she seemed pleased to report the new deeds were ready to go. She also said, "It's been very quiet without you." I wondered if she and Black Jack were still getting it on. The thought made my groin ache in jealousy.

J.J. drove me to the helipad, and assured me he'd take care of delivery of everything on this week's ferry to Hubba Hubba. I thanked him and suggested he improve his defense by buying a Humvee.

Then I was off. Sailing and smiling, thinking of Veronica, as I rose into the turquoise sky, free as a gull—or so I thought.

Little did I know that somewhere in the city below me, Charlie Schwabb Hubble was having the last laugh.

25.

Choosing sanity is not always as easy as it sounds. When I returned to Hubba Hubba, I felt like I'd entered a Caribbean Twilight Zone/Survivor show.

Shakey met me at the airstrip, and said: "Veronica, man, she try and kill Black Jack."

"What?" Veronica was one of the most laid-back people I knew.

"Is she alright?" Shakey started to laugh in the jiggly way he had, clicking his teeth. "She found out about Black Jack's steam cakes and went up da back found him wid Blanquita, and tried to cut him."

Steam cakes? "Jesus, Shakey! She used a knife?"

"Stay quiet, boss. She okay, now. Had a machete—so big. Tried to git his *cojones*, but missed. Da chief say he lucky he don't get kilt. Say it was self-defense."

"Self-defense?"

"He say Black Jack talk fart, and lie to his wife. He git what he deserve."

The anomalies in Hubba Hubba's system of justice got more mind-boggling every day.

Shakey added, "And Moses, he found da body, boss! Cabino climb a coco palm afore he died; got hisself all rigid, clingin' up there. Had to cut da tree down to git him on da ground. You free, man. Da doc says it be snake bite dat kilt him. Shor."

"That's good news." Is this what life would look like if Rod Serling and George Carlin were writing the script?

"Veronica she free too," Shakey said. "Both free as birds," he looked at me and grinned.

"Are you sure she's alright? Where is she now?"

"Down da courthouse, tryin' to pull da sequesters off da property."

"What sequesters? Oh never mind, I'll call her myself."

I did, but she didn't answer her cell phone. I left a message inviting her for a drink later on. Figured she'd need it.

At six-thirty, my lawyer/would-be-assassin/possible future paramour arrived just in time for sunset. I wondered if I should pat her down first?

I watched her walk up the hill. She had on big, gold, hoop earrings, and her hair, gathered in a ponytail on top of her head, was swinging behind her like a black horse's mane. She didn't look at all like a potential murderer and seemed happy to see me. She had on a white lacy blouse with a plunging neckline, tight jeans and short leather boots, definitely not business attire.

"Hello, Richard," she said shyly in greeting, and extended both hands to me.

"For someone armed and dangerous, you're looking very well."

"And I heard that Cabino tried to kill you," she gave me a serious look. "Why didn't you tell me?"

"Don't change the subject," I said, and led her up to the porch and gave her a passion fruit margarita.

"I know it sounds desperate what I did," she sipped at her drink and paused to see if I agreed or not. I didn't reply. "But I'm trying to solve this problem with Jack once and for all. Until I do, he'll keep trying to get even with me and you'll suffer, too. It's not easy."

"Surely, there are easier ways than a machete."

Her jaw set and her eyes glittered in hardness. "It wasn't about Blanquita, though everyone thinks so. My husband is a bastard, and I'm not going to tell you all of it. Just that he had it coming and it was time I gave it to him."

"It'll be tough for you to work for me if you're behind bars. They take your cell phone, don't they?" I tried a smile.

"This won't be over until my marriage to him is over. But no, I won't go after him with a machete again. The thing is, I don't love him, and he knows it. For another, we could never have children and he believes I'm holding out against him. That's a sin. The Church will actually grant annulments in Hubba Hubba to men whose wives can't, or won't, conceive."

Ah, good old Catholicism. "I hate to tell you this, dear Veronica, but choosing not to have children is not a sin, no matter how the local Padre wants to slice it."

She continued, "Jack won't divorce me anyway. He'd rather see me suffer, knowing I've known about his girlfriends for years, of course. But that's not why I attacked him."

"No?"

She looked like she had bad news. "I had all the title deeds ready, all five of them, and when I went to register them, they were all sequestered."

"Sequestered? You mean they had liens?"

"Legal liens, put there by my husband as President of the Municipal Council. The judge froze the titles pending a decision to see if Jack's action has merit or not."

"But what basis does he have?" If criminal laws were a matter of interpretation by the local police chief in Hubba Hubba, what did the civil law system look like?

"There's a little known law in Concepción that a foreigner cannot own more than fifty hectares of property on an island."

"But that's why we put everything in a corporation."

"Yes, but Jack is challenging it. He says the fact that you gave me a power of attorney is enough to show you're involved. So...the titles will be frozen until the judge decides."

"Well, he's certainly creative, I'll give him that."

Veronica explained that she was trying to have the action thrown out, or *tumbar*'d, literally tumbled to the ground. Meanwhile, she'd moved back in with George and Ella.

That was good news.

"You're my client, and my friend, Richard. I don't want you affected by my mess."

"There's no fear of that, and it's not your mess, it's mine. There are lots of other farms." I smiled at her. "And I've met bigger bullies than Jack Murillo. In my line of business, I've met many of them."

I gave her the box with the jewelry I'd bought in the city, and she took it from me with both hands, full of the pleasure of receiving a gift.

"Richard..." she began to admonish me. She undid the parcel slowly and expectantly, took out the necklace and her eyes glistened with real delight, then something else.

"Richard—I can't accept this." She put the necklace very carefully back in its box.

"Why ever not?"

"Firstly, I don't deserve it. Look what happened with Jack now, and you're buying me a present! Richard, I'm afraid he'll never quit. Jack is very determined, you know. Once he's got an idea in his head..."

I said, "Let's talk bottom line for a minute: Do you think the people of Hubba Hubba *need* a cruise ship industry here, Veronica? Are Black Jack and the municipal council the only ones who want it?"

"Of course, people want more money—look at how it changed my own family's life for the better! People want money, they need it. But most don't know how it will affect them, or even where they'll go once they've sold. If many people start moving here and buying up all the land, the happiness will go out of Hubba Hubba, I know it will. Jack only sees his own personal profit, not how it's going to impact everyone else."

"I agree." We sipped our drinks, and after a moment she said: "Mind if we change the subject?" She stirred her drink with one long finger, not really looking at me.

"OK."

"Do you still love your wife, Richard?" I definitely didn't see that one coming.

"No."

"That's it?"

I smiled. "No."

"Did you love her once?"

"I thought I did. But honestly, I think I was more in love with the idea of living in her world. Proving I could succeed in that world." I chuckled. "The money thing."

"Ah, yes. The money thing." She looked at me. "What about that?"

"It backfired." We both laughed.

"Do you think you'll stay in Hubba Hubba?"

I looked at her. "Yes, I do."

"Hmmm," she said. She wasn't convinced.

"Will you divorce Jack?" I asked.

"I think the Padre will give me an annulment after this."

"That's encouraging."

"Is it?" She looked at me with those big melting, almond eyes, and for the first time I saw a real spark of hope there.

"Very," I said, and we clinked glasses.

The next morning my stuff began arriving from the city, and René flew in to show me the plans for my new home. The engineer came with him to start setting up the electric plant and Shakey and I went to look for some new properties.

In the week ahead, we managed to put eight more farms under agreement, including the precious slice of white beach on the island's north side. I bought one six-hundred hectare parcel that had an old overgrown landing strip and three miles of golden sand beach. Another one of 350 hectares was a former cattle farm that looked like a golf course with meandering terrain, several ponds, and big stretches of degraded pastureland. Once we had a price agreement, we quickly closed on the deals, putting liens on them ourselves as we went—a defensive move by Veronica to prevent further sequesters. All went into a new corporation that showed ownership as fully Concepcionisto.

The setup was a great foil for Black Jack, and I was doing something that in my heart felt right: protecting miles of virgin Caribbean coastline from future development. Many indigent farmers who'd spent their lives breaking their backs raising cows and planting bananas could finally retire. The money I paid them benefited their families and filtered into the local economy. In cases where the families wanted to stay on, I let them, and Veronica handled the leases. The sequestered farms were put aside for the time being, pending a judicial outcome.

I also began getting many offers to purchase over-the-water properties in town, and had tossed around the idea of building one decent hotel and restaurant. The Boatel was a dying concern and the food at the Sum Fun, et al, was becoming monotonous to say the least. I bought three contiguous lots on the Calle Principal, and as the buildings were condemned anyway, had them torn down, opening a spectacular view to the east, right in the center of town.

Jack's tooth was gleaming a little less brightly these days when I saw him. But I still couldn't seem to make any romantic headway with his wife.

After many unsuccessful attempts, I finally got through to Elizabeth, and invited her to come for a visit.

"And sleep under a thatched roof? What about the snakes?"

I treaded lightly on that one. "Why not come down when my new house is ready—I know you're going to love it here. I want to talk to you about a conservation trust I'm putting in your name. What about Christmas?"

"Pierre's invited me to Gstaad over Christmas, dad. His family's invited me."

I tried not to sound disappointed. "But you don't like to ski."

"I've got to go somewhere. Mother wants to go to Palm Beach with Grandmother and Grandfather and I just can't face it. All they do is talk about what a bad person you are."

I thought I'd give that one a wide berth. The last thing I wanted was for my daughter to start choosing sides between her mother and me. I wondered if Michel was still on the scene but didn't want to ask. "Take care of yourself, sweet pea," I said. We promised to talk weekly.

I went to pay a call on Big Jim and Wanda after I'd heard that Jim tried to strangle the mayor with his bare hands. Both he and Mayor Fernando were now in neck braces, and Jim's progress with speech therapy had taken a big slide backwards. I offered to send him to the city for more treatment, and to my surprise, he agreed.

Shakey moved into the Boatel soon after.

My own daily routine started to have the semblance of predictability. With lots of prodding of Ezra, Zach and a whole crew of helpers hired by René, my new home—an elevated, open-air Balinese-style villa with wrap-around verandahs and hardwood floors and walls—began to take shape. After only two weeks, I had a foundation, enormous, vaulted thatched roof, and a roughed-in platform upstairs. To celebrate the completion of phase one, I invited Veronica, Joe and Patrice to dinner. I even called Daniel in New York to ask him how to make lobster thermidor on the household line.

He was very glad to hear from me. "Sir! How good to hear your voice!"

"Thank you, Daniel. How goes life at Foxglove Hollow?"

"Well, sir, to be truthful, there's not much cooking to do. The missus hardly eats, and now that young miss Elizabeth is away at school..."

"Have you seen my daughter?" I asked.

"She's beautiful, if somewhat thin. A little swan." I could just imagine. My daughter, with her bisque complexion and dark hair, had always been a beauty.

"Things good between her and Pierre?"

"Seem to be," I could hear reluctance in his voice. Was Pierre a gold digger, or did he really love my daughter?

"And Michel?" I had to know.

"Ooo. He's been a regular, too. They make quite a pair."

"Who? Hillary and Michel?"

"No, Michel and Pierre. The Dynamic Duo, I call 'em."

"Hmmm."

"But don't worry, sir. The fruit has fallen far from the tree in this case. Elizabeth's got much more sense than her mother, if you'll pardon my boldness."

"Thanks for clueing me in, Daniel. Obviously, this conversation is just between us..."

"You're tellin' me, sir! Where else can I get a job cooking with hardly any cooking involved? The missus says you're in a little country called Concepción. Let me know if you need me. You know I'd travel to the ends of the earth for you..."

He gave me the recipe I needed, and I went into my little kitchen and began to melt butter thinking back to my times in the kitchen with Daniel, and realizing they were some of my fondest memories of Foxglove Hollow.

We had dinner like a picnic on the upper floor of my new home that night: my two good friends, and one would-be inamorata, and me. I'd never been happier.

When I climbed into bed that night, I even forgot to check for snakes.

26.

The next morning, I left the crew under René's capable charge, and headed for town to check my email and stop at Lucky's to see if he had a few potholders; mine had become badly singed the night before.

Lucky and I were talking local politics, laughing about the mayor's new neck brace, when I heard the unmistakable sound of a chopper overhead.

"Invasion?" I asked Lucky, who actually looked worried.

"Hope not. Moses take my rifle last time. Don't give back." He folded up his crossword puzzle and looked skyward.

I continued shopping. "Hey, Lucky. What about these sinks, then? Do you have any that match the toilets, or just these pale blue ones?"

"Don't know." He was really sweating now.

The chopper sound stopped. Someone had landed, or left the area. We were only a half-mile from the airstrip here. Maybe I'd go have a look.

I left Lucky's. René could bring me up some matching bathroom fixtures on his next visit, I decided. I wandered into the street. Sr. Flores, former landowner, passed me in a shiny, red truck and stopped to pick up Sra. Flores from the Ina City Beauty Palace. Instead of her long fuzz, she now had dozens of tiny pearl-encrusted braids streaming from her head in a dark fountain, and a handbag to match.

Onassis, husband of Fermina Cordero, whose father had owned the golf-course farm, was also "cruising the strip." Onassis was now the proud owner of a white stretch limo with tinted glass that had a taxi sign on top of it lit like a big, square birthday candle.

Everywhere I looked, I began to see the changes, some obvious, some subtle. A lot of the children I passed now had on new shoes; mothers had new dresses. At least two new businesses had also popped up: one a paint store and chandlery, the other a mini-casino with slot machines.

Hubba Hubba was on the move, and for better or worse, I could see my impact.

People greeted me with the same friendliness as they had before, but now many wanted to talk about farms: farms they owned, farms their families had, farms they knew someone else was selling.

I also decided right then and there that enough was enough. Once we sorted out the problems on the Correa farm and the three others I'd agreed to in the beginning, I'd stop buying. Hubba Hubbans needed to decide their own future: about cruise ship ports, environmental impact, and which politicians to trust without further input from me. I'd continue to back the schools, the new library, the elderly poor house, but otherwise step aside. I was a stranger in paradise, after all.

I was just walking back through the park from the Kiss 'n' Tell—no more messages from Hillary, Harry or the lawyers—and mulling over my new environmental strategy, when I saw Shakey and Wanda heading my way. They seemed to be brimming with excitement, some news to tell me.

Wanda went first. "We have a surprise. Come and see, come and see!" Her old giddy self was on full display.

Shakey said, "Oh, you got friends, boss. Mighty fine."

"Friends?" I asked.

"You see," he grinned at me. "They's at the Dia y Noche."

It hit me, suddenly. Oh sweet Jesus. Not Charlie. And Leticia. If he moved here, I'd have to find another island. Maybe another country.

"Shakey...does my friend have a white hat and a colored shirt? Is he with a girl called Leticia?"

Shakey looked at me strangely. "Leticia? Nuthin' like that. You see."

And I walked into the little Hubba Hubba restaurant, and like something out of a drug-induced flashback, Helene du Pont came sailing toward me, arms outstretched, silk scarves flying, while behind her Martha Stuart, Frances Porter Dodge and Shelley Wurst all jumped up and sang out in unison: "SURPRISE!!!"

Which didn't begin to define my own state of mind.

I smiled to cover my shock and we all sat down.

"Isn't this *quaint?*" Helene exclaimed looking at the little pastry display, the steam table with shriveled hot dogs. "I don't believe I've ever seen anything like it!"

Shelley asked, "How did you find this place, Richard? It's extraordinary."

"You arrived by helicopter?" I asked.

"Of course!" Frances said. "We flew up from the city as soon as Charlie told us you were here."

"You *saw* Charlie?" He'd found me out then. The bastard.

"Actually he called us. We were visiting a spa on Curaçao—ever so boring. He said, 'You girls better get over here. You're missing all the fun,'" Helene told me. "Didn't you see him yourself?"

"Yes, as a matter of fact, I did. But I seem to remember distinctly *not* telling him where I was."

"Well, he knew. God knows how. And Hillary knows, of course. You could never hide from Harry and his snoops." They all twittered at this.

"We felt so bad," Martha said. "Thinking of you in Concepción all alone. We thought we'd come and cheer you up!"

"That's very kind of you," I said lamely. "Unfortunately, there's nowhere in Hubba Hubba to stay. And hardly anywhere to have a decent meal."

"Well, you don't look as if you're starving," Helene pointed out. "And this charming young lady...Wanda? Wanda has offered to let us have rooms in her Boatel. Isn't that sweet?"

Wanda beamed at me, the quintessence of the accommodating friend.

"Well, I guess it's settled then." I could see they weren't budging. "Did you bring your bags?"

"Shakey sent the limo to pick them up."

"The limo—you mean Onassis?"

"Is that his name? My God, if Ari were alive to see it himself, he wouldn't believe it!" Helene said. They laughed, silly as school girls.

We all got into the limo and Onassis sped off for the two full blocks it took to reach the Boatel, and braked so hard everyone slid forward.

They got out and looked at the Boatel, and after a moment's stunned silence began laughing.

"A great adventure," said Helene.

"It reminds me of the set of the African Queen," declared Shelley.

Martha said, "I'm not sure I can make it up the ladder."

To which Frances replied condescendingly, "I'll help you, dear."

"Me first," Helene said, as Onassis scrambled up in front of her and literally pulled her up onto the deck. The rest followed. I went last, feeling like I'd entered one of Dante's seven circles of hell. I'd thought just the sight of the Boatel would send them scurrying back to the airport. No chance.

"Well, Wanda," I said, full of false cheer. "Which cabins for our guests?" She'd done a good job of cleaning the place up, I had to admit. Since Jim's departure, the checked curtains had been replaced; she'd bought more fans, generally aired the place out.

"Do you have a suite?" asked Frances.

"Um," said Wanda. "There's the master stateroom."

"Perfect," said Frances, "I'll take it." She reached into her bag and produced a credit card. "Will this do?"

"Oh," said Wanda.

"Your money's no good here, Frances. Don't be silly. You are my guests. Anyway, there's nowhere in town that accepts credit cards."

"What?" they cried in unison.

"Only cash," I'm afraid. Maybe I could starve them out.

"Now where shall we have lunch?" Helene asked, moving right along. Foiled again.

"Well, I can offer you lobster and Cuba Libres at the Wreck Deck. Will that do?"

"A drink!" said Shelley. "What a grand idea."

"I don't suppose they have Maine lobster here," said the dour Martha.

"I just want to change out of this hosiery," said Shelley, "and slip into something more appropriate for the islands." They all nodded their approval at this idea, and so I went down to the limo. And waited.

Just under an hour later they sallied forth, dressed in large brimmed hats and colorful couture linens and we were ready. Onassis, with some coaching from me, was getting the hang of it now. Opening the door, not slamming it too hard. Not speeding off, and pumping the brake instead of standing on it. The day was full of miracles.

The Wreck Deck, unfortunately, was not empty. People gaped at us as if we were aliens, but Lovinia didn't bat an eye. She just smiled her usual warm smile, and took everyone's orders, five Cuba Libres, and told us it would just be a few minutes before a table was ready.

"What's all that over there?" Frances asked.

"You mean the stage?"

"They have entertainment?" Helene asked.

"Just about every night."

"Is it good?"

"I think so."

"Well, we'll have to come back then. No sense visiting a new culture without experiencing its traditional music."

Just then a boatful of men went by, the ferry workers. At the helm was the handsome Marinero, who gave us a big grin and waved as he passed.

"Who was *that*?" Frances wanted to know.

"He calls himself Marinero."

"Oh," said Frances, looking bowled over. Shelley shot her a look. "Now Frances..."

"I was just wondering," she said, and stuck her chin out. Lovinia, thankfully, showed us to our table.

"Well, that *was* enjoyable," Helene said, when we'd finished.

"I'd like a nap now," said Martha, "it's been a tiring day."

"Shelley and I will have a walk," Frances announced, "or a tour."

"In this heat?" Helene was like their scout leader. "You didn't even bring your parasols!"

"It'll be cooler later," I said. "Why not rest now and I'll call you later." I needed to figure out to get them back onto their helicopter as quickly and painlessly as possible.

"I'd like to have a look around," said Helene, coolly. "I understand you've been making some investments here, Richard."

I said nothing.

"Investing in land, Charlie said. Big tracts." Everyone grew silent and watched me.

"Investing is a big word, Helene," I said, trying to stay calm. Were they spying for Harry Goodman? And where the hell had Charlie gotten his information? "I've purchased some land for conservation purposes. That's it."

"Oil," said Shelley, who could never stop a thought from popping out of her mouth once it'd entered her brain. "Charlie said these islands could be the next Venezuela."

I suddenly knew how someone feels having an invading army camped out in their back yard.

"There is no strategy, Shelley. And no oil either. I'm sorry to disappoint you."

I could see they didn't believe me. And knew now why they'd really come.

A few hours ago they'd seemed like a flock of colorful, tropical birds, now they seemed like a band of turkey vultures.

"It seems you found this place en route to Venezuela," Helene point out. "Marty said so."

"Did he now?" So much for renewing my friendship with *him*.

Helene pursed her red lips together, a fatal clue. "Well, let's see how it works out, shall we, Richard? I mean, really. You can't keep *all* the best investments for yourself. You have to learn to share—with your friends."

I left them to their own devices after that. Dropped them back at the Boatel, and maintained my cordiality, but it wasn't easy. Without my hospitality and guidance, I didn't give them long. The Boatel's lack of luxury and comfort, the bumpy roads, the heat, the monotony of the food, would prove too much.

I gave them two days. Let them try the Ina City Beauty Palace just once, and they'd be scurrying back to Curaçao.

I vowed to stay away on my hill and wait them out. A coward's choice, perhaps, but there was nothing more I had to say to any of them. They'd come, uninvited, and on the guise of a visit, tried to encroach on my dream. They were a bunch of savvy old broads, but used to the crème de la crème of life. Soon gone, I told myself with a smile.

On day two—having regained my equanimity—I had a visit from Shakey.

"We got trabells, boss," he told me.

"What is it?"

"They's buying." He looked gravely distressed

"Who?"

"Yaw friends. The ladies."

"Who are they buying from?" My heart did a quick one-two beat.

"Black Jack, man. He's got 'em in that limo, cruisin' all over. Took 'em to the Boom Boom Room last night."

"The Boom Boom Room?" I was incredulous.

"The old one? She clingin' on to Black Jack like he was da second coming. Whassa matter wid doze white women? They sick?"

"Was it the tall one?'

"That be her."

"Helene."

Shakey said, "I went into da Boom to check it out. She said, 'Oh Jack, you just *mah-valous.*'"

That sounded about right.

"Well, Shakey. It's a free country. I guess everybody can buy land if they want to."

"Thing is, Jack sellin' the land hexpensive. He put da price up double, I'm hearin'."

"Those ladies have got plenty of money, Shakey. They can afford it. Where are they buying?"

"I'm hearin' Jack wanna sell dem da whole of Isla Esmeralda."

"You mean with the village and all those people on it?"

"Yep."

"Jesus." Helene was serious, then. This wasn't going to be a little property dabbling, but a major investment. Given the size of Isla Esmeralda, and Jack's greed, I figured we were talking millions.

"And boss..."

"What?"

"I hate to tell you this..."

"What is it Shakey?"

"Dat other friend of yaws, da one with da hat and da shirt? He came in, too. Flew in this moanin' wid my Leticia. Do you believe dat?"

"Leticia is Julie's sister, right?"

"Right." Shakey looked surprised I knew.

I tried to call Veronica on my cell phone, but couldn't reach her.

"Shakey, tell Veronica I'd like to see her. Ask her if she'll please come out here as soon as possible."

He left, and I sat down and looked out to sea and could envision it all. Hubba Hubba: the New Key West of the Caribbean. Pretty soon, there'd be an international airport, conch trains, and parasailing. The cruise ships would arrive, and there'd be miles of chaise lounges and bars with cutesy names. Jimmy Buffet tapes would be playing on loudspeakers and everyone would have giant pink cocktails in their hands. I felt the deep, pervasive horror of someone whose dream was about to be shattered.

The sun had just started its gentle descent when Veronica arrived. I passed her a cold beer and drained half of mine before we even spoke.

I asked, "What can we do?"

"I don't know," she said quietly. "If people want to sell, and your friends want to buy, how can we stop them?"

"Stop calling them my friends!" I yelled. "These are the people from my old life. They followed me here. It's a fucking nightmare." I drained the rest of my Ice. The sky was full of glorious color, but all I could see was red.

"It's only land," Veronica said, calmly. "I know it's important to you."

"It's everything to me! Can't people see how precious this place is...?"

"Everything?" Veronica repeated, looking at me.

"You know..." I said, "everything that matters, the only thing that has any real value any more..."

"Oh," she said, putting down her Ice untouched.

I looked over at her, sitting erect with her long legs curled under her, serene as a cat. She wouldn't look at me. For some reason, this infuriated me.

"So," I said. "Are you and Jack still getting it on?" I was on my third Ice and going strong.

"I have to go now, Richard," she said. But I didn't watch her leave. Just sat back with my beer and listened as she started up her little scooter and drove off down the road, leaving me alone. In the dark.

27

I spent a very maudlin few hours drinking beer, watching the now abandoned *servidumbre* in the silver moonlight, and laughing bitterly. With the full moon it was a perfect night for running drugs—so where was everybody? But Jack and his cronies would never have to work again. With the du Pont money, their cruise ship port would be a reality. Isla Esmeralda had a deep-water channel, too. They'd clear-cut the land, fill the bay with silt, kill the reefs and drive the fish away. Veronica, tired of being the town pariah, would start to come around. She'd loved Jack once. They'd begin seeing each other again. Maybe he'd go to her for legal advice, one thing would lead to another.

"Richard?" came a familiar voice. Luckily, male.

"Hmmm?" I answered from the depths of my gloom.

"Richard, it's Joe."

"Hey Joe. Grab a cold one. Don't just stand there."

Joe got a beer and sat down. "Got any candles? I can't see your face."

"Sure. Somewhere. In the kitchen, I think."

He came out with the candles and lit two of them. It was about all the light I could bear.

We both watched the flickering light and neither of us spoke.

At last Joe said, "I hear Helene du Pont is in town."

"You heard right."

"She's making some big deal with Jack Murillo."

"I heard the same thing," I snickered, "So, it must be true."

"There's no honor among thieves," Joe said.

I thought about this. "Helene du Pont as a common criminal is going to be a hard sell in every market I can think of."

"What goes around, comes around?" Joe ventured.

"If you're going to sit there and fill the air with a bunch of dumbass aphorisms, you might as well leave now."

"So, you're pissed."

"Of course I'm pissed! Wouldn't you be?"

"What pisses you off the most?" Joe sounded sincere.

I thought about it. "Losing everything."

"Losing control?"

"You think I'm a control freak?"

There was a tiny pause. "About this, yes."

I ignored him. "I guess I'm going to have to rescind Veronica's power of attorney."

"You don't trust her anymore?"

"Hell no! You know what she said to me a few hours ago? That there was nothing she could do. She's my lawyer, for God's sake! To tell you the truth, I think she and Jack are in bed together. Literally." I swigged my beer.

"Jesus!" said Joe, who rarely swore. "That girl is so crazy about you, she's one step short of ga-ga. She walks around with this big soppy grin on her face. I never even saw Veronica *smile* until you came here."

His voice startled me. Joe yelling?

"I..."

"Just don't blame her for your shit, ok?"

"OK," I said. Maybe if I agreed with him, he'd go off and leave me in peace.

But Joe kept right on sitting there. We both began breathing again. "It's going to be interesting."

"What's that?"

"Seeing what's going to happen. Du Pont and company have gotten Jack to sign over the mineral rights to the coasts here." He shook his head, and drained the rest of his beer.

I was stunned. "I didn't realize Jack had that kind of power."

"He doesn't. But the municipal council does. I hear it was unanimous."

"So, they really think there's oil here." I was descending into that gloomy place that feels like you've rolled in wet tar.

"Seems they do. The girls, that is. Jack Murillo can only see what he wants. The mineral rights are a worthless bargaining chip as far as he's concerned."

"Son of a bitch…"

"It was a big trade-off. This guy Charlie helped them put the deal together. I never knew anything could happen so fast."

"Trade-off?" I asked.

"They had to agree to buy all of Isla Esmeralda and fund that big cruise ship port the council wants to put out there in exchange. They've agreed to an investment of five million."

"It's only the beginning." I said. I knew Helene's capability. Not to mention the others'.

"Something tells me it's not going to be that simple," said Joe. He was like the eye of a storm. Which surprised me. I knew Joe loved Hubba Hubba as much as I did.

"This place is ripe for the plucking, just wait and see," I said.

"I intend to," Joe said.

"What's that?"

"Wait and see. If I learned one thing being a priest, it was that. Don't count on things working out the way you think they will."

"Expect the unexpected?" I said.

Joe said, "If you're going to sit over there and fill the air with dumbass aphorisms…"

I had the first laugh I'd had in three days.

The next morning, after a head-thudding sleep, I went into town. I couldn't hide out here forever.

I skipped the Dia y Noche, and went right to the Wreck Deck to see Lovinia. She'd learned to cook eggs the way I liked them, and was a better source of news than CNN.

I sat, and she gave me coffee.

"You no look so good, Meester Reech."

"Thanks, Lovinia."

"You wanna eat?"

"Definitely."

She started to make my breakfast. We were all alone. The Wreck didn't open officially until eleven or so.

"So, what's the latest?"

"She buy it all. Dat tall woman. But all dem peoples who lives over there? Where dey go?"

"I don't know."

"They got possession of dat land for years, Meester Reech. Land been in der families fifty, sixty year aback. Everybody got der chickens, der cows, der plantain. Gonna mow down da whole ting?" She shook her head in disgust and wiped a plate. "Bunch a *maleantes*."

"I'm sorry."

"It's not yo' fault, for goodness sake!"

"It doesn't feel that way."

She put the eggs and toast in front of me, and topped off my coffee. I'd just started to eat when I looked up and saw Frances and Shelley whizzing by in the middle of the channel. They sat, holding their hats, under the bright-blue bimini of a twenty-foot fiberglass boat with a new 75-hp Yamaha on the back. At the helm was Marinero, grinning from ear to ear.

Lovinia watched them and sucked her teeth in disgust. "That boy been wantin' that boat and motor so long, he's like a little boy at Christmas."

"They bought it for him?" Things were moving in Hubba Hubba at Amtrak speed.

"Shor," said Lovinia and showed her dimples. "They in heah last night dancin' to the Swinging Dicks. Learnin' the merengue."

"God help us."

"Uh-huh," agreed Lovinia.

I walked over to Kiss n' Tell to check my email, and was surprised Renata was nowhere to be seen. In her place was a tall, black man I'd never seen before.

At the risk of sounding too euphoric, I asked, "Where's Renata?"

"*Renata ha ido a Mejico con el alcalde.*" She'd gone to Mexico with the mayor? She must've really liked that caftan a lot. The mayor was obviously flush if they were both going. Helene must have made a good-faith deposit.

I went into the little booth, pleased to see I had a message from David Feldman. When I opened it, my heart sank. It said simply, *Richard, I need to get outta here. The Feds are heavy on my case about some of my offshore transactions. Can you help? David.*

I told him where to find me. What the hell. No sense trying to bar the cave door when everyone wanted to crawl in with me. I liked David, and he'd helped me when I needed it. Hey, maybe I'd send an engraved invitation to the IRS while I was in such a magnanimous mood. I could introduce them to Helene and company. They could all stay at the Boatel together. Maybe Wanda could add an extension?

I also had this cryptic message from Hillary. "*Richard, I've decided to leave New York for awhile. We need to meet to discuss our future plans, as you are obviously intent on staying away. I would therefore be willing to fly to Concepción to meet you in about a week's time. Is this agreeable? Hillary.*"

The plot thickened; so that's why I hadn't been hearing from the lawyers. Maybe she'd be waiting for me with Harry's lawyers and some burly bounty hunter with handcuffs. I doubted it. The tone of her message—I knew her so well—bordered on being conciliatory. The fact that the message had come from her and not the lawyers was also hopeful. If we could avoid a long, messy divorce, I was all for it.

I hit the reply button. *That's fine. I'll make us a booking at the Intercontinental. Two rooms, of course. Let me know your travel plans when you've made them. Richard.*

I walked across to the park and had a snow cone. It was purple, but tasted like pineapple. Oh well. Ever since the PJ parade, I'd discovered it was the best hangover cure on the planet.

I sat on a bench and sucked its sweetness and listened to the palacio bells strike the hour: twelve metallic gongs that still reminded me of toothaches and silver fillings. It was noon and the palacio began emptying out its employees, about three dozen of them. In Hubba Hubba, all of officialdom was under the same roof: the Judge, the municipal and circuit courts, the mayor's office, the sheriff, the police chief, the treasury, and of course, the Municipal Council itself.

I saw Black Jack coming out with his cronies, and they were laughing and carrying on loudly as though they'd all just hit the lottery. Which, of course, they had.

They began to cross the street to the Dia y Noche and then—was it just a coincidence? Veronica, who had just left her office, intersected with them, and Jack Murillo came forward and took his wife by the crook of her arm, and led her inside.

She didn't resist, though she didn't look happy about it, either. In fact, she seemed to have the exact same expression on her face she used to have, shut down and unsmiling; a sphinx with the most beautiful eyes I'd ever seen. Seeing her with Jack squeezed my heart and made my groin burn.

I got up and hailed a cab. There were a half dozen new ones since my purchase of the farms in northern Hubba Hubba. With Helene's investment in the area, we'd probably have a whole fleet of limos soon, and horses with little, frilly hats to carry the tourists around.

I went up to the airstrip to check out the action. There were two helicopters now, and a small, single-engine plane. Charlie must still be lurking around somewhere. I didn't want to see him, but didn't want to go home either.

Shakey had taken my truck on the ferry to Rambala to pick up a consignment of my stuff arriving by road.

Veronica was obviously off-limits for the moment, and I'd already been to the Wreck Deck. Wanda was busy with her new guests, and I hardly wanted to see Helene, Shelley, Frances, Martha or Charlie, in any case. So I did something that I been remiss about since my arrival, and went to call on George.

I arrived in a *panga*, feeling as if I was balanced on a log, which in a manner of speaking, I was. The trip to Little Conch was fifty cents, as usual. At least we didn't have rampant inflation yet.

George sat out in his front yard under a frond-covered roof shading a concrete pad that people in California called "lanais." George's "lanai" consisted of a standard issue pole construction and the requisite two worn, wooden chairs, numerous stumps and a banged together table. Seemingly, money hadn't changed George, at all.

He smiled and waved as I pulled up to his dock. I disembarked and went over and shook his hand, very glad to see him.

"And Miss Ella?" I asked.

"She inside, cookin' da turtle for lunch."

Turtle?

"Hope you can stay," George said, beaming at me.

"I will stay, but thanks. I just ate. Even had dessert."

"I can see dat," he said laughing. "Yo' lips all purple!"

I pulled up a stump and sighed. "There's trouble in paradise, George." And he was quiet, just looking at me.

"Seems like I started something here, and now I can't stop it." My guts were churning with a feeling I hadn't had in a long time.

George thought about this. "Since when God put *you* in charge?" he asked.

"Since He gave me this checkbook and my jet broke down?"

"You a reli-jus man?" George asked me.

"Not really."

"Then stop makin' jokes about da Lord. He watchin' you whether you thinks so, or not."

I was silent.

George said, "You know, I always thinks da same t'ing: Life she like a coco tree."

Uh-oh. "Meaning?"

"Da cocos they just drop—sudden like. Nobody knows when they gonna fall, and nobody can help if they standin' underneath when dey do."

This sounded a lot like the island version of "shit happens."

"But they's a plan too," George continued. "You gotta watch da signs."

"Like, if a coconut hits the beach and no one hears it does it make a noise?" I was in a New York state of mind.

"You's bein' too complicated," George said. "It's simple."

He picked up a splinter of wood and began chewing it, looking out to sea.

"It's not simple!" I said. "I thought it *would* be simple here, but it's not. I thought I escaped, and I didn't. It's like someone pushed the instant replay button."

"You's too angry to see it." George said, reminding me in his calmness of Veronica.

"I'm not angry," I said, angrily.

He was completely unruffled. He got up and started to walk away, then halfway to the house turned around and looked at me. "Ain't choo comin? It's time fo' lunch."

Ella gave me a warm welcome, and scattered about a dozen grandchildren out of the kitchen so we could sit down, just the three of us.

She carved up some meat that looked like pork, and then ladled gravy over it. I passed.

"Whatchoo been up to, Richard?" she asked, looking at me with Veronica's eyes.

"Holing up at the beach," I said.

"Mmm hmm," George agreed.

I could feel self-pity rearing its Medusa head. "I think I made a mistake ever coming here."

"Don't say such a thing!" said Ella.

"Hubba Hubba's so different from my old world, Ella," I said, and felt genuinely sad to admit it. "I feel like I don't belong here."

"That's ree-dicoolus," said George. "You a few coco short of a piña colada thinkin' like that."

Ella said, "Jus' cuz these peoples comes, cain't let 'em drive you out. No way." They looked at their plates where the turtle gravy was congealing. Children raced and screeched underneath the house. I could see them through the gaps in the floorboards.

"It's just not working out," I insisted, sitting firmly on the pity-potty now. "Veronica can't stand the sight of me..."

"Oh no...I don't think dat's true. Do you, George?"

"Ree-dicoolus," George repeated. He seemed to be getting quite cranky.

"Black Jack's deal with Helene du Pont is real. The cruise ship terminal will come; money isn't going to be an object any more."

"Dat all you think about? Whatchoo doin' wrong?" George put down his fork. "Think about things a little. It ain't yo' fault these peoples come. It ain't yo' fault dat cruise ships comin'. It ain't yo' fault Jack Murillo was born!"

Ella said, "You gotta let Him take care of things." She pointed skyward. "Don't hold on so hard."

George weighed in, "Make I say, it like shakin' a coco palm tryin' to make it drop its fruit."

The whole scenario had a familiar feel.

I was starting to get the picture.

And I didn't like what I saw one bit.

28.

Over the next few days, I stayed at the beach and thought about my choices. I could leave Hubba Hubba, go back to New York, make up with Hillary, and start working with Marty again. It wasn't too late to change my mind.

I could sail off with David Feldman for a few months.

I could murder Black Jack, and *then* sail away.

I could find another island.

I could try and co-opt Helene and company, or work to undermine their goals.

Or I could arrange to have the Boom Boom Room collapse one night while they were all doing the merengue.

Bottom line? I didn't want to run; I didn't want to hide; I didn't want to murder anyone. And I certainly didn't want Helene as a business partner.

That left the things I did want to do:

I wanted to make love to Veronica.

I wanted to live on this hill forever in a home I built myself.

I wanted to have Veronica on this hill with me, and laugh with her, and travel with her, and keep her by my side, always.

I never wanted to live at Foxglove Hollow, sleep with Hillary, play tennis at Piping Rock, or drive across the Throgs Neck Bridge ever again.

Things were getting simpler.

I called Elizabeth, and told her what I thought, too.

"Hello, Elizabeth. This is your father."

"I know who you *are,* Dad!"

"Well, that's good. Because if you don't come down here, you might not be seeing me for a long time."

This brought silence. "What?"

"It's simple, Elizabeth. You refuse to come down here; you seem to find my decision to change my life exasperating. Frankly, I think you're too spoiled to even consider my feelings, never mind my point of view."

"That's not true," she said, vehemently.

"I think it is. I'm sick and tired of walking on eggshells with you, Elizabeth. I thought you should know."

"I'm speechless!" she said, in a very good imitation of Hillary.

"And speechless you will stay," I said. "Until you come down here and see me in person."

"Is this an ultimatum?"

"Call it whatever you want, Elizabeth. I am your father, and I love you. I deserve a little respect."

Next I called Hillary.

"Hello, Hillary."

"Hello, Richard."

"I got your email. Did you get mine?"

"Yes. I've made my arrangements. I'll be coming in two days' time. I hope this is satisfactory."

"Yes, it is."

"I'll need you to book another room."

"For the bounty hunter?" I said.

"No, for Marty. He insists on coming with me. For moral support."

"That's fine." Marty as Hillary's moral support? Some things just got curiouser and curiouser.

Finally, I called Veronica.

"Hello, Veronica."

"Hello, Richard."

"I've called to apologize. I know I hurt your feelings, and I'm sorry. I overreacted."

"Thank you for saying so."

"Life in Hubba Hubba isn't as easy as I thought it would be."

She laughed. "'Sweet Hubba Hubba, full of juice and jive.' Don't you know? Hubba Hubba only keeps the people it wants. The rest, it spits out. But first it has to give you a good bite. See what type you are."

I was starting to wonder if George was right.

Veronica said very softly, "Please don't leave."

"I've got to go to the city for a few days to see my wife and finalize our divorce," I told her. I was finally going to clean up the mess and put it behind me. "Let's have dinner when I get back."

"Yes," she said, sounding happy.

"Your turn to cook," I told her, and hung up feeling more cheerful than I'd felt in days.

I finally saw Helene, Shelley, Martha and Frances at the airfield. They were standing around with the nattily-dressed members of the Municipal Council saying their good-byes before heading back to the city. Charlie was there too, and when I pulled up in the truck, everyone turned and stared at me.

At last Helene came over and I rolled down the window.

"Hello, Richard." She tried a superior smile, but it couldn't fully hide her embarrassment.

"Hello, Helene."

"Richard, I'm sorry for all our misunderstandings."

"Think nothing of it." I laughed.

"Well, I know you're against the cruise ship terminal. But really. It will have very little impact. You'll see."

"Yes," I said. "I will."

She tried another tack. "I know you don't think we *belong* here, Richard. But it's really not up to you, is it?"

I shrugged. "Let's see what Hubba Hubba thinks."

"What do you mean?"

"Make I say, what *type* you turn out to be." I bit the air hard, then swallowed. "Soon see," I said, and she backed up, looking frightened.

My chopper landed and Shakey hustled me into it, right past Black Jack. "Don't get lonely in da city, Meester Reech."

"Not a chance, Shakey. Wanda need anything beside the Jell-O and the hair color?"

"You might bring a few little clothes back."

"You're kidding!" I said. The blades were whirring over our heads.

He grinned at me. "Soon come. Six months to go."

I slapped him on the shoulder, and lifted off. I was almost free.

29.

I found myself back where I started, at the Intercontinental. Dominic and Aristides were both there. I was coming to think of them as the Gold Dust Twins.

"Mrs. Darlington has arrived, sir," Aristides told me.

"Bee-ootiful lady," added Dominic, trying not to leer.

"And Mr. Kahn?"

"He's here, too." I thanked them, and checked in. They gave me the same corner suite as before. I was beginning to think of it as my own.

I rang Hillary and she suggested I come to her suite, one flight up. Marty had gone on an errand and would be back soon.

I walked up the stairs with a strange mix of emotions in my gut, knowing that I wouldn't know until I saw her how I truly felt.

I knocked softly and she opened the door as if she'd been standing behind it. My wife of twenty years, standing in the doorway.

"Hello, Richard," she said, and put out her hand. She looked much more beautiful than I remembered, and there was something else. A new softness.

I took her hand and kissed it. Smiled at her. "Hello, Hillary."

She smiled back. Hopeful.

I followed her into the room and we sat on facing settees.

"So..." she said. She actually seemed shy.

"Thank you for coming, Hillary. I know you don't like to travel."

"It's not that..."

"Flying commercial?" I couldn't help but tease her.

"We did take the Lear," she admitted.

"No problems?"

"No, thank goodness. By the way, that was how we all knew where to find you. Before your calls to New York, when we are still in the frantic stage, Eric told Marty what happened. That you'd discovered this place. This Hubba Hubba."

"So you knew I wasn't off sailing…"

"We suspected you weren't. Marty and Elaine tracked you to Ft. Lauderdale after we went through those yacht brochures, and found David Felder's number. Then you spoke to Elizabeth and I found the country code in her directory…"

"You thought you'd reel me in that way?"

"Locate you," she smiled. "My first thought was that it was some kind of joke. I mean, the name! I couldn't believe a place could be called Hubba Hubba."

"Seeing is believing."

"Are the women all truly as large-breasted as Eric says?" She was genuinely curious.

"With big dimples, too," I said, laughing. "But that's not the reason I went there."

"I never realized you were so unhappy," Hillary said.

"Neither did I. But what about you?"

"I was unhappy, too."

"And now?"

"Now I'm in love."

Just then Marty came into the room. He looked the same, only thinner, and he'd started to grow a beard.

"Hey, Marty," I said, getting up. I went over to shake his hand.

"Hey, Richard." He gave me a quick, hard hug. "You look fantastic! Doesn't he look great, Hill?

"Your new life is agreeing with you," Marty said. "It really is."

Hillary nodded. She was more serene than I'd seen her in years.

We stood looking at each other, three people who'd known each other for a combined total of more years than I could count. I felt a great surge of hope. Maybe we'd have a happy ending, after all.

Marty got up to fix us a drink, and I excused myself to go to the loo.

And that's when I saw it. On the vanity, next to the sink; all the proof I needed, and then some: Marty's shaving kit.

Time stood still—literally—but when I looked at myself in the mirror, there was more surprise than anger. I washed my hands, and reflected on it. Everything made perfect sense now. I flashed suddenly to a silver-framed photo in her room, the one that always seemed like it didn't belong among the serious poses of her parents, our formal wedding shots; Elizabeth at different ages. It was a picture of a roguish-looking Marty with a full beard and long hair from his Berkeley days. She was in the photo, too: a young, fragile-looking blonde with large dark glasses and a long, flowery dress. Hillary had studied out there for a few semesters. She'd been on a French immersion course. And become immersed in something— someone—else.

I remembered our shotgun society wedding, Hillary's pregnancy. Everything fit. Why else would Harry Goodman let his little girl marry a nobody unless the nobody could cover up the truth?

When I came out into the sitting area, they were on the same settee, holding hands.

"Well, well," I said

Marty said, "Richard. We have something to tell you."

"I can see that," I said, but I wasn't angry. I was breathing pretty heavy, though, and trying to take it in.

"So, what happened to Depaulier?" I asked Marty.

"He went back to France."

"It was you that spied on them and took the photos?"

"Yes," he admitted. "It was me."

"What about Melanie?" I asked Hillary.

"She never suspected," said my wife, trying to suppress a smile while looking at Marty.

"Melanie was a passing fancy," Marty said. "She was never a substitute for the real thing. She was like...like a placebo."

Placebo?

311

I thought of Melanie and her wayward bears. I thought of a lone coyote on my lawn. Some creatures just didn't belong on the Gold Coast.

"What does your father think?" I could just imagine Harry's reaction to Hillary hooking up with Marty. A WASP/Jewish union would have him rolling in an early grave, which is why I'd become the chosen one in the first place.

"He's got cancer, Richard. Prostate," Hillary said. "The prognosis is good though." She looked at me hopefully. Her eyes were almost glassy; I wondered if she was on medication.

The man who'd threatened me with bodily harm, who'd played such a diabolical role in the past twenty years of my life, was now impotent. How fitting.

"I'm sorry," I said.

Marty said, "Can we just get it on with it?" My partner, the deal closer.

Hillary said, "We've decided to go to the West Coast, away from all the old memories." She looked at Marty with that infatuated look that Melanie had had. Did Marty have something other than an unlimited supply of pharmaceuticals?

"I'm happy for you both," I said.

"You are?" Hillary clapped her hands together in delight.

"I am. You have my blessings," I said. "You send me a reasonable settlement proposal, I'll accept it."

"Done," said my former partner. "I'll have the lawyer send yours the draft of the agreement we worked out. It's more than fair, Richard."

"Right, then," I said slapping my knees and standing up. "I'll be going now."

Hillary looked at me, a bit forlorn. "So soon? I thought we'd have dinner...catch up."

Marty said, "Stick around. We'll have a good time...like the old days." We shook hands.

"No, really," I said, "I've got to go."

"Why?" asked Hillary. She looked a bit desperate now.

"I'm in love too," I said, and turned and walked away. Leaving my old life, I hoped, completely, and irrevocably behind me.

30.

Aristides looked confused when I checked out.

"Not staying the night, sir?"

"No, Aristides. Just give me the bill."

"I won't charge you, sir. You've only been in the room a few hours."

"Thank you, Aristides. I'll see you again in a few weeks, then," I said, laying a fifty on the reception desk.

The helicopter people were getting to know me, too. One of the partners even approached me with the idea of partial ownership of one of the Bells. "There's a lot more traffic now to Hubba Hubba," he told me. "You're our best customer. It'd be a good investment."

"You wouldn't want me as a partner," I told him. He looked at me. "If I owned this place, I'd ground the fleet. Now, what good would that do?"

He smiled, tentatively. *Another rich weirdo*, I could see him thinking. He took my credit card and charged me for my flight.

I made my decision. "Add on an extra day, will you? Can the crew stay on like they did for Mrs. du Pont? Wait for me?" He assured me they could.

We headed north, over the city and tall buildings mixed with patches of fluffy green. I loved the contrast. Trees grew everywhere in Concepción. They weren't looked upon as a danger, or an inconvenience, but as natural adornment to a city block. We headed out toward the coast, and north to Hubba Hubba. It felt good to be airborne again, sailing through pure, fresh air. I made it back to Hubba Hubba before nightfall.

The next morning, I woke early, and called Veronica. I had a big day planned.

"I'm back," I said, when she answered. "Are you free?"

"Definitely," she said. "Are you?"

I laughed. "You have no idea."

I got out the V-Rod and went to find her. She had on her jeans, and in full view of the morning's pedestrian traffic on the Calle Principal, climbed on the bike behind me.

"Where are we going?" She seemed confident and relaxed. Trusting.

"On a tour."

We headed out of town, and up the north coast. In La Cabaña kids came running out, as they always did when I was on the bike, to wave and yell at me. Now they hooted wildly to see Veronica too.

We went past Coco Beach and through the farms I'd bought, over hard dirt tracks.

We stopped at a stream and I took her by the waist and spun her around.

"What do you see?"

"Pasture. Lots and lots of pasture."

"Exactly," I said.

We went to the end, as far as the beach in Drago Point, then doubled back. Everywhere there were these tracts of open land where cattle grazed.

By the time we reached the airfield, people were coming out of their houses to gawk at us; some of them looked a little frightened. Was that Mrs. Black Jack on the back of my motorcycle enjoying herself?

She wasn't so sure about the helicopter. "What if it falls?" she asked.

"It won't," I said.

"Are you sure?"

"I'd bet my coconuts on it." I grinned at her and she gave me a playful slap, and we got into the cabin and lifted off.

"Oh," she kept saying, "oh…"

"You'll get used to it," I said.

"It reminds me of the Ferris wheel at the *feria*," she said. I could see she was still breathless. "You can see everywhere. It's so beautiful!"

Indeed, it was a breath-taking day to be airborne in Hubba Hubba. We went all over the island. I wanted her to see the big picture.

There was my farm, the hill, the grid of coconut palms, and then there were the miles where the coconut palms had been. You could see the evidence from up here. The rotted stumps in a row, the toy cows grazing around them. Then there was the deep blue channel on the north end of the island where the cruise ships would *not* be.

We circled around, closer to the water then headed back, over the town. We flew across the channel to Little Conch Cay like birds, Veronica's face lit with delight. Her childhood home and George's ranch looked built by dolls, the people in the yard like tiny figurines. We sailed over to Isla Esmeralda. Inspected the bay where the future megaport was planned. Saw the village that Helene du Pont had "bought." Nothing could ruin this day for either of us.

I took her hand in mine and she looked at me, her face full of wonder.

"Have you seen enough?" I asked.

"I had no idea," she said. "It's like...like a fairy tale."

"Now you see what I see."

"Yes, I do," she said.

We went back to my place for lunch. Lobster again. With avocados fresh off the tree and bananas flambéed in rum and brown sugar for dessert.

I told her the story of Hillary and Marty. She was shocked.

"What did you say?"

"That they had my blessings."

She looked at me, skeptical. "Didn't you feel angry?"

"A little sad, but no. Not angry. In the past few days, the anger seems to have drained right out of me."

"A Hubba Hubba man would never say that."

"Black Jack?"

"Especially Black Jack." She was sitting on the settee again, legs under her, looking out to sea.

"Hey, let's see how the coconuts fall." I said in a good approximation of her father.

"Did my father tell you all those old coconut stories?" The smile came back to her face.

"Maybe we could write them all down, sell them as a self-help book: The Coconut Chronicles."

She laughed. "My daddy, famous at last..."

I said, "That morning? I saw you with Black Jack. I nearly incinerated in the park, snow cone, and all."

She said, "That must have been the same day I told him the church granted my annulment."

A charge ran through my veins. "You're divorced?"

"Just about. I just have to get the papers approved by the judge, but he does whatever the Padre wants. It's a rubber stamp."

"Tremendous!"

"That doesn't mean he's going to let go." She looked at me ruefully.

I went over and pulled her up, put my hands on her hips, and squared her off to me so I could get a closer look at those dimples.

"Richard...?"

"Don't say anything," I said. And kissed those full lips, at last, caressed that gorgeous long neck, and it was better than I'd ever dreamed. I was a love astronaut, free-wheeling in space.

EPILOGUE

We started planting coconuts and hardwood trees after Black Jack went to jail.

Moses finally caught up with him. He'd been right. It wasn't drugs that Jack Murillo was running late at night with all those flashlights; and it wasn't girlfriends. But guns. Guns in exchange for cash to a rebel group running cocaine and heroin into the U.S. from their jungle bases in Cassandra's Gap. Jack Murillo's plan had been to use the money to buy up the land and create his cruise ship super terminal. Helene du Pont's investment money had arrived too late, it turned out. Jack had been doing the dirty for years, according to Moses.

The judge sentenced Black Jack to twenty-five years, without parole. Since Concepción's last dictator had been extradited for crimes against humanity, the government didn't look fondly on caches of unregistered firearms, or arms dealers. From now on, he'd be dialing for dollars from his cell—if they allowed him his phone.

Veronica's divorce was a cakewalk.

Some members of the Municipal Council were also found guilty as conspirators, though they were given lighter sentences. The mayor, of course, simply stayed in Mexico. He had Renata with him, and I thought there was enough guilt-by-association to keep her away forever, too. What a shame.

Big Jim, on the other hand, died in a comfortable room with a morphine drip in his arm, probably happier and more comfortable than he'd ever been in his life. Wanda inherited the Boatel, of course, and Shakey moved in with her to raise their child, a girl they named Juanita.

We sent off some soil samples to an agricultural lab in the city, and they checked out fine. The soil was free of the bacteria that had decimated the coconuts in the early part of the century. And so we began planting again. Coconuts and tropical hardwoods. Lots and lots of them.

And getting rid of the cows.

Veronica and I were both gun-shy when it came to marriage, no pun intended. We were happy to live day-to-day getting to know each other: riding horses through the vast, protected green belt we'd set up, eating lobster and melted butter in bed, watching the coconuts grow. Our vision of restarting Hubba Hubba's economy from something other than fake trinket shops and duty-free perfume grew and grew.

And Aubrey showed up. With Leonard. Remember them? They'd heard about Hubba Hubba from Helene and came to check it out. One trip around the lagoon was enough to convince them. They invested over a million in purchasing and constructing on the three town lots I'd bought, and sent down a container of designer remnants from New York that was enough to fully furnish their eight-room hotel. They also began construction of a restaurant over the water, flying between Palm Beach and Hubba Hubba every month to oversee the project and bring more supplies. It became their hobby.

And Hubba Hubba just began to grow. By word of mouth, mostly. First the divers came, then the dive shops. Before you knew it, we had more restaurants and bars. The few locals who sold coconut oil in the street, settled down in little kiosks by the roadside and added beach towels, sunbrellas, straw hats and crafts.

The journalists began showing up too, and a "Paradise Found" headline in the *LA Times* Sunday supplement was followed by a six-page spread in *Islands Magazine*. The speculators began arriving in droves. The government paved the runway, and soon we had weekly, then daily, flights from the city. Americans of all ilks began arriving: homesteaders, dive masters, bartenders, and retirees. And the Europeans came too: an Italian hotelier and a French scientist who came to study the turtle nesting grounds and brought his family and friends.

Hubba Hubba got its own website, and a tourist building where you could send and receive email; and yes, Kiss 'n' Tell finally got around to offering wireless internet as well. One of the big non-profit biological institutes moved its Latin base to Hubba Hubba citing "the ecological and historical biodiversity" of the area. They built a bunch of laboratories and dorms and began running weekly seminars with titles like: "The Forgotten Sea Grasses," and "Habits and Habitats of the Leatherback Turtle."

Daddy Joe and Sister Patrice found that Hubba Hubba had gotten too civilized for their taste. They rented out their house and went a few islands further south on their sailboat. They bought a nice strip of primary jungle with a big hill and constructed a dock in front of it and parked the sailboat. "The coast isn't the only thing eroding," said Patrice, tapping her head. "I don't want to end up as an extra on *Survivor*." She giggled. Joe said: "I saw a red Hyundai taxi the other day…that did it for me." They did buy a cell phone though, so we could keep in touch.

David Felder also came to have a look but decided island life wasn't for him. He was a city boy and needed the pace and nightlife Concepción had to offer. He bought a big penthouse apartment with a sea view that overlooked the Concepción marina and opened up a little yacht brokerage office with a Spanish-speaking secretary. Linda and the girls came often to visit him but because of his tax problems, and the fact that he'd renounced his citizenship, he didn't go back to the U.S. again. And didn't want to. I visited him whenever I went to the city on business. He seemed happy and well adjusted in his adopted culture, and bought a SUV like J.J.'s. I liked David, but more importantly, I trusted him. A good basis for a lasting friendship.

With Black Jack gone, and half of the old municipal council in jail, Helene du Pont's power base had begun to erode faster than fresh snow on a black asphalt driveway. There were strikes and angry meetings among the locals about what had happened in Isla

Esmeralda. Lawyers began popping up like magic mushrooms in cow patties after rain. Many people had finally seen that a new taxi, or a wide-screen TV couldn't replace what had been created over generations. People wondered what they'd feed their children now that their fruit trees were being plowed into the ground and their land earmarked for future condo development. Many wanted their old lives back.

Helene called me at the zenith of this activity. Why wasn't I surprised? She sounded exactly the same as I'd remembered: rich, bored, deluded and superior. There were actually people who thought this was civilized.

"Hello, Richard," she said. "This is Helene du Pont."

"Hello, Helene."

"I hope you're well…"

I didn't reply.

She didn't let the pause intimidate her, though. In fact I wondered if she'd noticed it at all; Helene was used to being the center of the world. Other people existed only on the periphery of her consciousness. I pictured her in the drawing room of her magnificent home, having tea, the butler waiting just off to the side in case she wanted another small, hot slurp of Earl Grey, or a tiny cucumber sandwich. "I have a proposal for you, Richard. Perhaps you'll think I'm foolish…"

I'd like to break Black Jack out of jail. Maybe you can help me? "Go on," I said.

"We've had a meeting—all of us girls—and decided a new strategy is in order. As an investment, Hubba Hubba had its appeal. It would still appeal to some…."

"But not to you," I said. The conversation was beginning to give me that bloated feeling that comes from eating too many ripe mangoes.

"Not to me," she confirmed. "But what about you?"

Well, the woman had balls, I have to admit it. If she'd been a man, she'd have been hung like the Godfather.

"It's a little late to save Isla Esmeralda, Helene. And that's the only interest I have. I could offer you something nominal."

I imagined her bristle. Helene du Pont was very good at bristling. "We have seven million three of sunk funds so far...just what do you consider nominal?" She told me what was included: the cruise ship permits, the oil rights, the town, the land on the sea in front of the town. The deeds to the whole island, in fact.

I offered her a million and we settled on two point four.

Veronica drew up the contracts, and as my *de facto* attorney, she sent the instructions to Jarald McVey herself. There were some aspects of my former life I still refused to face.

And so, little by little the land was repatriated to its owners. Each family interested in repatriation was set up on a payback schedule. They'd had the money from Helene, after all, and had spent it in most cases. We set up an account so that the funds they paid back would be used to enhance the school system and other infrastucture of Isla Esmeralda. A satisfactory solution for everybody.

Waiting and seeing had turned out to be good advice, after all. And I never had to see Helene or the girls again.

But Charlie showed up. He was one of Aubrey's and Leonard's first guests. He took the corner suite and converted it into an apartment and installed Leticia in there with him. He rarely went out, and I heard he was suffering from some tropical fungus in his lungs. I heard he tried to divorce Penelope, but wasn't successful. Their assets were too intermingled. All those irrevocable trusts, you know.

And my daughter came, too. For spring break. She brought Pierre with her, and I must admit he seemed a genuine, thoughtful, young man, though not from the uppercrust background his Uncle Michel had claimed. He also seemed to love my daughter—which was what really mattered.

We finally sat on the hill together and she was as amazed by the view as I thought she'd be. She promised to try and come for the PJ parade next time, and we did get her over to Isla Esmeralda and she loved Blue Monday where the Swinging Dicks played rain or shine, fifty-two Mondays a year.

Elizabeth at twenty was something to behold. I thought she

was destined for great beauty with her porcelain complexion and dark glossy hair—she had the best of both her parents' features, and would always be my daughter, though her big brown eyes were no longer a mystery.

For me, life couldn't have been better. I hadn't been able to prevent Hubba Hubba's discovery, but at least I'd preserved a big chunk of it. The conservation trust we'd drawn up to protect the land allowing the planting and harvesting of coconuts and other fruit trees was cast in legal cement. It seemed fitting that the grandchildren of the original coconut workers now owned a cooperative on the same land where their grandparents had worked for "da company." The workers owned the fruit, with a small percentage of the harvest being turned back into a maintenance and rental account. The farms could therefore be self-sustaining, and also provide much-needed employment to the area. It would be a sustainable model for many years to come.

I was reflecting on this one night as Veronica and I sat on our chaises watching the sunset, drinking cold beer. The sun was a flaming melon ball backlit by a banana-colored sky, like a big fruit salad.

Nearby, a coconut thudded to the ground.

We both looked over at it. "It's funny about the coconuts here..." I began.

"What do you mean?" asked Veronica gazing out to sea, as usual.

"The size of them. They're so big. Much bigger than the same species grown in Hawaii, for example. It must be the soil."

"Mmm," said Veronica.

"Well, did you ever think about it?" Sometimes my new love could be so laid-back I had to give her a mental nudge to see if she was still paying attention.

"Of course," she said.

"And...?"

"They're just big, that's all. They've always been big up top. Just like the women of Hubba." She grinned at me.

I put down my beer and looked at her. "My God—do you think that's a coincidence...?"

Veronica just smiled at me.

"Richard," she said. "When are you going to learn to leave well enough alone?"

Made in the USA